THE PLANET EARTH HAD BEEN DESTROYED!

Only a small group of people—saved at the eleventh hour—managed to leave Earth and get to Bronson Beta. They thought they were the sole survivors of all humanity.

Alone in a strange world where a nameless race had once built magnificent cities, they faced the problem of survival.

Then they made a startling discovery—they were *not* alone on Bronson Beta. Were the others survivors of the People of the Past—or emigrants from Earth?

Most frightening of all was the knowledge that this unknown group was determined to see the Earthmen destroyed!

Also By Philip Wylie
and Edwin Balmer

WHEN WORLDS COLLIDE

AFTER WORLDS COLLIDE

BY PHILIP WYLIE and EDWIN BALMER

PAPERBACK LIBRARY
New York

PAPERBACK LIBRARY EDITION

First Printing: *December, 1963*
Second Printing: *February, 1965*
Third Printing: *November, 1966*
Fourth Printing: *January, 1968*
Fifth Printing: *June, 1970*

Library of Congress catalog card number 33-7382

This Paperback Library edition is published
by arrangement with J. B. Lippincott Company.

Paperback Library is a division of Coronet Communications, Inc. Its trademark, consisting of the words "Paperback Library" accompanied by an open book, is registered in the United States Patent Office. *Coronet Communications, Inc., 315 Park Avenue South, New York, N.Y. 10010.*

FOREWORD

EARLY in the middle third of the twentieth century a brilliant astronomer named Sven Bronson observed through a telescope in South Africa that two bodies were moving through space toward the solar system.

Bronson's calculations revealed to him that these wandering spheres would pass very close to the earth, make a circuit of our sun, and turn back toward space and infinity. The larger of the two wandering worlds would strike and annihilate the earth. Finer and more delicate calculations tended to show that the smaller body, which was of the same magnitude as the earth, would be "caught" by the sun and held in an orbit between the courses of Mars and Venus.

In other words, Bronson's discovery was an announcement of the end of the world.

It would be an end of the world preceded by the close passage of two mighty planets from some sun lost in the void—two planets which had been pulled from their pathways ages ago by a passing star. The world would be replaced by a new earth whose pathway would take it alternately out to the cold orbit of Mars and back again to the vicinity of Venus.

The bodies were named for their discoverer: the larger one, Bronson Alpha, and the smaller, Bronson Beta.

Sven Bronson knew the horrors that would attend the announcement of his awful findings.

He and Lord Rhondin, the Governor of the South African Dominion, summoned David Ransdell, a war veteran and flier, to carry the tangible demonstration to an American scientist, Cole Hendron. Ransdell started out with photographic plates which proved the discovery.

Cole Hendron, the greatest astrophysicist and engineer of the century, had already been notified of the approaching doom. He and his daughter Eve, who acted as his assistant, checked Bronson's calculations.

There was no doubt. The earth was doomed.

Hendron, Bronson and others united the foremost scientists of the world in a secret organization known as "The League of the Last Days" and these men kept the information from the public for some time. Among the first laymen to know, or guess the truth were Ransdell, the flier, and Anthony Drake, a young New York man-about-town who was in love with Eve Hendron.

Most of the informed scientists were ready to resign themselves to universal destruction. Cole Hendron, however, perceived a possibility of escape: if the planet which was to occupy the earth's position were habitable, and if a vessel capable of transporting human beings and their possessions through a few hundred thousand miles of space could be made, a small and select group of people might "jump" from the doomed earth to the new arrival in the solar system. This group could then set about reëstablishing mankind on a new earth.

Hendron and his assistants set to work at once. Atomic energy adequate to drive such a vessel exactly as a rocket is propelled was released in his laboratories. At first it could not be harnessed, as it fused everything with which it came in contact. Nevertheless Hendron persisted in his plans for the space ship. The "Ark" was the name given to the ship eventually built.

For its construction, Hendron established a vast manufacturing city in Michigan, and to it he took a thousand selected human beings—men and women with scientific training, healthy physiques, and great courage.

While Hendron labored frantically, the world found out what was in store for it.

Society disintegrated. The first, and relatively harmless "passage" of the Bronson bodies would be sufficiently close to cause vast terrestrial disturbances—tides, cyclones, terrific volcanic disturbances, and earthquakes. All the seacoast cities of the world were evacuated. New York, Boston, Philadelphia were cleared of their population, which was moved inland at the order of the President.

One bit of fortune came in the discovery of a new metal in the material forced from the depths of the earth during the great eruptions. Ransdell found it and brought it to camp where Hendron tested it. This metal proved able to withstand the heat of the atomic blast. The problem of propulsion of the "Ark" was solved.

In the fantastic days that followed, Hendron and his band manufactured the Ark, and found time and materials to make a second ship so that the balance of their heroic group could be transported to Bronson Beta and not sacrificed. The Michigan cantonment was attacked by bloodthirsty and hungry mobs. The first passage killed more than half of the people of the earth. Continents split apart. Seas rose. The internal fires of the earth burst to the surface. The moon was smashed to atoms.

Months afterward the celestial wanderers rounded the sun and returned. Hendron's two ships "took off" for Bronson Beta. Other ships, frantically constructed by other nations, also leaped into space as doom fell upon our world.

Bronson Alpha annihilated the earth and moved into the void.

Bronson Beta swung into a course about our sun.

Upon it, Hendron brought down the "Ark." With him was a company of a hundred and three human beings. Tony Drake was one of them, and his Japanese servant, Kyto. Eliot James, the diarist and historian of the party was in the "Ark." So was Dodson, the surgeon, and Duquesne, the French physicist who had been saved at the eleventh hour as the Ark stood ready to rise from Holocaust.

A safe landing was made. The air of Bronson Beta was found to be breathable.

But there was no word of the second ship—the vessel under Ransdell's command which had left with them. It was given up for lost. Ransdell, who also loved Eve, was presumed to have died somewhere in space with his brave companions—Jack Taylor, the college boy who had become one of Tony's best friends, and Peter Vanderbilt, the cynical and fearless New Yorker, and Greve and Smith, and four hundred others.

The arrivals on Bronson Beta could rouse no answer to their radio signals. They were forced into the awful realization that of all humanity they alone survived. They were alone on an unknown world where a nameless and dead race had once built cities—on a world which had been drifting through the absolute zero of space for nameless millenia. They faced the probem of survival. Responsibility for the future of the species was theirs.

Resolutely, they turned to their prodigious task.

CHAPTER I

THE FIRST DAY ON THE NEW PLANET

ELIOT JAMES sat at a metal desk inside the space ship which had conveyed a few score human beings from the doomed earth to safety on the sun's new planet Bronson Beta. In front of Eliot James was his already immemorial diary, and over it he poised a fountain pen.

He had written several paragraphs:

"*April*—what shall I call it? Is it the 2nd day of April, or is it the first? Have we, the last survivors of the earth, landed upon our new planet on All Fools Day? That would be ironic, and yet trivial in the face of all that has happened. But as I meditate on the date, I am in doubt about how to express time in my diary.

"The earth is gone—smashed to fragments; and the companion of its destroying angel, upon which our band of one hundred and three Argonauts holds so brief and hazardous a residence, is still without names, seasons and months. But April has vanished with the earth; and for all I know, spring, winter, summer and fall may also be absent in the new world.

"I have pledged myself to write in this diary every day, as Hendron assures me there will be no other record of our adventures here until we have become well enough established to permit the compilation of a formal history. And yet it is with the most profound difficulty that I compel myself to set down words on this, man's first morning in his new home.

"What shall I say?

"That question in truth must be read by the future generations as a cry at once of ecstasy and despair. Ecstasy because even while the heavens fell upon them, my companions remained firm and courageous—because in the face of earthquakes, tornadoes, bloody battles and the unimaginable holocaust of Destruction Day itself, they not only preserved whatever claims the race of man may have to majesty, but by their ingenuity they escaped from the earth to this new planet, which has invaded and attached itself to our solar system.

"And I am in despair not only because, so far as we can tell, all but one hundred and three members of the human race have perished, not only because my friends, my home, the cities that were familiar to me, the trees and flowers I knew, the rivers and the oceans, the scent of the wind and the accustomed aspects of the sky have forevermore disappeared from the universe, and not only because I am incapable of setting down the emotions to which those cosmic calamities give rise, but for another reason: as vast, as stirring, as overwhelming to the mind as those foregoing, the responsibility for half a billion years of evolution which terminated in man rests upon myself and one hundred and two others.

"They stand there in the sunshine under the strange sky on our brown earth—forty-three men, fifty-seven women, two children. They have been singing—a medley of songs which under other circumstances might seem irrelevant. Many of them are foreigners and do not know the words, but they also sing—with tears streaming down their faces and a catch in their voices. They sang 'The Processional' and they sang 'Nearer, My God, to Thee.' After that they sang 'Hail, Hail, the Gang's All Here.' Then they sang 'The Marseillaise' with Duquesne leading—leading and bellowing the words, and weeping.

"What a spectacle! Beside it, the picture of Leif Ericsson or Columbus reaching green shores at last is dimmed to insignificance. For those ancient explorers found the path to a mere continent, while this band has blazed a trail of fire through space to a new planet.

"Cole Hendron is there, his magnificent head thrown back, and his face grave under its thatch of newly whitened hair. No doubt replicas of Hendron's head will be handed down through the ages, if ages are to follow us. His daughter Eve has been near him, and near to Tony Drake. In young Drake one sees the essence of the change which has taken place in all the members of our company. The fashionable, gay-hearted New Yorker is greatly changed. So many times in the past two years has he resigned himself to death, and so many times has he escaped from it only through courage, audacity and good fortune, that he seems superior to death. His face is no longer precisely young, and it contains, side by side, elements of the stoniest inflexibility and the most willing unselfishness. I have no doubt that if this colony survives, when the time comes to bury our leader and our hero,—the incomparable Cole Hendron,—it will be Drake who supersedes him in command. For by that day I am sure the great person in that young man will have availed itself of all our technical knowledge as a mere corollary of his remarkable character.

"And now,"—the pen wavered,—"to what I imagine whimsically as the new future readers of my notes, I make an apology. This is our first day on Bronson Beta. My impatience has exhausted my conscience. I must lay down my pen, leave the remarkable ship wherein I write, and go out upon the face of this earth untrod by man. I can restrain myself no longer."

Eliot James stepped to the gangplank that had been laid down from the Ark. The earth around the huge metal cylinder had been melted by the blasts of its atomic propulsion-jets. But now it was cool again. A space of two or three hundred yards lay between the Ark and the cliff which beetled over the unknown sea. In that space were the planetary pilgrims. They had stopped singing. Half of them stood on the top of the precipice regarding the waters that rolled in from a nameless horizon. The others were distributed over the landscape. With a smile James noted the botanist, Higgins, leaping from rock to rock, his pockets and his hands full of specimens of ferns and mosses which he had collected. Every few seconds his eye lighted upon a new species of vegetation, and he knelt to gather it. But his greediness resulted invariably in the spilling of specimens already collected, and the result was that he continued hopping about, dropping things and picking them up, with all the energy and disorganization of a distracted bird.

James walked down the gangplank and joined Tony, Eve and Cole Hendron.

The leader of the expedition nodded to the writer. "You certainly are a persistant fellow, James. Some day I hope to find a situation so violent and unique that it keeps you from working on your diary."

"We have been through a number of such situations," James answered.

"Nevertheless—" Hendron said. He checked himself. Several of the people on the edge of the cliff had turned toward the Ark and were marching toward him.

"Hendron!" they hailed him again. "Hendron! Cole Hendron!"

Their hysteria had not yet cleared away; they remained in the emotional excitement of the earth-cataclysm they had escaped but witnessed, and of the incomparable adventure of their flight.

"Hendron! Hendron! What do you want us now to do?" they demanded; for their discipline, too, yet clung to them—the stern, uncompromising discipline demanded of them during the preparation of the Ship of Escape, the discipline of the League of the Last Days.

Too, the amazements of this new place paralyzed them; and for that they were not to be blamed. The wonder was that they had survived, as well, the emotional shocks; so they surrounded again their leader, who throughout had seen farther ahead and more clearly than them all; and who, through Doomsday itself, had never failed them.

Hendron stepped upon an outcrop of stone, and smiled down at them. "I have made too many speeches," he said. "And this morning is scarcely a suitable hour for further thanksgiving. It may be proper and pleasant, later, to devote such a day as the Pilgrims, from one side of our earth to another, did;

but like them, it is better to wait until we feel ourselves more securely installed. When such a time arrives, I will appoint an official day, and we shall hope to observe it each year."

He cast his eyes over the throng and continued: "I don't know at the moment how to express my thoughts. While I am not myself a believer in a personal God, it seems evident to me in this hour that there was a purpose in the invention of man. Otherwise it is difficult to understand why we were permitted to survive. Whether you as individuals consider that survival the work of a God, or merely an indication that we had reached a plane of sufficient fitness to preserve ourselves, is of small moment to me now. And since I know all of you so well, I feel it unnecessary to say that in the days ahead lies a necessity for a prodigious amount of work.

"Your tempers and intelligences will be tried sorely by the new order which must exist. Our first duty will be to provide ourselves with suitable homes, and with a source of food and clothing. Our next duty will be to arrange for the gathering of the basic materials of the technical side of our civilization-to-be. In all your minds, I know, lies the problem of perpetuating our kind. We have, partly through accident, a larger number of women than men. I wish to discontinue the use of the word *morality;* but what I must insist on calling our biological continuum will be the subject of a very present discussion.

"In all your minds, too, is a burning interest in the nature and features of this new planet. We have already observed through our telescopes that it once contained cities. To study those cities will be an early undertaking. While there is little hope that others who attempted the flight to this planet have escaped disaster, radio listening must be maintained. Moreover, the existence of living material on this planet gives rise to a variety of possibilities. Some of the flora which has sprung up may be poisonous, even dangerous, to human life. What forms it will take and what novelties it will produce, we must ascertain as soon as possible. I think we are safe in believing that no form of animal life can have existed here, whether benign or perilous; but we cannot ignore the possibility that the plant life may be dangerous. I will set no tasks for this day,—it shall be one of rest and rejoicing,—except that I will delegate listeners for radio messages, and cooks to prepare food for us. To-morrow, and I use an Americanism which will become our watchword, we will all 'get busy.' "

There was a pause, then cheering. Cole Hendron stepped down from the stone. Eve turned to Tony and took his arm. "I am glad we don't have to work today."

"No," said Tony. "Your father knows better. He realizes that, in our reaction, we could accomplish nothing. It is the time for us to attempt to relax."

"Can you relax, Tony?"

"No," he confessed, "and I don't want even to attempt to; but neither do I want to apply myself to anything. Do you?"

Eve shook her head. "I can't. My mind flies in a thousand different directions simultaneously, it seems. Where are those cities which, from the world—our ended world, Tony—our telescopes showed us here? What remains may we find of their people? Of their goods and their gods and their machines? . . . What, when they found themselves being torn away from their sun, did they do? . . . That monument beside the road that we found, Tony—what was it? What did it mean? . . . Then I think of myself. Am I, Tony, to have children—here?"

Tony tightened his clasp upon her arm. Through all the terrors and triumphs, through all their consternations and amazements, instincts, he found, survived. "We will not speak of such things now," he said. "We will satisfy the more immediate needs, such as food—deviled eggs and sandwiches; and coffee! As if we were on earth, Eve. For once more we are on earth—this strange, strange earth. But we have brought our identical bodies with us."

"Sardines!" Duquesne said. He patted his vast expanse of abdomen—an abdomen which in his native land he had often maintained, and was frequently to assert with pride on Bronson Beta, consisted not of fat but of superior muscle. Indeed, although Duquesne was short of stature and some fifty years of age, he often demonstrated that he was possessed not only of unquenchable nervous energy, but of great physical strength and endurance. "Sardines!" He rolled his eyes at half a dozen women and several of the men who were standing near him. He took another bite of the sandwich in his hand.

Eve giggled and said privately to Tony: "All this expedition needed to make it complete was a comedian."

Tony grinned as he too bit a crescent in a sandwich. "A comedian is a great asset, and a comedian who was able even years ago to help Einstein solve equations, is quite a considerable asset."

"So many things like Duquesne's arrival have happened to us," Eve said. "Purely fortuitous accidents."

"Not all of them good."

"Who's in charge of lunch?" Eve asked a moment later.

Tony chuckled. "Who but Kyto? He, and an astronomer, and a mechanical engineer, and a woman who is a plant biologist like Higgins, are all working in happy harmony. Kyto seems to understand exactly what has taken place. In fact, there are moments when I think he is a high-born person. I had a friend once who had a Japanese servant like Kyto, who after seven years of service resigned. When my friend asked him what he was going to do, the Japanese informed him that he had been offered the chair of Behavioristic Psychology at a Middle Western university. He had been going to Columbia at night for years. Sometimes I think Kyto may be like that."

Eve did not make any response at the moment, because Duquesne was again talking in his loud bombastic voice. He had attracted the attention of Cole Hendron and of several others, including Dr. Dodson.

Dodson's presence on the Ark was due to the courage of a girl named Shirley Cotton. On the night of the gory raid on Hendron's encampment, Dodson had been given up for dead by Tony. The great surgeon's last gesture, in fact, had been to wave to Tony to carry his still living human burden to safety. However, before the Ark rose to sear and slay the savage hordes of marauders, Shirley Cotton had found the dying man. In the space of a few moments she had put a turniquet around his arm, partly stanched a deep abdominal wound, and dragged him to a cellar in the machine-shop, intending to hide him there. It saved both their lives, for soon afterward the whole region was deluged by the atomic blast of the Ark as it rose and methodically obliterated the attackers of the camp.

Dodson had recovered, but he had lost one arm. As Tony was Hendron's chief in the direction of physical activities, Dodson became his creator of policies. He listened now to Duquesne.

"A picnic in the summer-time on Bronson Beta, children," Duquesne boomed. "And it is summer-time, you know. Fortunately, but inevitably from the nature of events, still summer. My observations of the collision check quite accurately with my calculations of what would happen; and if the deductions I made from those calculations are correct, quite extraordinary things will happen." He glanced at Hendron.

The leader of the expedition frowned faintly, as if Duquesne were going to say something he did not wish to have expressed. Then he shrugged.

"You might as well say it. You might as well tell them, I suppose. I wasn't going to describe our calculations until they had been thoroughly checked."

Duquesne shook his head backward and forward pontifically. "I might as well tell them, because already they are asking." He addressed those within earshot. "We will have a little class in astronomy." He put to use two resources—the smooth vertical surface of a large stone, and a smaller stone which he had picked up to scratch upon the bowlder.

As Duquesne began to talk, all the members of the group gathered around the flat bowlder to watch and listen.

"First," he began, "I will draw the solar system as it was." He made a small circle and shaded it in. "Here, my friends, is the sun." He circumscribed it with another circle and said: "Mercury." Outside the orbit of Mercury he drew the orbits respectively of Venus, Earth and Mars. He looked at the drawing with beaming satisfaction, and then at his listeners. "So this is what we had had. This is where we have been. Now. I draw the same thing without the Earth."

He repeated the diagram—this time with three concentric circles instead of four. A broad gap was left where the earth's orbit had been. Again he stepped away from the diagram and looked at it proudly. "So—Mercury we have; Venus we have; and Mars we have. The Earth we do not have. Bear in mind, my children, that these circles I have drawn are not exactly circles. They are ellipses. But they vary only slightly from circles. Mr. Cole Hendron's associates will give you, I do not doubt, very fine maps. This rock-scratching of mine is but a child's crude diagram. I proceed. I set down next the present position of this world on which we stand—Bronson Beta."

Every one watched intently while he drew an ellipse which, on one side, came close to the orbit of Venus, and on the other approached the circle made by the planet Mars on its journey around the sun.

"Here is our path, closer to the sun than the Earth has been; and also farther away. The hottest portion of this new path of this new planet about the sun already had been passed when we fled here. This world had made its closest approach in rounding the sun, and it had reached the point in its orbit which our earth had reached in April. Now we are going away from the sun, but on such a path that—and under such conditions that—only slowly will the days grow colder."

"They will become, when we get out on that portion of our path near Mars," a man among his hearers questioned, "how cold?"

Duquesne called upon his comic knack to turn this question. He shivered so grotesquely that the audience laughed. "The most immediately interesting feature of our strange situation will be, my friends, the amazing character of our days. Many of you have been told of that; so I ask you. Who will answer? Hands, please!" He pretended to be teaching a class of children. "How long will be our days?"

They nearly all laughed; and several raised their hands. "You, Mr. Tony Drake. You, I know, have become like so many others a splendid student of astronomy. How long will be our days?"

"Fifty hours, approximately," replied Tony.

"Excellent! For what determines the length of the day? Of course it is the time which the planet takes to turn upon its own axis. It has nothing whatever to do with the sun, or the path about the sun; it is a peculiarity of the planet itself, and inherent in it from the forces which created it at its birth. Bronson Beta happens to be rotating on its axis in approximately fifty hours, so our days—and our nights—will be a trifle more than twice as long as those to which we have become accustomed. Now—hands again—how long will our year be? Let one of the ladies speak this time!"

"Four hundred and twenty-eight days!" a girl's voice said. Her name was Mildred Pope.

"Correct," applauded Duquesne, "if you speak in terms of the days of our perished planet. It will take four hundred and twenty-eight of our old days for Bronson Beta"—Duquesne, not without some satisfaction, stamped upon it—"to circle the sun; but of the longer days with which we are now endowed, the circuit will consume only two hundred and five and a fraction. It tears up our old calendars, doesn't it? We start out, among many other adventures, with new calculations of time. So we will rotate in some fifty hours, and swing in toward Venus and out toward Mars, in our great elliptical orbit, making a circuit of the sun in four hundred and twenty-eight of our old days—which will live now only in our memories—or two hundred and five of our new days. Around and about, in and out, we will go—let us hope, forever."

His audience was silent. Duquesne let them study his sketches on his natural blackboard before he observed: "A few obvious consequences will at once occur to you."

Higgins, who had dropped his plants while he listened, gave his impromptu answer like a grade boy in a classroom: "Of course: our summers will be very hot, and our winters will be very cold and very long."

Duquesne nodded. "Quite so. But there is one fortunately favorable feature. What chiefly determined the seasons on the old earth," he reminded, "was the inclination of the earth upon its axis. If Bronson Beta had a similar or a greater inclination in reference to the plane of its orbit around the sun, all effects would be exaggerated. But we find actually less inclination here. Whether that may be a favorable feature 'provided' for us by some Power watching over this singularly fortunate party, or whether it is one of innumerable accidents of creation which have no real causative connection with our destinies, the fact remains: The equinoxes on Bronson Beta will not march back and forth on the northern and southern hemispheres with such great changes in temperatures. Instead, as we round the sun at its focus."—he pointed with his chubby finger,—"there will be many, many long hot days. Perhaps our equator at that time will not be habitable. And later, as we round the imaginary focus out here in space so near to the orbit of Mars, it may be very cold indeed, and perhaps then only the equator will be comfortable. So we may migrate four times a year.

From the Paris of our new world to its Nice—I mean to say, from the New York City to its Miami. Does one think of anything else?"

Hendron was looking tentatively from one face to the next of his Argonauts. He had been reasonably sure that Bronson Beta would travel in the ellipse Duquesne had described; and from the behavior of the celestial bodies at the time of the collision, he had formed his calculations; but he had not wanted to worry them with thoughts of excessive heat and extreme cold in their new home, and he had enjoined the other mathematicians, astronomers and astrophysicists to say nothing. He was pleased with the reaction of the people. There was no fear in their faces, no dismay. Only a great interest.

The silence was broken by a question from Dodson: "How close will we come to Venus and Mars?"

Duquesne shrugged. Eve turned to Dodson and said: "If my figures are right, it will be three million miles at periods many, many years apart. Three million miles from Mars, and at the most favorable occasion about four from Venus."

Dodson's eyebrows lifted. "Is that dangerous?"

Eve shook her head. "The perturbations of all three planets will, of course, be great. But as far as danger of collision is concerned, there is none."

The group was thoughtful.

"There will be a great opportunity," Dodson said slowly, "to study those two planets at close range. We must build a good telescope."

"Telescope!" The word burst from Duquesne. His eyes traveled over the members of the group standing in front of him to the tall, shining cylinder of the Space Ship. There they remained; and slowly, one by one, the people turned to look at the Ark which had carried them from Earth to Bronson Beta. They realized the meaning of Duquesne's steady gaze. There would be an opportunity in the future not only to study Venus and Mars at close range—but to voyage to them.

Duquesne dropped the stone with which he had been drawing, and stepped away from his diagram.

Eliot James walked over to Tony and Eve. "That is something I didn't think of," he murmured. "Something I didn't think of. Stupendous! Colossal!"

Eve smiled. "Father and I thought of it independently a long time ago. It will make your journey around the United States after the first passing seem pretty trifling."

James shook his head in agreement. "I'd want Vanderbilt with me again if I went on such a trip. And Ransdell." Abruptly he stopped. Vanderbilt and Ransdell had been lost on the other Space Ship. James flushed, as he looked at Eve. "I'm sorry, Eve. For an instant I forgot."

"It's all right." She took Tony's arm. "I want to go over and look at the ocean. It's a funny thing—looking at the ocean. Every time I stared out to sea on earth, I always expected to see a shark's fin, or a big turtle, or a jellyfish, or a sail, or the smoke of a steamship; and I keep looking for such things on this one. And yet there can be nothing. Nothing at all." Her eyes traveled the expanse of ocean, and then she sighed. "Let's take a walk."

"Let's go back and look at that road in daylight."

Eve started. "We've left it all this time! Did you tell Father about it?"

"Not yet."

They went over to Cole Hendron. "Last night," Tony said, "Eve and I were out walking, and we found a road."

Ten minutes later every one was gathered around the highway. It was made of a metal-like substance. It ran to the bluff along the sea and then turned south. Except for that single curve—a graded curve, which suggested that the vehicles that once traveled the road moved very swiftly, there was no other turn. In the opposite direction it drove straight toward the dim and distant hills. Its surface was very smooth. As the Argonauts had gathered around Duquesne's natural lecture-platform, so they now gathered around the metal monument Tony and Eve had seen in match-light on the previous evening. Way was made for Bagsley, the paleontologist. He bent over and looked up with a curious smile.

"That isn't a job for me." His eyes were fastened on the inscription the metal slab bore. "You see, this is such a thing as might be found in the future of our earth, but not in the past. No ancient civilization in our world could make a road such as this, or use metal so skillfully."

"How about the writing?" some one asked.

Bagsley replied: "It's beautiful, isn't it? I wonder if we won't find that the curves in all those letters are mathematically perfect? That is, if they are letters. But I couldn't give you the faintest notion of what it says. It is not remotely related to Sanskrit, or Chinese, or Mayan, or cuneiform, or hieroglyphics, or runes; and it is equally remote from any modern writing."

Duquesne was taking again. "Anyway," he said, "whoever lived here had a language to write, and eyes to read it. They had roads to travel and vehicles to go upon them. So they had places to go and to come from. The cities we saw, or thought we saw, must have been real. My friends, great as our adventures have been, there lie ahead adventures infinitely more astounding."

In the face of so many necessities and so many unknown possibilities, any normal person would have lacked adequate judgment to do the right things in the right order. The colonists of Bronson Beta succeeded in a logical procedure because they had been chosen from a multitude of human beings better than normal.

On the first day of their sojourn they had rested.

On the evening of that day Bronson Beta had exhibited another phenomenon. Soon after dark, when more than half the members of the colony had gone to sleep from fatitgue, a colossal meteor blazed across the sky and disappeared over the edge of the sea. It passed so close to the place where the Ark rested, that they had been able to hear a soft roar from it. It left a blaze upon the sky—a livid pathway of greenish-white fire which faded slowly. It was followed by another smaller meteor, and then half a dozen.

During the ensuing two hours countless thousands of meteors hurtled across the atmosphere of Bronson Beta in the vicinity of the Ark, and many of them fell to earth within the visual range of that spot.

Tony and Eve were outside when the aërolites commenced to fall. At first they were spellbound by the majesty of the spectacle, but when a great hurtling mass of molten material splashed into the sea less than a mile offshore and set the ocean boiling all around, so that clouds of hot steam drifted over it, they became alarmed. Hendron and Duquesne were alseep, but there were twenty-five or thirty people outdoors.

In the afternoon of that day Tony had made his way some distance down the coast, and he had found a precipice carved by an ancient ocean from living rock. At its base were shallow cave-like openings, and above it three or four hundred feet of solid stone.

When several of the great masses of material had hit the earth so hard that it trembled beneath their feet, Tony quickly commanded the little knot of people who were standing together, watching the spurts of fire across the sky, to go to these holes in the rock wall. They started, with Eve leading the way. Tony then entered the Ark and woke Hendron, whom he found lying on the padded floor in sound, exhausted slumber.

Hendron sat up. "What is it?"

So effective was the insulation of the ship that the fall of meteors was not perceptible on its interior.

"Meteors," Tony answered. "Three of them have landed within a mile of here in the last few minutes. Big ones. Any one of them would annihilate this ship if it hit it. There were about thirty people outdoors. I sent them up the coast to some shallow caves at the foot of a basalt cliff. I thought it was safer there."

As he said the last words, he was following Hendron down the spiral staircase. They debouched on the gangplank; and as they did so, a dazzling, dancing illumination and a crescendo roar announced the fall of another meteor. It hit on the brink of the cliff overlooking the sea some distance down the coast. A million bright, hot particles splashed over the barren landscape, and an avalanche of melted metal crashed into the ocean. Hendron looked up at the sky, and saw a dozen more of these spectacular missiles pursuing each other. He turned instantly to Tony. "If one of those things hit the cliff where you sent the people, would it knock the cliff down?"

"I don't know. It's safer than the Ark, anyway."

"Right." Hendron rushed up the stairs, followed by Tony.

"How about the animals? Should we try to get them out?"

The living creatures—mammals, birds, insects—had been tended and fed but not yet moved. Where, outside, could they yet be established?

"The animals," said Tony, "will have to take their chances here."

But Hendron and he awakened all the pilgrims who had been asleep. They were commencing to leave the Ark in an orderly but fast-moving line. Hendron was at the door of the Ark, and as the people emerged, he divided them into groups of five, and sent each group running in a different direction, thus dispersing over a wide area those of the colonists who were not hiding under the rim of the cliff.

The number of the astrolites increased with every passing minute, until the sky seemed full of them. The terrain was as brightly illuminated as by daylight; and from the gangplank Tony could see the little bands scurrying in their appointed directions.

When they had all emerged, Hendron said to Tony shortly: "You go to the cliff and disperse the people there. I'll stay here with the last five."

The air was filled with parched, hot odors and clouds of steam. In the distance, around the craters made where the meteors had struck earth, there was a red glow. Half an hour passed. The pyrotechnics stopped. During that half-hour Cole Hendron had been busy in the upper control-room of the Ark with two electrical engineers; and when after five or ten minutes of normal darkness, interrupted only by spurts of the soft multi-colored aurora which frequently flickered on Bronson Beta, a few of the groups of five began to return to the Ark, they were halted by Cole Hendron's voice—a voice broadcast from the Ark by a mighty loud-speaker. It carried distinctly for a distance of two or three miles—a distance much greater than that which separated any of the bands.

"You will stay where you are," Hendron's voice commanded, "in groups of five for the remainder of the night. Try to sleep, if possible, but keep a long distance from the party nearest to you. I will summon you when the time comes."

Tony had rejoined Eve in a group of five along the base of the precipice. Eliot James was in that group, and two women—one of them Shirley Cotton, who was already a prominent person among the hundred and one odd people who had been prominent on earth. The two men and the three women slept fitfully on the hard earth that night; and in the morning with the first rays of dawn, Hendron's voice summoned every one together again.

No more meteors had fallen after the shower had ended. The human beings who trekked back over the bare landscape to the Ark were a little more grave than they had been on the previous day. Once again the frailness of their hold upon their new home had been made plain. Once again they had been reminded of the grim necessities by which they would have to live. For in order to insure that some of them, at least, would be safe, they had been compelled on a moment's notice to desert all that they had brought with them from the earth, and run like dislodged insects into the night, into hiding.

All of them, because of their weariness, and in spite of the hard ground, had slept. Most of the bands had kept one member awake in turn as a watchman. Since the night on Bronson Beta was longer than the night on earth, they had used the additional time for rest. Hendron first summoned them by calling on the loud-speaker; and then, for those who had marched out of sight of the Ark, he gave an auditory landmark by broadcasting over the powerful loud-speaker a series of phonograph musical records. The men and women in clothes now earth-stained, the former not shaven, and the latter not made up, straggled to the Ark to the music of "The Hymn to the Sun" and of Schubert's "Unfinished Symphony."

They answered a roll-call. No one had been harmed. The Ark was unscathed. They sat down to breakfast.

Hendron explained the unexpected dilemma of the previous night. "Unless I am greatly mistaken, our new planet passed through a cluster or path of fragments of the moon, destroyed, as you know, months ago. They would find orbits of their own about the sun; and we have approached again an area where we might encounter fragments of any size. I believe that the meteors which fell last night were débris from the moon—débris scattered and hurled into space by that cosmic collision.

"In the future we will probably be able to chart the position of such fragments, so that we will know when we are coming within range of them. It is my opinion that the phenomenon was more or less local here, that we attracted to our surface a unified group of fragments scattered along a curve coinciding with our orbit, so that they dropped virtually in one place.

"I regret that the night which I had planned should be so

peaceful for all was so profoundly disturbed. You are courageous. I would like to extend our period of rest to include this, our second day, on Bronson Beta. But so divergent and so pressing are the necessities of our work here, that I cannot do so. We will start immediately after breakfast to construct a cantonment which will be adequate at least temporarily."

CHAPTER II

CIVILIZATION RECOMMENCES

SUCH isolation, such solitude, such courage in the face of the unknown never before existed. One hundred and three people ate their breakfast—one hundred and three people laughing, talking, saluting each other, staring often at the ocean and the greenish sky, and still more often at the shining cylinder standing on end in their midst.

Cole Hendron walked over to Tony and Eliot James and his daughter, who were breakfasting together.

"Right after breakfast," he said, "I want you, together with Higgins, to start prospecting for farm lands."

Tony nodded. Two years before, the assignment would have appalled him. He would not have known whether beets were planted an inch under the surface of the soil or three feet, and whether one planted tubers or seeds; but he had been for a long time in charge of the farm in Michigan, and he was now well equipped for the undertaking.

"Bring back soil-samples. You understand the nature of the terrain which will be required—level and free from stones. It may be that you will find nothing in the vicinity that will be adequate; and if that is true we will consider moving the Ark. It is still good for a few hundred miles, I guess."

Eliot James grinned. "Or a few hundred million? Which?"

To the surprise of all three, Cole Hendron did not respond with a smile. Instead he said simply: "I'd risk taking it up if we had to move in order to find a suitable place to raise food."

Tony understood that the leader of the expedition was entirely serious, and said with sudden intensity: "What's the matter with the Ark?"

"In the laboratory tests," the gray-haired man answered, "and in the smaller furnaces and engines we designed, Dave Ransdell's metal did not fuse or melt. But under the atomic blast, as we came through space, it commenced to erode. About eighteen hours after we had started, we went off our course because, as I discovered, the lining of one of the outside stern jets was wearing out more rapidly than the others. I used one of the right-angle tubes to reëstablish our direction, and I made some effort to measure the rate of dissipation of Ransdell's metal. I couldn't be very accurate, since I could not turn off the jets, but I was not at all certain that the material would stand the strain until we had reached the point where we started falling on Bronson Beta."

"You mean to say," Eliot James exclaimed, "that we barely got here?"

Cole Hendron smiled, and yet his face was sober. "It turned out that we had a little margin. I examined the tubes yesterday, and I dare say we could use them for a trip of another five hundred miles. But at both ends of the ship our insulation is nearly gone. We could not, for example, circumnavigate this globe."

The writer looked depressed. "I had imagined," he said, "that we would be able to cruise at will on the surface of the planet from now on."

Hendron turned his face toward the ship, which represented the masterpiece of his life of engineering achievements. He regarded it almost sadly. "We won't be able to do that. In any case we would move her over the surface of the planet only to find good farm land, because we've got to take her to pieces."

"To pieces!"

Hendron assented. "We designed her for that very purpose. Those layer sections on the inside wall will be taken down, one by one, and set up again on the ground. The top section will be made into a radio station, so that we can make accurate measurements of our orbit and also study meteorological conditions. The next section below that will be a chemistry laboratory. The one below that will be a hospital, if we need it. The next three will be store-rooms, and we will turn the last section into a machine-shop. The steel on the outside hull will be our mineral source for the time being, and out of it we will make the things we need until it is exhausted."

His eyes twinkled. "I had anticipated we might have a great deal of trouble in finding a source of iron ore and in mining it, but I dare say that some of the meteorites which fell here last night will not have buried themselves very deeply, so that we may have many tons of first-rate metal at our disposal when we need it."

"An ill wind," Eliot James said. "Still, I hate to think of the Ark being torn down. I had imagined we would go hunting for the others in it."

Tony spoke. "I'd been thinking about that. It seems to me that if anybody had reached here, we would have heard some kind of signal from them by now."

"I agree with you," said Hendron.

"And when I thought about looking for them, it seemed darned difficult. After all, Bronson Beta has an area of more than five hundred million square kilometers, and any one of those five hundred million would be big enough to hide a ship like the Ark. Besides, we don't even know where the land is, except in a general way."

"I've got maps made for telescopic photographs," Eve said, "but they're not very good. Bronson Beta was mighty hard to observe—first with its atmosphere thawing, then its water. You could get a peek through the perpetual clouds at a little chunk of water or a small area of land now and again, but all the photographs I collected don't give a very good idea of its geography." She reached in her pocket and took out a piece of paper. "Here is a rough sketch I made of the East and West hemisphere; it isn't very good cartography, but it will give you some idea of what little we do know of the planet's surface."

They bent over the map for a few moments. Hendron said: "It would be like looking for a haystack on a continent, so that you could look for a needle in the haystack when you found it."

"And besides," Tony continued, "you might go over the place, where the people you were looking for were, at night, and in that case your jets would completely annihilate them."

Cole Hendron's face showed amazement. Then he said:

"By George, Tony, you're quite right! And do you know that although I spent a lot of time thinking about looking for other human beings here, and although I originally considered we would probably make long excursions in the Ark until I realized it would be more sensible to take it down at once, it never occurred to me for an instant that our jets would be dangerous to anybody underneath, even in spite of the fact that I used it to wipe out that army of hoodlums that attacked us. It just goes to show what you may omit when you think. Still, I am of the opinion that we arrived here alone out of all the expeditions. If our crops fail us entirely because of too much heat, or because it gets cold too soon, or for reasons we cannot anticipate now—" He paused.

"Twenty-five or thirty of us might get through the winter on the provisions I've brought. But all of us couldn't."

With the injection of that grim thought into their breakfast conversation, the meal was brought to an end.

"It therefore behooves me," Tony said, "to look for farm lands, and get some sort of crops in."

Half an hour later Tony started out with Higgins. Tony carried a knapsack in which there was food enough for two days for both of them. He also carried a pair of blankets and a revolver. He had objected to the revolver, as it had been his wish to appear in complete possession of himself. Reason argued that there would be no phenomenon on the new planet which might make firearms useful, but imagination made the possession of a gun a great comfort, and Hendron had insisted he take it.

As the two men started, the sound of hammering was already audible inside the Ark, and most of the members of the company were engaged in useful work.

A few watched their start. Tony reached into his pocket and took out a quarter. "I've carried this from Earth," he said to

Higgins, "for just such emergencies. Heads we go inland; tails we go along the coast."

The coin landed with the eagle up. Tony flipped it again, saying as it spun in the air: "Heads we go north, tails we go south." Again the eagle. Tony pointed toward the coastline and said: "Forward."

The people who were seeing them off waved and called: "Good luck!"

"You'll have to abandon your botanical pursuits, I'm afraid," Tony said to the elderly scientist. "I usually hit a pretty fast pace. If I go too fast, let me know."

"Very well," Higgins said, and he chuckled dryly. "But I'd like to tell you, young man, that I've spent three sabbatical years climbing mountains in Tibet and Switzerland and the Canadian Northwest, and I dare say I'll be able to keep up with you."

Tony glanced at the scrawny, pedagogical little man at his side, and once more he felt almost reverent toward Hendron. Who would have thought that this student of plants, this desiccated college professor, was also a mountain-climber? Yet, since a plant biologist of the highest capabilities was essential to the company of the Ark, how much better it was to take a man who not only knew his subject magnificently, but who also could scale rugged peaks!

For an hour they walked along the bluff that faced the sea—a continuation of the landscape upon which the Ark had landed. It was rocky and barren, except for such ferns and mosses as they had already observed. Of dead vegetation there seemed to be nothing which had grown as large as a tree or indeed even a bush. The whole area appeared to have been what on earth would have been called a moor—though Higgins could recall no earthly moor of this character or evident extent. The ground inland was a plateau ranged with low hills, and in the remote distance the tops of a mountain-range could be seen.

At the end of an hour they saw ahead of them an arm of hills that ran at right angles down to the ocean and extended out in a long rocky promontory. At the foot of the promontory was a cove, and in the cove were beaches. They climbed to the highest near-by elevation and surveyed the arid, rock-strewn plateau.

"I don't believe," said Tony, "that there is any farm land in this area."

Higgins shook his head. "I think if we can find a place to get down over the cliff to the edge, we can go around that point at water level."

They continued along a little way, and presently Higgins pointed to a "chimney" in the precipice. He looked at Tony with a twinkle in his eyes. "How about it?"

Tony stared into the narrow slit in the rock. It was almost perpendicular, and only the smallest cracks and outcroppings afforded footholds and handholds. He was on the point of suggesting that they find a more suitable place to descend, when he realized that the older man was laughing at him.

Tony set his jaw. "Fine!"

Higgins started down the chimney. He had not let himself over the edge before it was apparent that he was not only a skillful climber, but a man of considerable wiry strength.

Tony had always felt an instinctive alarm in high places, and he had no desire for the task ahead of him. Perspiration oozed from him, and his muscles quivered, as he lowered himself into position for the descent. It was ticklish, dangerous work. Two hundred feet below them lay a heap of jagged rocks, and around that the beach. Tony did not dare look down, and yet it was necessary to look for places to put his feet; and from the corner of his eye he was continually catching glimpses of the depth of the abyss below. His composure was by no means increased when the Professor below him called: "Maybe I should have gone last, because if you fall where you are now, you'll probably knock me off."

Tony said nothing. Twenty minutes later, however, he felt horizontal ground under his feet. He was standing on the beach. He was covered with perspiration; his clothes were soaked. His face was white. He looked up at the precipice which they had descended; and he said, with his best possible assumption of carelessness: "I thought that was going to be difficult. There was nothing to it."

The Professor gave him a resounding clap on the back. "My boy," he exclaimed, "you're all right! That was one of the nastiest little jobs I've ever undertaken."

There was sand under their feet now, and they slogged through it up to the end of the promontory, where the sea rolled in and broke in noisy gusts.

They walked around it. Before them was a vast valley. It stretched two miles or more to another series of hills. It disappeared inland toward the high mountains, and down its center meandered a wide, slow river.

Tony and Higgins stared at the scene and then at each other. The whole valley was covered with new, bright green, where fresh vegetation had carpeted the soil!

They ran, side by side, out upon the expanse of knee-deep verdure until they arrived, panting, at the river's edge. The water was cold and clouded. After they had regarded it, they turned their heads in unison toward the distant range; for they realized that this, the first river to be discovered on Bronson Beta, was the product of glaciers in the high mountains. Higgins stepped back from the bank a moment later, and pulled up a number of mosses and ferns, until he had cleared a little area of ground in which he began to dig with his hands. The soil was black and loamy, alluvial and rich. He beckoned Tony to look at it. They knew then that their mission had been fulfilled; for here, not more than half a dozen miles from the Ark, along the valley of this river, was as fine a farm land as could be found anywhere on the old Earth. Here too water would be available for irrigation, if no rains fell.

There were no tides on Bronson Beta to make the river brackish at its mouth. Some one in camp had already announced that the sea was salt, saltier even than the ocean on Earth. Now Tony went to the river's edge, scooped up a handful of water and tasted it. He was mindful as he did so that he might be exposing himself to an unknown spore or an unheard-of bacterium, but recklessness had so long been a part of necessary risk, that he did not heistate.

Higgins raised his eyebrows.

"Fresh," Tony said. "Fresh and cold." He unstrapped his canteen, poured out the drinking-water they had brought, and filled it with water from the river.

"We might as well go back," said Tony, "and tell them."

They collected samples of soil, then started back, side by side, avoiding the chimney by turning inland and following a gentle rise of ground over the promontory. They walked eagerly for a while, as they wished to hurry the news of their discovery to the camp; but they fell to talking, and their pace unconsciously slowed. It was not unusual that ardent conversation would occupy the colonists of Bronson Beta, for their problems were so grave, their hazards were so little understood, that they were constantly found in large or small groups, exchanging plans, suggestions, worries and ideas. Higgins was inclined, like many people of his type, to be pessimistic.

"My interest," he explained to Tony, "in finding various new forms of plant life on Bronson Beta was purely scientific. I regard their discovery as a very bad omen."

"Why?"

"Wherever ferns and mosses will grow, fungi will grow. Fungi are parasitical. The seeds we have brought from Earth have been chosen through countless generations to resist the fungi of earth. But many of them, if not all of them, will doubtless fall prey to smuts and rots and root-threads and webs, which they have never encountered before and against which they have no resistance. It would have been better if what I had always maintained to be true were a fact."

"Which was what?" Tony asked.

Higgins snorted. "I wouldn't have believed it! For years I have been teaching that the theory that spores could survive absolute zero was ridiculous. I have had some very bitter quarrels with my colleagues on the subject. In fact,"—he frowned uncomfortably,—"I fear I have abused them about it. I called Dinwiddie, who made experiments with spores kept in liquid hydrogen, a pinhead. It is unfortunate that Dinwiddie has not survived, although I can imagine nothing more detestable and odious than to have to apologize to such an egotist. Dinwiddie may have been right about one matter, but he was indubitably wrong about hundreds of other theories."

Tony grinned at this carry-over of this curious man's prejudices and attitudes. They surmounted the central ridge of the promontory and scanned the landscape. Tony's eyes lighted on a feature which was not natural, and he suddenly exclaimed: "By George, Higgins, we should have followed that road! It went south a little inland from the coast, and there it is."

Higgins grunted. "So it is! But we'd have missed that splendid little climb of ours."

They walked together to the road and stepped upon its smooth hard surface.

"It will give us a perfect highway from that valley to the Ark," Tony said jubilantly. "Let's go back a few hundred yards."

They returned along the highway to a point from which they could see its descent into the river valley, where it turned and ran west along the side of the watercourse. Having satisfied themselves that it served the valley, they turned again toward the Ark, following the road this time.

For several miles they came upon no other sign of the creatures that had lived upon the planet in the past ages—not even another of the slabs of metal neatly engraved with the unreadable writing. The road curved only when the natural topography made the problem of grading it very difficult. As a rule the Bronson Betans had preferred to cut through natural barriers or raise up a high roadbed over depressions rather than to curve their road around such obstacles.

"It looks," said Tony, "as if they built these roads for speed. They didn't like curves, and they didn't like bumps. They went through the hills and over the valleys, instead of up and down and around."

There were a few bends, however; and upon rounding one of these, they came abruptly upon an object which made both of the men scramble from the road and stand and stare silently. The object was a machine—or rather what was left of a machine. It was crushed against a pinnacle of rock at the end of one of the rare curves in the road. The very manner in which it stood against the rock wall suggested how it had arrived there: it had been one of the vehicles which the creatures of the planet drove or rode, and rounding the curve at too high a speed, it had shot off the highway and smashed head-on into the wall of stone.

The two men looked at it, then went closer and looked again.

They bent over it and touched it. They exchanged glances without speaking. The thing still glittered in the sunlight—the metal which composed it being evidently rust-proof. The predominating color of that metal was crimson, although many parts were steel blue, and some were evidently made of copper. An unidentifiable fragment lay on the ground beside it; and Tony, picking it up, found to his surprise that it was extremely light, lighter even than aluminum. The engine was twisted and mangled, as was the rest of the car. It was impossible to guess what the original shape of the vehicle had been, but it was conceivable that an expert, examining the débris, might decide what type engine had driven it.

Tony could not tell. He could see that it had not been a gasoline engine. It was not a reciprocating steam engine, or a turbine. Furthermore, it was not an atomic engine. There were wires and connections which suggested an electromotive force, but that was all. For a long time they looked at this mute record of age-old reckless driving. They could find no sign of the driver or of his clothing. Tony picked up the loose fragment of crimson, iridescent metal, and they went on down the road, for a while silent and thoughtful.

"An automobile," Higgins said at last.

"With an engine like none I have ever heard of."

"I know very little about such things. It looks like drunken driving, though."

"It must have been going frightfully fast."

"Did you see the wheels?"

"They were big."

"They didn't have pneumatic tires, just a ribbon of some yielding material around them."

"You wouldn't need rubber tires on a road as smooth as this."

"There were no people."

"Would they have been—people?"

Neither of them could answer that question. They walked quickly now and by and by in the distance they saw the summit of the Ark.

They ran to the encampment, bringing their news. . . .

Naturally the colonists were excited—even ecstatic—to know that apparently good farming land had been found within a few miles of the Ark. The value of the discovery was understood clearly by all of them. But they were human. It was the report of the strange machine wrecked by the roadside which set them ablaze with curiosity.

Even Hendron made no pretense of concealing it.

"The importance of finding the valley unquestionably outweighs your other discovery by a thousand to one. However, I share the feeling of every one else here. The minute you said you had found a vehicle, a score of questions burst into my mind. No matter how badly wrecked it is, we can certainly tell what its motive force was, and more than that, we can get some idea of the creature or creatures who operated it. We can tell from the position of its controls how big they were and how strong they were. In fact, although it had been my intention to postpone archæological research until we were more comfortably situated,"—Hendron smiled,—"I know that I, for one, cannot stay away from that machine, and I am going to let everybody who feels they would like to see it, accompany me with you to the spot at once."

An hour later nearly every one from the Ark was gathered around the machine. Bates and Maltby, who were perhaps the best engineers and mechanics among them, except Hendron, stepped out of the circle of fascinated onlookers. Behind them walked Jeremiah Post, the metallurgist of the company. These three men, together with Hendron, began painstakingly and slowly to examine the wreck. They worked without spoken comment, although occasionally one of them would point to a connection, or trace a cable with his finger; and even more frequently questioning looks and nods would be exchanged. They studied particularly the twisted and battered remnants of what had been the controls.

Finally Hendron, after a brief *sotto voce* colloquy with Post, Bates and Maltby, addressed the crowd of people, who had remained far enough away to leave room for those inspecting the discovery.

"Well, friends," he said simply, "until we have had time to take this apparatus back to camp and study it more thoroughly, we will be unable to make a complete report on it. But we four are agreed on a good many things that will interest you. In the first place, judging from the area of space for passengers and the division of that area, whoever occupied and operated this machine could not have been much larger or much smaller than ourselves. You will note,"—he walked over to the wreck and pointed,—"that although the force of the crash has collapsed this portion of the vehicle, we may assume that its operator sat here.

"I say sat, because this is manifestly a seat. The vehicle steered with a wheel which has been broken off. This is it. The braking mechanism was operated by either of two flat pedals on the floor; and on what corresponds to a dashboard there were manual controls. Whether the creatures on Bronson Beta had hands and feet like ours cannot be said. However, that they had four limbs, that they were able to sit upright, and that their upper pair of limbs terminated in members which could be used precisely as fingers are used, is very illuminating. In fact, I won't say that the builders of this very interesting and brilliant vehicle were human beings; but I *will* say that if the vehicle were intact, it could be operated by a human being."

He paused for a full minute, while a babble of conversation swept his audience.

The talking stopped, however, when he continued: "As for the machine itself, it was made very largely of beryllium. Beryllium was a very common element on earth. It is, roughly speaking, about half as heavy as aluminum, and about twice as strong as what we called duraluminum. It was rare and valuable in a pure state only because we had not as yet perfected a way of extracting beryllium cheaply. The brilliant coloring of the metal is due to the addition of chemicals during its refinement and smelting, and I think it is safe to assume that the color was added for decorative rather than for utilitarian purposes. It is interesting to remark in that connection that the metal, which was rust-proof and tarnish-proof, is very much superior to the enamel finishes which we used for similar purposes.

"The principle upon which this vehicle was propelled is obvious in the sense that we have all agreed upon what was accomplished by its engine, although further study will be necessary to reveal precisely how it was done.

"For the sake of those who are not physicists or engineers, I will explain that except for the atomic energy which we ourselves perfected, all terrestrial energy was thermal energy. In other words, it came from the sun. Oil represents the energy stored up in minute vegetation. Coal, the sunlight stored in larger plants. Water-power is derived from kinetic energy in water elevated by the sun to high places. Tidal energy may be also excepted, as it was caused by the attraction of the moon. Since we found electricity a more useful form of energy, we bent our efforts to the changing of thermal energy into electrical energy. Thus we burn coal and oil to run steam turbines, which in turn run dynamos, which generate electricity. We run other turbines by water-power, not to use their force directly, but in order again to generate electricity.

"All those systems were inefficient. The loss of energy between the water-fall and the power line, between the fire-box and the light bulb, was tremendous. It has been the dream of every physicist to develop a system whereby thermal energy could be converted directly into electrical energy. For most of you it will probably be difficult to understand more than that the engine of this vehicle of the ancient inhabitants of Bronson Beta was run by that precise method. Its machinery was capable of taking the energy of heat and turning it, in simple steps, into electricity."

Cole Hendron glanced at Duquesne and Von Beitz, who stood near the vehicle. He spoke as if to them: "A stream of superheated, ionized steam was discharged at a tremendous velocity upon a dielectric, and the induced current ran the driving motor." He turned to the others. "We must go back and go to work. As soon as we can spare the time, I will have this machine studied in complete detail." He smiled. "I'd like to do it myself, as you can all imagine, but just now planting beans is more important. One other thing before we go back to our labors: you will probably all be interested to know that the reason this car is in such a demolished condition is that it must have been able to attain a speed of at least three hundred and fifty miles an hour."

CHAPTER III

SOLITUDE

IN Eliot James' diary appears the following anecdote. It is dated Day No. 14:

"Higgins has classified most of the local flora, and in that connection an amusing thing happened.

"For the first two weeks of our stay here he hopped around like a madman, gathering specimens; and except for his expedition with Tony, it was impossible to make him do anything else. The whole group was at lunch outdoors one day when he came running in with some miserable little fragments of vegetation, yelling: 'I've got the brother of one we had on earth! Identical! Identical in every way. One of the *Pteridophyte*. Light-pressure has probably carried these spores all through space. It is the *Lycopodium Clavatum*. Found a sample with a Prothallus bearing young sporophyte, with a single sporangium and adventitious roots!'

"Even among our learned company this burst of botanical terminology caused a ripple of laughter. Hendron took the plant gravely from Higgin's hand, stared at it and said: 'It's club moss, isn't it?'

"Higgins nodded so that he nearly shook off his little goatee. 'Exactly Hendron. Precisely. Club moss. We had it on earth.'

"Hendron then turned to his comrades and said: 'Dr. Higgins has brought up a principle which I have long intended discussing with you.' He held up the plant. 'Here is an insignificant bit of vegetation, which was known on earth as club moss, and also by the three jawbreakers the eminent Doctor has pronounced. To my mind, *club moss* is a fine name. To my mind, the use of Latin as a basis for terminology of the sciences is a little silly, especially since the last vestige of Rome is now reduced literally to atoms. So I was going to suggest that for the sake of the headaches of all future generations of students, as well as for the convenience of the human race which can memorize *club moss* more readily than *Lycopodium Clavatum*, we base the nomenclature of our new sciences, and reëstablish the terminology of the old, upon English.

" 'We will have plants which belong to the genus *Moss*, the cohort *Rock Moss*, the species *Club* or *Creeping Moss;* and instead of *cohort* and *genus* we will say *class* and *type*. The main artery in the arm will not be known as the axilliary, brachial and radial, hereafter, depending upon just what part of the artery is meant, but it will be known as the main artery in the arm at the armpit, the elbow and the wrist. Of course, I speak carelessly now, and our simplification will have to be made so that no name-value is lost. But since we are going to be a strictly scientific civilization, I see no reason why science should remain esoteric; and I wish as much effort would be made to use familiar terms for our scientific facts and features as will be made to introduce scientific terms into common speech.'

"Higgins stood before Henderson, crestfallen, amazed. 'It couldn't be,' he said suddenly, almost tearfully. 'Why, I've spent years acquiring my technical vocabulary!'

"Hendron nodded. 'And you call a skunk—*Mephitis Mephitica?*'

"Higgins said: 'Quite so.'

" 'And what does *Mephitis Mephitica* mean?'

"Higgins flushed. 'It means something like—a—er—smelliest of the smelly.'

"Everybody giggled. Hendron, however, was serious. 'Quite so. Now, I think *skunk* is a better name than *the smelliest of the smelly,* so if we find any skunks on Bronson Beta—a discovery I seriously doubt,—we will call them not *Mephitis Mephitica,* but just plain skunks. And in our classrooms we will teach the fact that they are nocturnal, burrowing meat-eaters, but we will ignore the *Mephitis Mephitica.*'

"Higgins shook his head sadly. 'It will mean the reorganization of all science. It will mean beginning at the bottom. It will be tragic. I suppose, my dear Hendron, that you will forget the *Laminariæ* and the *Fuci,* and call their ash *kelp.*'

"Hendron nodded again. 'I shall certainly have different names from *Laminariæ* for them, but whether we shall call their ashes *kelp* or not, is for the simplifier to say. Maybe we could just call them *seaweed ashes* and let it go at that.'

"But perhaps my penchant for summarizing at anniversaries should be given a little chance to function. We have been here two weeks. We have been working furiously.

"Great cranes surmount the top of the Ark. Already the uppermost layer has been removed and reassembled on the ground. Our settlement looks like a shipbuilding yard, but I think all our hearts are heavy with the knowledge that we are not building, but wrecking our ship. We have cut off escape to anywhere else. We have committed ourselves to life here.

"The peril of the planets in the sky on Earth, and the last tribulations of civilization, were great nervous driving forces in the days before the destruction. Those stimuli exist no longer. We sweat. Our atomic winches purr, and chunks of metal clank to the earth. At night our forges glow, and rivet-hammers ring.

"The food we eat is monotonous. No dietitian could give us

a better balanced diet; but on the other hand, none of us is able to gratify those daily trifling appetites, which were unimportant on earth, but which up here assume great proportions. I saw Lila Parker become hysterical one day because she couldn't have olives with her lunch. It was not that she wanted olives so badly, but just that she was making an expression of the frustrations of all of us in such respects. Bread and beans and johnny-cake and oatmeal, and bacon and lentil soup and sweet chocolate and rice, together with yeast which we cultivate and eat to prevent pellagra, and other vitamins which we take in tablets, form a diet nourishing beyond doubt, but tiresome in the extreme.

"Some of us still sleep in the Ark. Some sleep in the observatory, and some in two different groups of tents. We remain scattered because of the possibility of a recurrence of the meteoric shower.

"One of the small atomic engines Hendron brought has been converted into the motor of a tractorlike machine which pulls a flat four-wheeled trailer back and forth to the river valley.

"Tony and twenty other men and women live in that river valley. They have used the tractor to plow, and already they have several hundred acres under cultivation. They work frantically—not knowing how long the growing season will be—knowing only that our survival depends upon their success. The sun has been very hot these days, and the heat increases through a strange, tremendous noon. Several of the people, particularly the women, have been severely sunburned, as the actinic rays appear to be much stronger on Bronson Beta than they were upon Earth.

"None of us has yet adjusted himself to the difference in the length of the day, so that the hours of light seem interminable, and we reach darkness exhausted. I have seen workers on the Ark, and men and women on the farm, fall asleep at their jobs in the later afternoon. On the other hand, since we are accustomed to sleeping at the most nine or ten hours, we are apt to wake up long before dawn. We have ameliorated this problem somewhat by dividing the labor into eight-hour shifts, with eight more hours for recreation. But this brings the free periods of all of us frequently in the dark hours, and there is little in the way of recreation available then, or any time; so we go on working, although nearly always a number of those who are enjoying a rest-period may be found in the circular observation-building, watching Von Beitz or one of the other electrical engineers as they continue their long and manifestly hopeless vigil at the radio-receivers. They occasionally vary that vigil by sending out into the empty universe a description of our position and an account of our situation.

"The soil at the farm was judged excellent by the chemists. Bacteria have been sowed in it. Ants have been loosed there. Our grasshoppers are fattening on the local flora; their buzzing is the only familiar living sound except our own, and the occasional noises of the animals we tend. Every day the tractor brings over the Other People's road an iron tank of drinking- and cooking-water from the river. We had at first utilized sea-water, which we distilled; but the water in the river was found to be pure and apparently without bacteria, so we have given up our distillation.

"We would like to restock the sea with fish, but we are doubtful about the possibility of establishing a biological economy there. We have numerous fishes in an aquarium on the Ark, and perhaps at some later date we shall make the attempt.

"Shirley Cotton has fallen more or less in love with Tony. I would not enter this in a diary that is perhaps to be history, except for the fact that she announced it to every one the other day, and said that she was going to move for a system of marriage codes by which she could compel him to become her mate as well as Eve's. It must have saddened Eve, although she has said nothing about it, and appears not to mind. But Shirley has pointed out what every one has often thought privately—there are thirteen more women than men. All the women but five are under forty years of age. Nearly half the men are more than fifty. Our other party, which appears lost, contained more of the younger people.

"So at the end of two weeks we find ourselves disturbed by many questions, working hard, and realizing slowly the tremendous difficulties to be conquered.

"Yesterday and the day before it rained. The days were like any rainy ones on earth, with gray skies and an incessant heavy drizzle that crescendoed to occasional downpours. The river at the farm rose. The earth around us became a slough of mud, and we tramped in and out of the Ark dejected, despondent, soaked and uncomfortable. When the skies cleared, however, Tony was jubilant. His wide acres were covered with even rows of green, and indeed, the farm was a beautiful spectacle. Hendron ordered Kyto to serve a meal which was an anticipatory thanksgiving.

"We have moved our animals to the farm and put them in stockades where some—the most valuable, fortunately, the cows and sheep—thrive so far, on the ferns and mosses which we have mixed with the last of the fodder brought from earth. Other of the animals do not do so well; and if they die, it is the last we shall see of their species. But shall we ourselves survive?

"On reading the above, it seems that my tone is melancholy; and I feel that it cannot be otherwise. Pressure of work and the reaction to our months of strain and danger, and contemplation of the awful though splendid perils of the flight from earth, have brought about this state of mind. We may be—are, for all we know—the only living, intelligent beings in all the cosmos; one hundred and three of us,—many past the prime of life,—stranded in this solitude with two cows and a bull, two sheep and rams, two deer, a few ants, grasshoppers, fungi, bacteria and bees that we have brought with us. We are now feeling the grinding despair that cast-aways must know, except that we cannot have the hope of rescue, and still worse, we have abandoned the hope of any other fellowship than our own. Solitude—exile—loneliness!

"The children—the little boy and girl whom, thank God, we brought—are the bright lights in our emotional gloom. Their eagerness, their amusing behavior, their constant loyalty and affection, point us more powerfully than anything else to an untiring hope.

"If there were more children—if babes were born among us, new members of our race, this awful feeling of the *end* might be lifted. But who would dare to bear children here? Eve? Shirley?"

Eliot James, on this despairing note, interrupted his record.

Two matters recommend themselves for comment at this point. One concerns Kyto, the quick-witted, obedient Japanese, who had so honorably, as he would have said, followed his master's cause and was now one of the mysteries of Bronson Beta. Everybody talked to Kyto. Naturally, the little Jap was no longer Tony's servant. No one would have servants again. His handiness in the matter of the preparation of meals had made him gravitate to the commissariat in the first few days. But it began to appear at once that Kyto was more than a good cook.

On the third day, when Shirley Cotton had been instructed to inform Kyto on the matter of vitamins and balanced diets, she discovered that he knew fully as much about the subject as she. His budgeting of the food supply was a masterpiece. Unaided, he organized a storeroom system and made plans for its transference. Indeed the eventual discoveries about Kyto surpassed even the wildest guesses of the colonists.

The other matter concerned Hendron:

Others beside Eliot James had observed, and with concern, the change in the leader; and they began to discuss it.

Tony knew that he himself was talked of as a candidate for commander of the group—governor of the camp—if Hendron was to be replaced; so Tony was especially careful to refrain from criticism. In addition to his sincere loyalty and devotion to Hendron, there was the further fact that Eve became even more fanatically devoted to her father as his difficulties increased.

"Tony," she asked him, "what do they—the opposition—say about Father?"

"There's no real opposition," Tony denied. "We'd be crazy to oppose each other; we'd be stark insane! A hundred and three of us upon an empty planet. Surely we've more sense than that."

"Tony, tell me," insisted Eve, "what you hear them say! Father's through? They want another leader; isn't that it?"

"No," denied Tony. "They want him to *lead* again; that's all. He's not doing it now as he did, you know."

"But he will again!"

"Of course he will."

"They're so unfair to Father!" Eve cried. "How much more can they expect of a man? He brought them—those who criticize him—he brought us all through the greatest venture and journey of mankind; and they complain that now he rests a little, that he does not immediately explore. Does it occur to nobody that perhaps Father is too wise to explore or to permit others to wander off—exploring?"

"I've told them I agree with your father," Tony said. "I agree that our first procedure should be to establish ourselves where we are by hard work."

"But do you really agree, Tony?"

"Well," said Tony honestly, "it would certainly be more pleasant to explore."

"But it must not be done now; not yet. And you know why."

"Yes," said Tony; for he too was familiar with Hendron's fears—which were these: since the spores of certain plants had manifestly survived upon Bronson Beta, it was probable up to the practical point of certainty that spores of disease-inducing bacteria also had survived. These would be found where the previous "hosts" of the bacteria had dwelt and died—that is, in the villages and the cities of the Other People.

So Hendron, in this new mood of his, feared the finding of dwellings of the Other People; he forbade, absolutely, further exploration.

Hendron was tired; he had borne too much. He had brought his people over through space, having dealt with and conquered the most tremendous risks; and now he would risk no more. He became obsessed with a passion to preserve and keep safe these followers of his, whom he considered the last survivors of the human race.

Yet, against all his care and caution, death came to the camp. On the morning of the twentieth day, after the slow, dragging dawn when the sun so leisurely arose, two men were found lying in a strange stuper. They were Bates and Jeremiah Post. Before sunset of that long day, twenty more—both men and women—were afflicted, and the physicians had isolated all the sick and ailing.

The epidemic, while somewhat resembling the "sleeping sickness" of earthly days, differed from it in important aspects. It might be, Dodson announced, due to an infection carried from the world and which had developed on this new planet, and which, in the strange environment, exhibited different characteristics. It might be caused by some infective agent encountered on Bronson Beta.

Was it significant that Bates and Jeremiah Post, who had dug from the soil the wreck of the Other People's vehicle, were the first affected? And Maltby soon afterward was sick. Twenty-six persons altogether fell ill; and three died—Bates, and Wardlow, a chemist, and one of the girls who had served as a nurse to the sick—Lucy Grant. The rest made complete recoveries; no one else was later affected; the strange plague passed from the camp.

But of the hundred and three emigrants from earth—perhaps the sole survivors of humanity in all creation—three were dead. And Tony Drake ordered the breaking of the strange soil of Bronson Beta for the first burials of Earth People! Three new interments to add to the uncountable graves of the Other People who were yet to be discovered!

Hendron, who himself had not fallen sick, was by far the most disturbed by these deaths that had come to the camp; thereafter he doubled his restrictions.

It was Higgins the botanist, who at length openly defied the leader.

Higgins took four of the younger men—and under other circumstances Tony unquestionably would have joined them—and went off. At that time Hendron was endeavoring to make a new set of gears, and a chassis and a body, for a second atomic-engine vehicle, using metal from the wall of the Ark; and although he engaged more than twenty people in the operation, it was progressing very slowly. Moreover they had just passed through another three days of heavy rain, and while it was good for the gardens, nevertheless the people who lived in tents were extremely miserable. They were studying the possibility of having to live altogether in one or two of the round sections of the Ark during the coming winter, as it would be impossible to erect metal houses by that time; and every one was dejected over the idea of passing nearly two earth years sleeping on the padded floor of a chamber in the Ark in one great communal group.

Higgins and his party were gone for four days, and anxiety about him became so acute that music was played on the great broadcasting machine constantly during the day, and at night a searchlight shot into the air a vertical beam which was visible for many miles.

Late on the afternoon of the fourth day the exploring party returned.

The five came down the Other People's road from the west, walking with rapid, swinging strides, plainly in triumphant excitement.

Higgins reported for them all when they halted, surrounded by their friends:

"We covered about seventy-five miles. We saw a great desert. We went into a valley where a mighty tangle of fern trees is beginning to rise toward the heavens. We saw glaciers on the top of those distant mountains. I have seen excavations in an old pit where the fossils of animals that were extinct during the civilized period on this planet were being dug out. And we encountered, not ten miles from here, on the Other People's road, something that will very largely relieve one of our great difficulties."

With that he unstrapped his pack, opened it, and dumped out at Hendron's feet a dozen objects upon which Hendron dropped eagerly.

They were wood, chips of wood. Hard wood—soft wood. Finely grained wood, and wood with a coarse, straight grain.

"Is there much of it?" Hendron asked, as he examined the chips.

Higgins nodded. "It isn't related to any of the wood on earth, and there are many interesting features about this vegetation which I will outline in a monograph later, but it is vegetation. It is wood. It comes from the trunks of trees, and there is enough of it standing, seasoned, perfectly preserved, to supply us with all the lumber we can use for generations.

"You have assumed," he continued, speaking directly to Hendron, "that this planet upon which we stand was long ago drawn away from its orbit about some distant sun—some star. We had assumed that, for uncounted ages, this planet followed its prescribed course about its sun until, by the close passing of some other star, its orbit was disturbed, and this planet, with its companion world which destroyed our earth, was cast out into space and cold and darkness.

"The appearance of the forest that we found completely accords with your theory of this planet's past history. There stood a great forest of many varieties of trees, none exactly resembling those of our world, yet of their general order. They seemed to have been deciduous trees mostly; their leaves had fallen; they lay on the ground; the boughs were bare.

"There must have been a long, last autumn followed by a winter without parallel on our world and previously on this planet. All water froze; air froze, preserving the forest as it was at the end of that awful autumn when no thaw came through the millions of years in outer space until this planet found our sun.

"I have said that the trees I examined were unlike the trees on earth; yet their trunks and boughs were wooden; their leaves encumbered the ground. Here are a few of the leaves. . . . I am taking the liberty of calling this one maple, and this one oak, and this one spruce, and this one elm."

The exiles from earth pushed close to finger the leaves and bits of wood, so strange and yet suggesting the familiar. These promised them homes, rooms of their own, chairs, tables, cupboards and book-shelves and writing desks, and a thousand other things dear to their emotional memories. And yet it was odd to see Duquesne, the great French physicist, weeping, and Dodson, the dignified dean of New York surgery, hurling an old felt hat into the air and yelling at the top of his lungs, simply because a wiry little man with a goatee had showed them a few chips of wood.

Tony drew close to Eve. "We'll be outcasts no longer—outcasts!" he emotionally murmured. "We'll have a house and a wood fire again!"

"We?" whispered Eve. "We? You and I? We'll be allowed to marry and live by ourselves?"

They were near to Hendron, but he seemed not to hear them.

"Did you go to the other edge of the forest?" he asked of Higgins.

"There was no sign of the edge as far as we went. The road we followed went through the forest, and before we came to the woods, there were two crossroads. We considered both of them; but we went on, as we have told you, deep into the forest; and returned, as you see."

They were all sitting around a fire on that night, after those first moments of gentleness and of affection when they had been brought electrically back to the happy past, when once again their hopes had risen.

It was night, and dark; and there was no moon. Nor would there ever be a moon. They had been singing softly; and one of their number—Dimitri Kalov—had slipped away from the fire and talked to Hendron, and gone to the Ark and come back with a piano-accordion strapped around his shoulders. No one had seen him return, but suddenly from out of the darkness came a ripple of music.

The singing stopped, and they listened while Dimitri played. He played old songs, and he played some of the music from Russia which his father had taught him. Then, between numbers, when the applause died and a hush fell over the group, as they waited for him to begin again, there was a sound.

It was soft and remote, and yet it transfixed every one instantly, because it was a sound that did not belong to any human being. It was a sound that did not belong to their colony. A sound foreign and yet familiar. A sound that rose for a few instants, and then died out to nothing, only to return more strongly than before.

One by one they turned their faces up, for the sound was in the sky. It approached rapidly, above them, in the dark. There was no mistaking it now. It was the motor of an airplane. An airplane on Bronson Beta! An airplane piloted by other human beings, or perhaps—they did not dare to think about the alternative.

Nearer and nearer it came, until some of them could discern the splotch of darkness against the stars. But then the ship in the heavens seemed to see their fire on the ground and be alarmed by it, for it switched its course and started back in the direction from which it had come.

Hendron rushed toward the observatory and shouted to Von Beitz, who was on duty at the radio, to turn on a searchlight. Von Beitz must have heard the airplane too, for even as Hendron shouted, a long finger of light stabbed across the sky and began combing it for the vanishing plane. It caught and held upon the ship for a fraction of a second before it plunged through a sleazy cloud, but that second was not long enough for any one to tell what manner of ship it was, or even whether it was a ship such as might have been made by the people of the earth. A speck—a flash of wing surface. And the clouds.

They sat, stricken and numb. Surely, if there had been human beings in that ship—surely if it had contained other refugees from the destruction of the earth—it would have circled over their fire time and again in exultation.

But it had fled. What could that mean? Who could be in it? What intelligence could be piloting it?

The pulsations of the motor died. The light was snapped off. The colonists shuddered.

They were not alone on Bronson Beta.

CHAPTER IV

WHAT WAS IT?

SOMEBODY threw a log onto the fire. It blazed up freshly, and illuminated the strained, immobile faces of the emigrants from earth. Nobody spoke. They only looked at each other.

Out of the night, out of the darkness, out of the remote, infinitely distant, impersonal Nowhere, had come that humming, throbbing reality. Somewhere on Bronson Beta there were other human beings. Another still more dreadful thought curdled the imaginations of the people who sat around the camp-fires: were those other beings human?

Hendron, the leader of these brave people, had never felt upon himself pressure for greater leadership—had never felt himself more incompetent to explain the mystery of that night.

He moved among his fellows almost uncertainly. He walked up to the camp-fire and addressed his comrades. "I think," he said slowly, "that the thought now engraving the imaginations of many of you may be discarded. I mean the thought that the plane which approached our camp was piloted by other than human beings."

Eliot James interrupted, speaking with a confidence he did not feel. "It looked like an ordinary airplane."

Cole Hendron shook his head. "From the glimpse we had, no one could say. What we saw was merely a glint upon some sort of material. However, we must use our reason to rescue us from impossible conclusions. We must infer from our glimpse of that machine in the sky, and from the sound of its flight, that some other party on earth was successful in completing a ship capable of taking the leap from Earth to Bronson Beta; and that, also, they were fortunate in the flight; and that they have succeeded, as well as we, in establishing themselves here."

"They must be established very well," somebody else said grimly. "We haven't got a plane."

Hendron nodded. "No; nor did we include an airplane in the equipment of our larger Ark. Therefore it could not have been our comrades from our own camp on Earth whom we heard in this sky. Were they the English, perhaps? Or the Russians? The Italians? Or the Japanese?"

"If they were any people from earth," Jeremiah Post countered, "why should they have approached so near, and yet not give any sign they had seen us?"

Cole Hendron faced this objector calmly. He was aware that

Post was one of the younger men who believed that he, the leader of the party on earth, and the captain on the voyage through space, had served his purpose. "Have you come to believe," he challenged the metallurgist, "that any of the people native to this planet could have survived?"

"I believe," retorted Post, "that we certainly are not safe in excluding that possibility from our calculations. As you all know," he continued, addressing the whole group now rather than Hendron, "I have given extended study to the vehicle of the Other People which we have found. Not only in its mechanical design and method of propulsion was it utterly beyond any vehicle developed on earth, but its metallurgy was in a class by itself—compared to ours. These People had far surpassed our achievement in the sole fields of science from which we yet have any sample. Is it not natural to suppose that, likewise, they were beyond us in other endeavors?"

"Particularly?" Hendron challenged him.

"Particularly, perhaps, in preservation of themselves. I will not be so absurd as to imagine that any large number of them could have survived the extreme ordeals of—space. But is it utterly inconceivable that a few could?"

"How?" said Hendron.

"You know," Jeremiah Post cast back at his leader, "that is not a fair question. I suggest a possibility that some people of this planet may have survived through application of principles or processes far beyond our knowledge; and then you ask me to describe the method. Of course I can't."

"Of course not," agreed Hendron apologetically. "I withdraw that question. However, in order that each of us may form his and her own opinion of the possibilities, I will ask Duquesne to acquaint you with the physical experience of this planet as we now perceive it."

The Frenchman readily arose and loomed larger than ever in the flickering flare of the fire:

"My friends, it is completely plain to all of us that once this world, which has given us refuge, was attached to some distant sun which we, on the world, saw as a star.

"That star might have been a sun of the same order as our sun, which this world has now found. If such were the case, it seems likely that Bronson Beta circled its original sun at some distance similar to our distance from our sun; for the climatic conditions here seem in the past to have been similar, at least, to the conditions on earth.

"There are two other alternatives, however. The original star, about which Bronson Beta revolved, might have been a much larger and hotter sun; in that case, this planet must have swung about that star in an enormous orbit with a year perhaps ten or fifty times as long as our old years. On the other hand, the original sun might have been smaller and feebler—a 'white dwarf,' perhaps, or one of the stars that are nearly spent. In that case, Bronson Beta must have circled it much more closely to have obtained the climate which once here prevailed, and which has been reëstablished now that this planet has found our sun.

"These are fascinating points which we hope to clear up later; we can only speculate upon them now. However, whether the original sun for this planet was a yellow star of moderate size, like our own sun, or whether it was one of the giant stars, or a 'white dwarf,' this world must have been satisfactorily situated with regard to it for millions and hundreds of millions of years.

"Orderly evolution must have proceeded for an immense period to produce, for instance, that log—the material which we burn before me to give us, to-night, light and heat; and to produce the People who made the vehicle which my colleague Jeremiah Post so admirably has analyzed.

"Beings of a high order of intelligence dwelt here. We have evidence that in science they had progressed beyond us—unfortunately for themselves. Poor fellows!"

Dramatically, Duquesne stopped.

Some one—it was a girl—did not permit him the full moment of his halt. "Why unfortunately?"

"Their science must have showed them their doom so plainly and for so frightfully long a period—a doom from which there scarcely could have been, even for the most favored few, any means of escape. Theirs was a fate far more terrible than was ours—a fate incomparably more frightful than mere complete catastrophe.

"Attend! There they were, in some other part of the heavens, circling, at some satisfactory distance, their sun! For millions and millions of years this world upon which now we stand went its orderly way. Then its astronomers noticed that a star was approaching. A star—a mere point of light on its starry nights—swelled and became brighter.

"We may be sure that telescopes upon this world turned upon it; and the beings—whose actual forms we have yet to discover—made their calculations. Their sun, with its retinue of planets, was approaching another star. There would be no collision; we do not believe that such a thing occurred. There was merely an approach of another sun close enough to counteract, by its own attraction, the attraction of the original sun upon this planet, and upon Bronson Alpha.

"The suns—the stars—battled between themselves from millions and perhaps hundreds of millions of miles away; and neither conquered completely. The new sun tore the planets away from the first sun, but it failed to capture them for itself. Between the stars, this planet and its companion, which we called Bronson Alpha, drifted together into the darkness and cold of space.

"The point is, that this must have been a torturingly prolonged process for the inhabitants here. The approach of a star is not like the approach of a planet. We discovered Bronson Alpha and Bronson Beta only a few months before they were upon us; the Beings here must have known for generations, for centuries, the approach of the stranger star!

"Knowing it, for hundreds of years, could any of the inhabitants here have schemed a way of saving themselves? That seems to be the question now before us.

"I cannot say that they could not. I can only say that we could not have devised anything adequate to meet their situation. Yet—*they* might have. They knew more than we: they had much more time, but their problem was terrific—the problem of surviving through nearly absolutely cold and darkness, a drift through space, of a million or millions of years. If any of you believe that problem could have been met by the Beings here, he has as much right to his opinion as I have to mine."

"Which is?" Jeremiah Post demanded.

"That the People here tried to solve that problem," replied Duquesne without evasion, "and failed; but that they made a magnificent attempt. When we find them, we will find—I hope and believe—the method of their tremendous attempt."

Shirley Cotton stood up. She always moved with an almost languid voluptuousness. Now, in these tense moments, her actions were seemingly doubly calculated to be slow and indolent.

"What, M. Duquesne," she inquired, "would be the attitude of the Beings if they survived and found us here?"

The Frenchman shook his head. "Before imagining their attitude, I must first imagine them surviving. I have confessed my failure at that task."

"But *if* some of them survived?" Shirley persisted.

"Their attitude, after awaking from a million years' sleep, would combine, among other elements, surprise and caution, I should suggest," the Frenchman concluded courteously. "But, engaging as such speculations may be, our position demands that we be practical. We must assume that aircraft we saw in these skies came from earth. If there are other people from our world upon Bronson Beta, we prefer to be friends with them. That attitude, besides being rational, is our natural inclination. However,"—he shrugged his huge shoulders eloquently,—"it does not therefore follow that another party of emigrants from earth would want to be friendly to us. We cannot assume that the same emotions sway them. It is possible that, finding themselves here, they prefer private possession of this planet."

Eve, sitting beside Tony, leaned toward him and whispered: "I can imagine that. Can't you?"

Tony nodded. "That's what I've been doing. I was in Russia during the days on earth," he said, and repeated, *"during the days on earth,"* feeling how it seemed an epoch long ago, though it was not yet a month since they fled before the final catastrophe; and as Duquesne had reminded them, it was less than two years since they all had been living on the world unwarned that its end was at hand. Only a little more than two years ago, Tony had traveled as he liked on the world, and had visited, among other countries, Russia.

"Suppose that a Russian party made the hop," Tony continued. "Since we did, why not? They worked along lines of their own, but they had some of the world's best scientists. If they made it, you may be sure they packed their ship with first-class communists—the most vigorous and the most fanatic. When they found themselves here, what would they feel most?"

"I know," Eve nodded. "They'd feel that they had a world to themselves, where they could work out the millennium according to their own ideals."

"And," Tony finished for her, "that they must beat down, at the very outset, possible interference."

They were whispering only to each other; but many heads bent near to listen; and Hendron, seeing that Tony caught this attention, called to him: "You have a suggestion?"

"Two," said Tony, rising to his feet. "I suggest, Cole, that we organize at once an adequate exploring expedition; and at the same time, prepare defenses."

Nobody in the encampment had ever before called Hendron by his first name. Tony's use of it was involuntary and instinctive. Having to oppose his leader in again urging exploration, he took from it any air of antagonism by addressing him as "Cole."

Hendron appreciated this.

"Will you lead the exploring party—and choose its members?" he asked Tony.

"Gladly."

"I," said Hendron, "will be responsible for the defenses here."

The people about Tony pressed closer. "Take me! . . . Me! . . . Tony, I want to go! Take me!"

From the gloom, where Eliot James sat rose his calm, twangy voice: "So we have come to the end of our honeymoon!"

Eve reached for Tony's arm and clung to him as he moved out of the group gathered about him.

"Take me too, Tony."

"Not you."

"Why not?"

"I wouldn't on earth; why would I here? Besides, I want to come back to you. I want to feel, when I'm away, I'm risking whatever we happen to risk, for you. You see, I love you. It's like on earth, when I'm with you away from the others. See the stars up there." The clouds were cleared from a patch in the sky. "There's Cepheus and the Dragon; and Vega and the Swan, as we've always seen them. And the earth hard and cold at our feet; so comfortably solid and substantial, this earth, which came to us torn from some distant star for a couch, sometime, for you and me!"

Night deepened. The company of emigrants from the earth heaped higher the fire with the wood from the forest which had leafed on this land of Bronson Beta a million years ago. Some of the company—men as well as women—shivered with a chill not instilled in their veins by the sharpness of night, as this side of the planet turned away from the sun it had found at the end of its incalculable wandering. Slowly, lazily, the stars swung in the sky; for this planet rotated much less swiftly than the earth upon its axis. The earth people had learned not to lie down too soon to sleep, but to wait out the first hours of the long night in talk; and doubts, terrors, phantasms, easier to dismiss by day, plagued them.

That night, as Eliot James had said, they felt "the honeymoon over." The triumph of their flight, the enormous excitement and relief at finding themselves safe on the new world, could suffice them no longer. Others besides themselves were on this world.

Survivors of the People of the Past! That idea would not down. Contrarily, it increased with the night.

Survivors of the People of the Past—or other emigrants from Earth who had made the journey safely, established themselves and already were exploring, and who, having found this encampment, had swung away again to report. Report what? And to whom?

Nothing happened.

Days passed—the long, slow days of Bronson Beta. The murmuring specter of the sky put in no further appearance; but the consequences of its evanescent presence continued. The camp was roused to a feverish activity which reminded the emigrants of the days of the Ark-building on earth. Indeed, this was Ark-building again, but on a far smaller scale; for the Ark was being taken down, and its materials—especially the last of the lining of the propulsion tubes—were being adapted to an exploration ship.

In the section of building which had been originally dedicated to research, rivet-hammers now rang, and metal in work glowed whitely. The crew that manned the farm was still at its post. Lumber was still being brought from the forest. But the most skillful and the most energetic members of the colony were working upon a small metal jet-propulsion ship hastily designed to travel in Bronson Beta's atmosphere—a ship with lifting surfaces—but a ship with an enclosed cockpit; a ship which could travel very rapidly through the atmosphere of the new planet, and which could rise above that atmosphere if it became necessary.

The throbbing of the motor of the strange plane had changed the entire tempo of the lives of the colonists; it had rearoused them to themselves. If they were to preserve the intelligent pattern of their plans, it was essential to learn at once what interference threatened them. They could look upon themselves no longer as law unto themselves. Some other beings—survivors of the People of this planet or others from the earth—shared this new world with them.

Hendron's people no longer could endure delay in learning, at whatever risks, what lay beyond these silent horizons.

On the morning of the fifty-sixth Bronson Beta day after their arrival, the airship was ready. Streamlined, egg-shaped, with quartz glass windows and duraluminum wings, with much of the available Ransdell-metal lining its diagonally down-thrust propulsion tubes, it stood glittering in the sunshine five hundred yards from the half-wrecked cylinder of the Ark. At about noon of that day Tony and Eliot James climbed into the hatch of the ship after Tony, under Hendron's tutelage, had been familiarizing himself with the controls.

They were to make the exploration alone; the ship had been built only for pilot and observer. Both carried pistols.

It was proof of Hendron's high practicality that, among the implements cargoed from earth, were pistols and ammunition. Policing might have to be done, if there were no other use for arms; and so there were pistols not only for Tony and Eliot James, but for others who remained in the camp.

As long as the explorers stayed in their ship, they possessed, of course, weapons far more deadly than pistols—the jet-propulsion tubes which had proved their terrible deadliness on the night of the raid on the camp in Michigan.

The camp here owned the same weapons; for all of the tubes from the Ark had not been broken up to supply the little exploration ship. Hendron, keeping his word to prepare defense for the camp, had had the extra tubes prepared and mounted almost like cannon—which he hoped never to use. But he had them.

Hendron watched Eliot James establish himself in the cockpit beside Tony; then he beckoned him out. Hendron would make one last trial flight with Tony at the controls. So James reluctantly stepped out; Hendron stepped in, and the ship rose.

It rose—shot, indeed, crazily forward, spun, jumped still higher and finally rushed southward along the coast till the camp was nearly out of sight. Then Tony brought it back, pushing away Hendron's hands that wanted to help him. He made a landing on the barren acres selected a mile from the camp; and after waiting a few minutes, Tony and then Hendron leaped over the hot earth which surrounded the ship, and went to meet the people hurrying from the camp.

Eve was with the first of them; and Tony saw her pale and shaken. "Oh, Tony!" she exclaimed. "You nearly—"

He looked at her and grinned. "I certainly nearly did whatever you were going to say."

Hendron said: "He did well enough."

"All right now?" asked Eliot James eagerly.

"All right," said Hendron; and yet he held them, reluctant to let them go. "I've had everything put in place—everything you are likely to need. In all our observations from the earth, we made out a great continent here nearly two thousand miles wide and seven thousand in length. We believe we landed about the middle of the east coast of that continent."

He had reviewed this time and time again with Tony and Eliot James, separately and together; yet he had to do it again at the last moment before he let them go:

"Your charts have spotted in them the sites of the cities that we thought we observed. Go to the nearest points first, and then as much farther as—as circumstances dictate.

"If you get into any kind of trouble, radio us. We may not be able to help; yet it is essential to us to learn what may be happening to you. Remember you have a deadly weapon of defense in your tubes.

"Remember, if you come upon survivors of the original People of this planet, their first impulse may be to protect themselves against you. I cannot myself imagine how any of the People of this planet could have survived; yet I must admit the possibility. If they live, they probably have weapons or materials of defense and offense utterly strange to us. . . . Far more probably, you may find other people from earth. If you possibly can, avoid conflict of any sort with them. Nothing could be more tragic than warfare between us here. Yet—if they attack, you must defend yourselves. Fight to kill—to annihilate, if need be! May the God of this world go with you!"

He stepped back and, for a moment, Tony merely stared at him. No moment since they had gained the ground of this strange planet had been as pregnant with the emotions of the Earth. Fight to kill—to annihilate, if need be!

It was the sensible thing: and for it, Tony was himself prepared. Yet it was shocking to hear it announced on this desolate world resuming life again after its long journey through dark and cold.

Eve broke the spell. She stepped forward. "Good-by, Tony."

She gave him her hand; and he longed to draw her to him, and though before them all, to clasp her close and kiss her again. Suddenly, defiantly, he did it. She clung to him. It was another very earthly moment.

His eyes caught Hendron's and found in her father's—in his leader's—no reproach. Hendron, indeed, nodded.

Shirley Cotton spoke to him; he grasped her hand, and she kissed his cheek. She kissed also Eliot James. Others crowded about.

Eliot himself saved the situation.

"It's awfully nice of all you girls to see me to the train," he half declaimed, half chanted, in his comedy twang, a refrain of years ago. "So long, Mary!"

Then Hendron signaled men and women alike away from the ship. Tony and Eliot climbed in; but they waited until their friends had retreated nearly half a mile before they set the jet-propulsion tubes in action.

There was a tremendous roar. The ship bounded forth and took the air. A few moments later it was out of sight; a spark in the sunshine—then nothing.

Eve sat down and wept. Hendron knelt beside her, encircling her with his arms, and remained there staring toward the west in silence.

Travel in the hastily contrived combination of rocket-ship and airplane was not pleasant. Its insulation and cooling systems were inadequate, so that its interior became hot.

Tony flew at a height of five thousand feet. At this height the blast of the Ark would have seared the earth underneath, but the less powerful jets of the airship were dissipated before they reached the ground and caused no damage.

They followed the Other People's road inland. When they had been flying for a few minutes, Eliot James pointed downward; and Tony, looking through a quartz window in the floor, had a fleeting glimpse of a magnificent metal bridge which carried the road across a deep valley. A little later they both concentrated their gaze upon a vast green thicket that reached to the horizon—a cover evidently composed of ferns. They soon left it behind them, and the mountains loomed directly ahead.

At their base was a desert valley some twenty miles in width. From the far side of the valley the mountains rose precipitously to the level at which Tony was flying. They were craglike raw mountains of red and bronze-colored stone, bleak and forbidding. The spore-generated vegetation did not seem to grow upon them, and as far as the fliers could tell, nothing had grown there even before disaster had wrenched Bronson Beta from its parent system.

Tony tilted the nose of the plane upward and gained sufficient altitude to clear their summits by a few thousand feet. He could see, as he looked downward, the direct course of the Other People's road through these mighty mountains—a road that leaped great chasms on spectacular bridges, a road that vanished occasionally in the bowels of some bronze or henna spur or shoulder.

Both men as they flew were particularly absorbed in their immediate uncomfortableness, but still more occupied by the same thought: what would lie upon the other side of this mighty range of mountains? Up to that moment they had seen nothing which gave any indication of the existence of living intelligence. The Other People's road was a monument in a dead world—and for the rest, all that lived and grew was vegetation.

They rose higher to surmount still loftier peaks, penetrating the upper altitudes of the thin greenish atmosphere of Bronson Beta. For almost half an hour they flew straight west across the mountains, and then, far away, they saw a break in the turmoil of upthrust peaks. The mountains turned into hills of lesser altitude which finally gave way to a broad flat plain. It was a plain that seemed endless and through its heart, like an arrow, ran the metal road.

Tony occupied himself with the business of losing altitude for a few moments and abruptly felt his arm gripped by James' hand. Once again he followed the outstretched finger of his companion and he drew in his breath in astonishment.

CHAPTER V

THE OTHER PEOPLE

FAR away on the horizon, blazing in the pathway of the sun, was a mighty iridescent bubble. From the windows of the plane it appeared to be small, and yet its distance was so great that the senses immediately made the proper adjustment in scale. It was like half of a soap bubble, five or ten miles in diameter, sitting on the earth. Its curvature was perfect. It was obviously not a natural formation. The road pointed toward it and Tony followed the road. What it was he could not guess.

As they flew, they shouted conjectures to each other, meaningless guesses. Tony said: "It looks like some kind of giant greenhouse." And Eliot James hazarded a notion: "Perhaps the people of Bronson Beta lived under those things when they began to drift out in Space."

The bubble stretched out laterally before them as they flew, and quite suddenly they were able to see in the opalescent glitters of its surface what was within it. It was about six miles in width and more than a mile in height at its center. Inside it, completely contained by it, was a city—a city laid out in a circular geometrical pattern, a city which had at regular intervals gigantic terraced metal skyscrapers—a city with countless layers of roads and streets leading from one group of buildings to the next—a city around the outer edge of which ran a huge trestled railroad.

It was so perfect a city that it might have been a model made by some inspired artist who was handicapped by no structural materials and who allowed his orderly invention no limitations commensurate with logic. Architecturally the plan of the city within that bubble was perfect. The materials of its composition harmonized with each other in a pattern of shimmering beauty.

Tony flew directly to the bubble and circled it at a short distance from its perimeter. The men looked down in stunned silence as the ship wheeled slowly round the great transparent bubble. Both observers realized that the city had been enclosed for some such reason as to keep out cold or to keep its internal temperature unchanged.

Dimly Tony heard James shouting: "It's magnificent!" And in an almost choked voice he replied: "They must have been amazing." In the majestic streets beneath that dome no living thing moved. No lights glowed in those streets where the setting sun allowed shadows to fall; no smoke, no steam, no fire showed anywhere, and although their motor made hearing impossible, they knew instinctively that the colossal, triumphant metropolis below them was as silent as the grave.

Eliot James spoke: "Guess we'd better have a look-see."

Tony nodded. He had already noted that several metal roads led up to the bubble which covered the city, and that the bubble itself was penetrated by gateways. He tipped the nose of the ship toward one of the gates and a few moments later rolled up to a stop on the smooth metal roadway which entered through the locked gate. The two men sat for a moment staring at the spectacle before them, and then, arming themselves, they climbed out of the ship to the ground.

When they put their feet on the ground and looked toward the city, one gate of which was now only a few rods from where they stood, its majesty was a thousand times more apparent than it had been from the air.

When the roar of the motor of their plane had died, when the ringing it left in their ears had abated, when they stood finally at the gate of the city in the sunset, their imaginations were staggered, their very souls were confounded with the awful silence and lonesomeness of the place. They looked at each other without speaking, but their words might very well have been:

"Here are we, two men—two members of a race that appeared on a planet which is no longer—untold millions of miles away from their home—the scouts of their expedition, their eyes and ears for the unknown peril which overshadows them. Here are we, facing a city that we do not understand, facing dangers that are nameless—and all we have is four frail hands, two inadequate minds."

However frail their hands might have been in comparison to the task to which they must be set, however weak and inadequate their minds were in comparison to the Titanic problems confronting them, it could be said that they did not lack in resolution. The haunted expressions left their faces. Tony turned to Eliot James and grinned.

"Here we are, pal!"

"Sure. Here we are. What do you suppose this is—their Chicago? New Orleans? Paris, Bombay, Tokyo?"

"Search me," said Tony, trying to down his awe. Suddenly he shouted, yelled; and Eliot James joined in his half-hysterical cry.

Partly it was a reflex from their wonder, partly a confession that their feelings subdued their intelligence. They knew that this was the city of the dead; it must be. But, standing there at its gate, they could not feel it.

Their eyes searched the curved slope of the great glass dome over the geometrical angles of the metal gate. Nothing stirred; nothing sounded. Not even an echo returned.

They looked down at each other; and on their foreheads glistened the cold sweat of their awed excitement.

"Maybe everybody's asleep," said Eliot James, and knew he made no sense. "Maybe everybody's taking a walk."

"We'll find them inside. We must find some of them inside," said Tony.

"Dead, of course," said Eliot.

"Yes," agreed Tony. "Of course, they're dead." But he had never been further from believing it.

The city stood so in order that it seemed its inhabitants *must* be going about within. It seemed that, down the wide road to this gate, some one must be coming.

Tony suddenly spun about, startling Eliot who jerked around, also.

No one and nothing approached. The wide, smooth, hard road remained utterly deserted.

Again they looked at the gate.

"How do you suppose we can get in here?" Eliot asked.

"There's something that looks very much like a knocker right over there." Tony pointed to a heavy metal ring which was apparently fitted in the end of a lever in a slot at the side of the gate. They walked over to it. The gate itself was perhaps thirty feet in width and forty feet high. The ring was about at the level of Tony's eyes. Above it was an inscription in the unknown language of the unknown inhabitants of Bronson Beta. Tony took hold of the ring and pulled it. Much to his astonishment two gates quietly and swiftly separated. Air blew from the city with a gusty sound, air that seemed age-old, and continued to blow as they hesitantly walked through the gate.

Inside, under the mighty glass dome, they were confronted by a stupendous spectacle. Straight through the heart of the circular city ran a highway along the edge of which were two rails, so that by leaning over they ascertained a moment later that underneath this top street were other thoroughfares at lower levels. On both sides of the street, which was wider than the main avenue of any of the earth's cities, towered colossal buildings. The tallest of them, in the center of the city, must have been more than half a mile in height, and they were made of materials which took brilliant colors, which gave back in the sunlight myriad glittering hues. Exquisitely suspended bridges connected these buildings which rose at intervals of about a quarter of a mile. From their airplane the city had looked like a spangled toy town, but from its own streets it looked like the royal city of Titans. There was no sound in it. Except for the air that whispered through the open gates, not a murmur, not a throb, not a tinkle or a pulsation—just silence. Nothing moved.

A few feet from the gate by which they had entered was a big poster in bright red and white material which was covered by the strange writing of the inhabitants of Bronson Beta. They walked forward almost on tiptoe after looking at the runes beside the gate.

They stared down the avenue ahead of them and aside along the ways that crossed it.

"Where are they, Tony?" Eliot James whispered. He meant not, "Where are living beings?" For he knew the people who built this city must be dead; but he expected, at least, their bodies.

Tony, too, had failed to drive away such expectation. If not living, where were the dead? He could not help expecting the streets to be, somehow, like those of Pompeii after the débris and ash of Vesuvius was cleared away; he could not help expecting to see bones of the Beings, fallen in flight from their city.

But conditions here had been the opposite of those in Pompeii. There it was sudden destruction of fiery blasts, and burial from volcanic ash, that had overwhelmed the people and caught and buried them. Here, instead of sudden, consuming heat, had come slow, creeping cold—cold and darkness, of the coming of which they had been warned for generations. Such a death could have caught no one unprepared on the streets of the city.

"Where are they, Tony?" Eliot James whispered again, as his senses reminded him of the situation. "Where did they go to die? Did they stay in their homes, do you think? Will we find them in these buildings?"

"I don't think so," Tony tried to say steadily, improving his tone above a whisper.

"Where will we find them, then?"

"We won't find them—any of them here, I think," Tony said.

"Why? What did they do?"

"What would such people do?" Tony returned. "Such people as could build this city? What would they do against annihilation which they could see coming for a century?"

"They eliminated themselves, of course: they ceased to reproduce themselves; they ceased to have children."

"That," said Tony, "seems certainly the logical thing to do; and these people appear to have been logical. But there must have been some group who were the last. They could scarcely have buried themselves after they died. Somewhere we will find—somebody."

"It's marvelous," said Eliot James, "how they left this city. They'd covered it over and closed it almost as if they meant to preserve it for us."

"How could they dream of us?" challenged Tony.

"Of course they didn't. Shall we move on?"

"All right," agreed Tony, and ended their paralysis of amazement. "This was a store, I suppose," he said, turning from the stupendous vistas of the streets to the building beside him.

The face of the building was glass, streaked but yet remarkably clear over much of its surface. Behind the glass was an empty area which suggested space for display of goods; but none showed behind the huge high window. The ceiling was perhaps twenty feet high; and above, up and up, stretched glass divided by sills and panels of the multicolored metals.

"Did they live up there, do you suppose?" Eliot James appealed to Tony. Staring up, staring about, but keeping close together, they walked on the silent, utterly empty street. "Did they die up there? If we climbed, would we see—them?"

"The street," said Tony, "might have been swept yesterday."

"They swept it before they left—or died in here," Eliot replied. "They drew their gates and shut out the wind. After they left—or died—what else could disturb it? But, my God, they were neat. No rubbish, no litter."

"And everything locked," Tony said, having halted to try a door. The order of everything, and the utter stillness, was getting his nerves again. "Where've they gone? Where'd they go—leaving it like this?"

Eliot James did not answer; he had run ahead.

"Tables!" he called. "Tables and chairs! This was a restaurant!"

His nose was pressed against the glass, and Tony swiftly joined him. Within stood rows of metal tables and what were, unquestionably, chairs of metal. All bare; and all, of course, empty. It resembled nothing so much as a restaurant; and looking in, no one from earth could doubt that that was what it had been.

The place looked immaculate, as if put in order an hour ago —and then deserted.

"Where are they?" Eliot James appealed again. "Oh, Tony, where did they go?"

"What were they?" Tony countered. "That's what I want to know. Were they huge ants? Were they human-brained reptiles? Were they—"

"They sat in chairs," said Eliot James. "They ate at tables. They ran a car that steered by pedals and a wheel. Their equipment would fit us; their floors and steps are on our scale. Let's break in here."

He tried the door, which was fitted with a handle; but this did not turn or budge, however pulled or pressed. There was no keyhole; no locking device was anywhere apparent; but the door was to be moved no more than those that they had tried before.

Tony looked about. A shudder convulsed him. A thousand windows looked down on this stretch of the silent street; a thousand pairs of eyes once had looked down. It seemed to

Tony that they must—they must do it again. Eyes of what? Huge, sentient, intelligent insects? Reptiles of some strange, semihuman sort?

What lay dead by the tens of thousands in those silent rooms overhead?

Tony was pulling at his pistol. Somehow, it reassured him to hold it in his hand. He reversed it, and beat the butt on the great glass pane behind which stood the strange metal tables and chairs.

The glass did not give way. It twanged, not like glass but like sheet metal—metal utterly transparent.

Tony caught the butt in his palm, and he pulled the trigger. The shot roared and reëchoed. But the metal pane was not pierced. The bullet he had fired lay at Tony's feet. Hysterically, he emptied his pistol.

With the last shot, he jerked about again and stared up at the rows and rows of windows. Did something up there stir?

Eliot James jumped and pointed; and Tony stiffened as he stared.

Something fluttered a hundred yards overhead and farther down the street; something light, like a cloth or a paper. One way, now another, it fluttered as it fell in the still air of that strange sealed city. It reached the street and lay there.

Ten thousand eyes gazed down, it seemed to Tony. It seemed to him that if he could look up twice as quick, he would catch *them* at their windows gazing down at him. But he never could catch them. Always, when he looked up, *they* had anticipated him; *they* were gone; *they* had snatched their heads away.

So he never saw anything but glass and metal—and the single fluttering object which had fallen down.

"We'll go see what that is," he said to Eliot James, wetting his dry lips so he could speak.

But before they gained the object, they forgot it. A window, evidently the vitrine of a gallery of art, confronted them; within the glass was a portrait.

Simultaneously, Tony and Eliot saw it. They stopped as if they were struck; and their breath left them. Breath of relief, and wonder!

They looked at the likeness of a woman!

She was a young woman, strange and fascinating. She was not fair; nor was she dark of skin. Her hair and brows were black—hair arranged with an air that might be individual but which, these discoverers of her felt, was racial.

And of what race?

Not the Caucasian, not the Mongolian; not the Ethiopian, surely; not the Indian. She was of no race upon earth; but she was human.

More than that, she had been sensitive, eager, filled with the joy of living. Her bosom and body were like that of a lovely woman on earth, slight and graceful. Her eyes were wide apart and gray; her cheek-bones were very far apart; and her lips, which were bright red, perhaps because they had been rouged, were pleasant and amiable.

"So," said Eliot James, who first succeeded in speaking, "so they were human! By God, you feel you'd like to know her."

Tony relaxed his hands, which had clenched. "Where did she live, do you suppose, Eliot? Did she live up behind one of these windows?"

"She had a name," said Eliot James. "And surely she had lovers. Where are they?"

"Dead," said Tony. "Dead with her—maybe a million years ago. Let's go on."

"Why go on?" demanded Eliot James. "Why? To pick up a scarf on the street? We've got to get into one of these buildings somewhere. We can break in somehow—with nobody to stop us. We might as well begin here."

So together they attacked the door, which, like those they had pushed and pulled at before, showed no lock, yet was secure.

The door, like the walls of the buildings, was of metal and glass. Indeed, it was difficult to distinguish by texture between the glass and the metal. The panes appeared to be transparent metal. Jeremiah Post had spoken conservatively when, after the examination of the wrecked vehicle discovered near camp, he had said that the People of Bronson Beta had far surpassed any people on earth in metallurgy.

This door evidently was designed to lift; it should rise and slip into the metal wall overhanging it; but no pushing or straining at it, no hammering and pounding, could cause it to budge. And the glass in it—the panel of transparent metal—was not to be broken.

Weary and sweating from their straining at it, Tony and Eliot stepped back.

Their own blows, their own thudding and their gasping for breath, had made the only sound in the silent city.

Repeatedly, while they had worked at the door, each of them had spun about for a glance over his shoulder. The metal seemed so new—some one *must* be about this city standing all in such order.

Tony kept trying his game of looking up quickly, without warning, to catch the heads of the people behind the upper windows who always—so he felt—had jerked back in time.

Now, as the two men from earth stood side by side staring about them, the slightest of sounds reached them; and a door—not the door at which they had pushed and pounded, but a door some twenty steps beyond—began rising.

Tony and Eliot shrank closer together. They pulled out their pistols, which they had reloaded. Up, up steadily, slowly, the metal door was lifted.

"Counterbalanced!" exclaimed Tony to his companion; but his voice was husky. "It was counterbalanced, of course! Our pounding affected some mechanism inside!"

It was the reasonable, rational explanation. For the people of this city could not be alive; it was impossible that they had survived! Yet, here in their city, you could not believe that.

"They're human, anyway," whispered Eliot James.

"Yes," said Tony, his eyes fastened on the aperture under the rising door. "See—anything?"

"Say it, Tony," returned Eliot James. "Or I will."

"All right," said Tony hoarsely. "See—*any one?*"

"There's nobody there," argued Eliot, with himself as much as with his comrade. "They all died—they all died a million years ago."

"Yes," agreed Tony. The door was ceasing to rise; it had reached its limit and stopped, leaving the way into the great metal building open. "They all died a million years ago. But where did they go to die?"

"Who cares?" Eliot continued his argument. "Can a ghost live a million years? I don't believe they can. Come on in, Tony. They can't even haunt us."

"A minute," said Tony.

"Why?"

"I want to look around once more." He was doing it. "All right now!" They approached the open doorway together; and together, neither in advance or in the rear of the other, they entered it, pistols in hands. That was wholly irrational; and both knew it; but neither could help himself.

So, side by side, revolvers ready, they entered the door of the Million Years Dead.

The walls of the hall in which they found themselves were vemilion. It did not appear to be paint. Like the colors of the exteriors, the hue was a quality of the metal. Vermilion surrounded Tony and Eliot—vermilion and gray, in vigorous, pronounced patterns.

There was no furniture in the hall; no covering upon the floor. Perhaps there never had been one; the floor was smooth and even and of agreeable texture. It was not wood nor metal, but of some composition. It might have been meant to be a dance-floor or for a meeting-hall. Nothing declared its use. An open doorway invited to an apartment beyond; and side by side, but with their pistols less at alert, Eliot and Tony stepped into this.

It was blue—ultramarine, they would have called it on earth, with slashes of silver. Great long-beaked, long-legged birds, suggestive of cranes, flew across a marsh—a decoration done by some superlative artist.

But this room also was empty.

Tony and Eliot James went on.

"How do you feel?" demanded Tony, after they had entered the fifth great room in gay colors, with marvelous decoration, but empty.

"Feel?" repeated Eliot. "It feels to me that we're in a building that never was used, into which they never moved."

"Perhaps," said Tony, "that goes for the whole city."

"Too soon to say, much too soon to say. How do you go up, d'you suppose?"

"Elevators behind one of these doors, probably. No sign of stairs."

"How do you open the doors?"

"Pound on one of the others, probably," suggested Tony, "judging from recent experience."

"How about the one we opened?" said Eliot. "Is it still up, d'you suppose?"

"What'd lower it?"

"What lifted it?" returned Eliot. "I'll go back and look. Want to go with me?"

"No: I'll stay here and try some of these."

But he had accomplished nothing with any of them when Eliot came back.

"That closed, Tony," he reported soberly.

Tony started. "You didn't close it?"

"No."

"All right!" Tony almost yelled. "Go ahead. Say it!"

"Say what?"

"What you're thinking. Remote control of some sort! Somebody saw us, opened the door, let us walk in, closed it again."

"Somebody!" said Eliot. "Let's be sensible, Tony."

"All right," said Tony, jittering. "You be! . . . Damn it, look at that door. Look at it! That's opening now!"

For a door at the farther edge of this room now slowly was rising.

"Were you working at it?" Eliot whispered.

"Yes."

"Then, that's it. You started another counterbalance working."

"Sure," said Tony. "Sure."

They stepped to the opening. Utter darkness dropped below them. There was a shaft, there—a shaft which, under other circumstances, might have showed machinery. Now it was empty.

Tony and Eliot James knelt side by side at its edge. They shouted, and no voice came back to them.

Tony took a cartridge and dropped it. For so long did it fall silently that they were sure, as they listened, that it must have struck something which gave no sound; then they heard it strike. Tony dropped another, and they timed it. One more they timed, and they stepped back from the shaft carefully.

"Half a mile below!" said Eliot. "They went down almost as far as up; perhaps farther. Why?"

They stepped back from the shaft's threshold carefully.

"There's some control to these damn doors," said Tony, "that probably made it utterly painless to operate them when everything was working. You maybe merely had to stand before them, and some electric gadget would work that's jammed now because the power isn't on. These doors can't all be to shafts."

About fifteen minutes later, they had opened another that exposed a circular passage, leading both upward and downward.

"Ah!" said Eliot. "This is the stuff. No machinery. They probably had it for emergencies."

Tony, awakening, stretched, rubbed his eyes and gazed up at the ceiling. His eyes followed mechanically, forgetfully, the graceful, tenuous lines of decoration which traced down over the walls of the pleasant, beautiful chamber.

He still did not fully recollect where he was, but he realized that he was lying on a couch of soft, agreeable material. Then he saw Eliot James, in trousers and shirt but without his coat, seated at a table, writing. And Tony remembered.

Eliot and he were in the Sealed City—the amazing, stupendous metropolis of the Other People, the People a Million Years Dead.

The light diffused through this chamber, so pleasantly and evenly—it seemed to be spread and intensified somehow by its refraction through the peculiar metal-glass of one wall—was the light of the dawn of the third long Bronson Beta day since Eliot James and Tony Drake, refugees from earth, had discovered and entered the Sealed City.

The amazements of their two days of exploration passed through Tony's mind like reviewing a dream; but they remained reality; for instead of becoming dimmer and dimmer as he sought to recall them, they became only sharper and clearer. Moreover, here before him in a heap upon one of the tables of the Other People, and piled also on the floor, were the proofs of the actuality of what Eliot and he had done. Here were the objects—some of them understandable, more of them utterly incomprehensible as to their purpose or utility—which they had collected to carry with them back to Cole Hendron and the camp.

Eliot was writing so intently and absorbedly that he did not know that Tony was awake. They were in utter stillness; not a sound nor a stir in the Sealed City; and Tony lay quiet watching his companion attempting to deal through words with the wonders they had encountered.

What could a man say that would be adequate?

Tony fingered the stuff of the couch upon which he lay—material not wool, not cotton, not silk. It was soft, pliant fiber, unidentifiable. How old? A million years old, perhaps, in rigidly reckoned time; but not five years old, probably, in the practical period of its use.

It might have been new a million years ago, just before Bronson Beta was torn from its sun; thereafter the time that passed merely preserved it. It was in the utter cold and dark of space. Not even air brushed it. The air was frozen solid. Then this planet found our sun; and time which aged materials, was resumed.

So it was with all the stuff which Eliot and he had collected; those objects might be a million years old, and yet new!

Eliot halted his writing and arose; and glancing at Tony, saw he was awake.

"Hello."

"Hello. How long you been up?"

"Quite a while."

"You would be," complained Tony admiringly. It had been late in the long night, and both had been utterly exhausted, when they lay down to sleep. "It's the third day, isn't it?"

"That's right."

"We ought to go back now."

"Yes," agreed Eliot, "I suppose so. But how can we?"

Tony was sitting up. "How can we leave?" he agreed. "But also, how can we stay—without letting Cole Hendron and the rest of them know?"

"We can come back, of course," Eliot James reluctantly assented.

"Or we may find another city or something else."

"By 'something else,' do you mean the place where 'they' all went, Tony? God, Tony, doesn't it get you? Where did they go? Not one of them—nor the bones of one of them! And all this left in order."

He stood at the table and sifted in his fingers the kernels of a strange grain. Not wheat, not corn, not rice nor barley nor rye; but a starchy kernel. They both had tasted it.

"There's millions of bushels of this, Tony. Should we say 'bushels' or, like the Bible, 'measures'? Well, we know there's millions of measures of this that we've already found. If it's food—and what else could it be?—we've solved our problem of provender indefinitely. And it's foolish to have our people improvising shelter and equipment when all we have to do is to move into—this. Here's equipment we never dreamed of!"

"Yes," said Tony. "Yes." But he remembered that contest

that already had divided the camp. Did the emigrants from the earth dare to move into the city when found? Also, could the people from the earth sustain themselves on this grain or other supplies left by the vanished people? Though the kernels might have been preserved through the epoch of utter cold, had the vitamins—essential to life—remained?

But that was a matter for the experts of the camp to test and to decide. Tony could not doubt his duty to report the tremendous discovery.

"We'll leave to-day, Tony," Eliot pleaded, "but not until later. Let's look about once more."

And Tony agreed; for he too could not bear yet to abandon the amazements of the Sealed City.

It was later than they had planned, when at last they had loaded their ship with the objects—comprehensible and incomprehensible—which they had chosen to carry back to Hendron and his comrades. The sun—the old sun of the shattered world, the new sun of Bronson Beta—was low when Tony drew down once more the great metal ring which closed again the gate of the Sealed City.

"Let's not fly back to the camp by the path we came," said Eliot James.

"No," agreed Tony. "Let's loop to the south before we cut back to the seacoast."

They were in the air again, supported on the rushing golden stream of fire that emerged from their rocket-tubes. They flew through the darkness, occasionally casting upon the ground underneath the bright ray of their searchlight, and still more often thrusting it ahead of them into the gloom. There were no lights anywhere beneath them to indicate that people lived or moved or had their being there.

Long after midnight they flew across what they judged to be either a huge lake or a great inland arm of the sea.

Toward morning they were planning to alight and rest before continuing their adventures, when suddenly they were transfixed. Not in the east, where the first gray bars of the rising sun might be expected to appear, but ahead of them, to the south, a single finger of light pointed upward to the sky—the only light except their own, and except the weird inhuman illumination of the great domed city, which they had seen on the surface of the planet.

CHAPTER VI

SALVATION

THEY were approaching the vertical beam of light at a high speed, but no sooner had its unnatural appearance made a mark in Tony's consciousness than his hands leaped for the controls, and the plane slowed as much as was possible—he'd cut down its elevation.

He turned to James: "What do you think it is?"

"It looks like a searchlight pointed straight up in the air."

"There seems to be a ridge between us and where it comes from."

"Right," James shouted back to him. Tony made a gesture which outlined the process of landing the plane, and James nodded.

When they had come upon the great bubble that covered the city, it had been daylight, and there had been no sign of life about it; but light implied an intelligent agency, and besides, it was night, and their sense of caution was stirred by the very primordial influence of darkness.

Now the plane was skimming low over the empty desert, and in the light of their abruptly switched-on beacon, they could make out racing beneath them a flat aridity.

There was no choice of spots on which to land. The thunder of the tubes had been cut off as Tony turned a switch, and his voice sounded very loud when he said: "How about it?"

"Let 'er go!" James answered, and an instant later they were racing over the ground, stirring up a cloud of dust that had been undisturbed for millennia.

They stopped. They stepped out.

The night around them was warm and clear. Its distant darknesses were weaving with the perpetual aurora of Bronson Beta. Far ahead of the waste in which the plane lay, the single finger of light pointed unwavering toward the stars.

"Shall we wait for day?" Tony asked.

Eliot James looked at the illuminated dial of his wrist-watch. "It'll be several hours in coming yet," he said after a pause. He grinned. "I've learned how to tell time by this watch in a mathematical process as complicated as the theory of relativity."

Tony did not smile at James' whimsy. He was staring at the light. "I should say, from the way it spreads, it must come together in some sort of a lens or reflector a couple of hundred feet below the other side of the ridge. If there's anybody around the base of it, I don't think they saw or heard us coming. If they saw anything, it could easily be mistaken for a meteor." He was silent.

James spoke his thoughts in the quiet of the desert night. "It may be four miles away—it may be six. The walking's pretty good; but the point is—shall we leave our ship?"

"I wonder—have we got time to get there and back before it's light?"

"Meaning the top of the ridge?"

"Exactly."

James squinted at the barren black edge of land traced upon the brief width of the light beam. "Plenty."

Tony made no further comment, but started walking through the night. They walked steadily and rapidly. The ground was sandy, and there were no large stones in it, although once or twice their ankles were nearly turned by large pebbles. They said no more. It might have been interesting to their biographers to note also that neither of them had mentioned their safe landing in the hazards of darkness and unknown terrain. That was like each of them. When you had to take a chance, you took it. When you made it, there was nothing more to be said.

They walked for half an hour before the flat plain, the arid waste, began to rise. In the dark they noticed the inclination more by the increase of their breathing than by the change in the strain on their muscles. Presently, however, the upward pitch became steep, and they realized that they were traversing a series of bare undulant ledges. They went more cautiously then, in their imaginings and their fears, not daring to use flashlights, but feeling for each step—sometimes even moving upward with the aid of their hands.

They knew for several minutes precisely when they would reach the top, and they slowed their pace to a crawl.

A breeze fanned their faces. They stepped up over the last rocky surface, and unconsciously moving on tiptoe, crossed it so they could look into the valley beyond.

Because neither of them was conventionally religious, because both of them were thunderstruck by what they saw, they cursed, fluently and sibilantly, in the night on the ridge.

At their feet, not more than a mile away—so close that the purring of machinery was faintly audible—a single searchlight turned its unwinking eye upon the heavens. In the diffused light around the great lamp they were able to see many things. A huge cylinder, a cylinder like their own Ark but larger, lay toppled upon its side, crippled and riven. Near the cylinder was an orderly group of shelters. Standing beside the searchlight, apparently talking to each other, were doll-like figures of human beings.

"It's our Other People!" Tony said, and his voice choked.

Eliot James gripped his arm. "Maybe not."

"But it must be!"

"It's about the same size, but how can you be sure? Those people who flew over a few nights ago and didn't like us, may have come up in it. All the ships that were built to attempt this flight have looked more or less alike."

"Come on," Tony said.

"Quietly, then."

The minutes were like hours. Both men found themselves slipping down the opposite side of the ridge, holding their breath lest their panting might be overheard in the distance, and trembling whenever a fragment of rock fell. Their thoughts were identical. If the space ship which lay wrecked beyond the searchlight was the carrier of enemies, their presence must never be known. But if it was the ship which had embarked from Michigan with themselves—if that beacon stabbing the night was a signal of distress—and what else could it be?—then—

Then they dared not think any further. They were on level ground now, sluicing through the blackness like Indians, alert, ready to run, ready to throw themselves on the ground. They were half a mile from the two figures at the light. Both of them were men; both of them had their backs turned.

At that distance Tony and Eliot could see how horribly the space ship had been mangled when it descended. There was a great scar on the earth where it must have struck first and tipped over. Its forward end had plowed into the ground, cutting a prodigious furrow and piling at its nose a small mountain of earth and stone. The metal of which it had been made was cracked back in accordion-like pleats. Whether they were friends or enemies, their arrival on Bronson Beta had been disastrous.

That quarter-mile was cut to three hundred yards. They could see each other's faces shining palely in the radiance of the searchlight. They crept forward; the three hundred yards became two.

Suddenly, to the astonishment of Eliot James, Tony emitted a wild bellow which woke echoes from every corner of the night, rose to his feet and rushed across the earth toward the light. Eliot James followed him—and presently understood.

Tony's first shout had been inarticulate, but as he ran now, he called: "Ransdell! *Ransdell!* Oh, my God! It's me—Tony! Tony Drake! We've found you at last!"

And Eliot James, running like a deer, saw one of the men at the light turn around, lift his hand, try to say something, fall forward in a faint.

Ten minutes later, only ten minutes, and yet to three hundred and eighteen human souls that ten minutes had marked the beginning of salvation. They were all out now on the bare earth of Bronson Beta. Everyone was awake—all the lights were shining. The cheers still rose sporadically. Ransdell had come to, and was still rocking in the arms of Tony when he did not unclasp him long enough to embrace Eliot James. The crowd of people, delirious with joy, was trying to touch them and talk to them. All the crowd, that is, except those who had not yet recovered from the terrible smash-up of the landing—and those who would never recover.

Ransdell had fainted for the first time in his life out of pure joy, pure ecstasy, and out of cosmic fatigue. He had scrambled to his feet in time to meet Tony's rush toward him. They had not exchanged many coherent words as yet—just, "Glad to see you," "Great!" "Are you all right?" Things like that. Ransdell had managed to say, "Hendron?" Tony had been able to answer, jubilantly: "Made it all right. Everybody well and safe."

Then Ransdell succeeded in reducing his command to a momentary quiet. He said: "Tony has told me that the Ark made the trip and landed safely."

Again the cheering rose and echoed in the night. Again people rushed forward by the score to shake Tony's hand. Jack Little was there, bandaged and grinning. Peter Vanderbilt, apparently calm but blowing his nose in a suspicious manner. Jack Taylor was there too, and Smith and Greve and a hundred other people whose faces had become the faces of friends for Tony and Eliot James in the past two years. Somebody brought from the mêlée of dunnage that had spilled out of the split-open space ship two tubs. Upon them Tony and Ransdell stood.

By waving their arms and smiling in the flood of light which had been turned on over the encampment, they made it plain the whole night could not be spent in cheering and crying. They made it plain by shouting through their dialogue that they had better trade information.

CHAPTER VII

REUNION

TONY felt it utterly useless to attempt to speak to the throng; the people were too hysterical. More than three hundred of them were able-bodied, though many of these still bore bandages that testified to the injuries from which they were recovering. They had thought themselves recuperated from shock; but this intense excitement betrayed them.

Ransdell, restored from his faintness, proved the superior quality of his nerves by attaining composure first. He went to Tony and drew him away from the excited throng which continued to clamor about them.

"Eliot!" shouted Tony to his companion in this flight of exploration. "You try to tell them—as soon as they give you a chance."

"O. K.!" Eliot yelled, and he stepped up on the tub which Tony had quitted. He shouted and made gestures and caught the crowd's attention. Only a few trailed after Tony and their own leader, Ransdell.

Tony could not yet quiet his own inner tumult. He felt an arm about his shoulder, and found Jack Taylor beside him; and he thought how he had traveled on a train along the Hudson, back on the earth, on his way to Cornell University to meet this young man and ask him to become a member of Hendron's party.

On the other side of him walked Peter Vanderbilt; and Tony thought of Fifth Avenue, and its clubs and mansions, so staid, so secure! Or they had felt themselves so. Now where were they?

Reveries of some similar sort were running through Vanderbilt's head. His eyes met Tony's, and he smiled.

"Tony, I woke up laughing, a night or so ago," Peter Vanderbilt said.

"Laughing at what?" Tony inquired. They had passed from the noise of the crowd.

"At my dream. I dreamed, you see, Tony, that I was back on earth. Not only that, but I was on earth before the time these delectable Bronson Bodies were reported in the night skies. I was attending the ceremonies of installation of somebody's statue—for the life of me, I can't say whose—in the Hall of the Immortals! After I woke up, a meteor crossed this sky. I couldn't help wondering if it mightn't have been part of that statue! . . . Well, why not sit here? You can tell us a little more of what happened to you."

So the four friends sat down on the ground close together, seeing each other in the distant radiance of the lights in the camp; and interrupting each other as they told, they traded their experiences in the flight from earth.

The account that Tony heard was far more tragic, of course, than that which he had to tell. The technicians under command of David Ransdell had made their calculations accurately, and the journey through space had been little more eventful than that of the ship in which Tony and his comrades had traveled. However, the second Ark had been built more hastily, and its greater size increased its difficulties; as it approached Bronson Beta, it become evident to its navigators that the lining of its propulsion-tubes was being rapidly fused. It approached the planet safely, however; and like its sister ship, found itself over the surface of a sea. Fortunately, the coast was not far away, or the great vessel would have dropped into the water and all aboard perished.

The coast which the second Ark approached—the coast upon which it now lay—was fog-bound. "In spite of the fog," Ransdell said to Tony, "we had to land at once. Of course, the jets cleared away the fog below us, but only replaced it with a brilliant cloud of gases. We were flying 'blind,' and had to land by instrument. I ordered everybody to be strapped to the floor, and gave the command to set down the ship under the added pressure of the blast required for the delicate business of landing. Three of our tubes fused almost simultaneously. The ship careened and almost tipped over. In trying to right it, we rose perhaps fifty feet above this desert." He swept his hand toward the surrounding darkness. "And then we crashed."

Tony nodded. Ransdell went on: "Every bit of apparatus that was in the least fragile was, of course, demolished. On top of the crash, one of the jet-tubes burst, and its blast penetrated the storeroom. That might have been much worse; it might have annihilated half our party. Perhaps it did so, indirectly—it fused or destroyed more than half our stores and equipment. Since landing, we have not found it possible to construct even a radio. That is why you have heard no signals from us. We had more than we could do, for the first weeks, taking care of our injured and burying the dead—and salvaging and making usable what supplies were spared, in part. The searchlight you saw to-night was the best effort we accomplished."

Suddenly Ransdell's voice failed him. He cleared his throat and continued very quietly: "To tell the truth, Tony, we wondered whether we should try to communicate with Hendron's party—assuming you had come through safe. We are so without supplies or resources, that we could only be a burden to you. We knew that at best you could barely manage for yourselves. It was that, as much as anything else, which stopped us from making efforts to find you. We decided not to drag you down and perhaps cause you, as well as ourselves, to perish."

"You would," said Tony. "You would decide that—Vanderbilt and Taylor and you, Dave. But thank God, that point's past. I haven't told you half the news. Eliot James and I didn't come from our camp to you. We came from a city!"

"City?"

"Of the Other People, Dave!"

"Other People? . . . What Other People? . . . Where?"

"I mean a city of the old inhabitants of this planet!" Tony cried. "For it was inhabited, as we thought. And by what people! Eliot and I spent three days in one of their cities!"

"But not—with Them?"

"No," agreed Tony. "Not with them! They're gone! They're dead, I suppose—for a million years. But wait till you hear what they left behind them! And what the cold and the dark of space saved for us! Food, for one thing. Dave! Peter! Jack!" In their excitement, they were all standing up again, and Tony was beating each of them in turn upon the back. "Food—grain and other things saved for us by Space's wonderful refrigerator of absolute cold. Cheer up! Food—something to fill you—no longer's one of our troubles. Their food—if it doesn't kill us all. And it hasn't killed Eliot or me yet. . . . Listen! What's that?"

For there was shouting in the camp.

"I suspect," said Peter Vanderbilt, "that James has got to that point too. He's been telling them of the food you found. Perhaps now we better rejoin our comrades and—the ladies."

Eliot James *had* reached that point; and it started a new hysteria; for they believed him, and had faith in the food-supplies he reported. The immediate effect was instinctive and practical; they ordered their own sparse supplies distributed more satisfyingly than on any occasion since the terrible landing on this earth.

It was indeed salvation which Tony Drake and Eliot James had brought out of the night—salvation and the end of some of the hardships heroically borne. Tony did not realize then the extent of those hardships; but when half an hour later coffee was served for all of them in the improvised dining-hall, he was made to realize it by a simple statement of Ransdell's. "This is the first ration of coffee we have served, except to those in most desperate condition, since the day after we landed."

It was a hilarious midnight picnic in the impromptu dining-hall, where the men and women dared to eat as much as they wanted for the first time since their epochal journey—where they sang hymns, shouted snatches of gay songs from lost days on the vanished earth, wept and laughed again, over-hilariously. Tony found himself compelled to repeat again and again details of the city which Eliot James and he had found; again and again he had to iterate how Hendron and Eve and all their people had fared; and now he told how the three had died from the strange disease.

In return he gained other items from this and that of his companions, who enabled him gradually to piece together a more coherent account of the experience of the second band of Argonauts. Each detail was made vivid by the various narrators. The horrible day of the landing as the fog cleared away, revealing moment by moment the magnitude of the disaster which had overtaken them; the groans of the wounded; the crushed and mangled bodies of the dead; the desperate efforts of the doctors and surgeons among them to save those who were not beyond hope. Hastily constructed operating-tables under a sun which had once shone on the earth, and which now cast its radiance into the greenish-blue skies of Bronson Beta. The gradual emergence of order. The tallying of the lists of stores and tools. The shocking discovery that every one of the seeds so carefully stored on the ship had been burned by the unleashed atomic blast. The necessary destruction of the animals which had survived the crash, and the utilization of them for food. Rationing, then, and hunger. Long and weary expeditions on foot in search of sustenance. Efforts to find vegetation on Bronson Beta for food—efforts which in more than one case had led to illness, and twice had brought about death. The erection of the searchlight. The nights and days of waiting and hoping, complicated by fear to be found, because of the burden their discovery might constitute to those who discovered them.

"For a while," said Jack Taylor, "we believed that nobody else—no other ship from earth—got over. We felt that, desperate as our situation was, yet we were the luckiest."

"But two weeks ago—two weeks of these peculiarly prolonged days, not to mention the similarly protracted nights," put in Peter Vanderbilt, "two weeks ago, we began to believe differently."

"Why?" asked Tony.

"Airplane," replied Vanderbilt succinctly.

"Where?"

"Where would it be?"

"I mean," said Tony, "it didn't land?"

"Not it. Nor too plainly appear."

"Neither did ours," said Tony.

"You mean you sent it? It was your machine?" Ransdell swiftly demanded.

"Not two weeks ago," Tony denied. "We had nothing in

the air then. I mean, an airplane visited us too; and it didn't too plainly appear."

"But you saw it?"

"We got a glimpse of it— a glint of light on a wing through the clouds," explained Tony. "Did you see more here?"

"Yes," said Ransdell. "We got a shape—a silhouette. Queer type; we couldn't identify it. Long, back-pointing wings. Like larks' wings, somebody said. It looked like a giant lark in the sky."

Tony looked up from Ransdell to Eliot James, who had joined the circle.

Eliot softly whistled.

"Well," said Tony to Eliot.

"Well yourself!" Eliot James retorted. "You say it."

"Say what?" demanded Ransdell impatiently. "You know whose plane it was? What party brought that type over?"

"No party," said Tony bluntly.

"What do you mean?"

"What I say. No party from earth brought that ship with them. It wasn't brought over."

He had gone a little pale, as he spoke; and he wiped his forehead and then his hands with his handkerchief.

"What—the—hell!" whispered Jack Taylor with awed deliberation.

"I said," iterated Tony solemnly, "it wasn't brought over. On the edge of the city of the Other People, of which we've been telling you—under the great glass dome, but near an edge where they could be run out, easily—was a sort of hangar of those things. We saw a—a hundred of them. Like larks, they'd look in the sky—all-metal larks of marvelous design. They had engines. Did you tell them of the engine in that car we found wrecked before we went off to find the city?" He appealed to Eliot James.

Eliot nodded; and several voices urged Tony on with: "Yes; he told us. . . . We know."

"Well," said Tony, "they had engines of that same small, powerful type. We recognized it; but we couldn't get one going. We tried to."

He stopped, wet his lips.

"Go on! For God's sake, go on!"

"All right," said Tony. "But where do I go from there? What am I to tell you? I can tell you this; for I know it. I saw it. I saw the machines; and I felt them with my hands; and as I told you, I tried to make the engine work, but Eliot and I couldn't."

"The Other People—the People a Million Years Dead—the inhabitants of Bronson Beta—had aircraft that would look, in the air, like nothing we had on earth but a lark. They had small, economical and evidently exceedingly powerful engines that propelled them by a motive-power we haven't learned to employ."

"I believe it was one of those machines which flew over you—and over us."

"Flew?" repeated Peter Vanderbilt calmly. "Of itself? No pilot?"

Tony shook his head.

"A pilot perhaps," pronounced Vanderbilt softly, *"a million years dead?"*

Tony nodded; the inclination of his head in this affirmative made them jump.

"You don't believe it!" Peter Vanderbilt rebuked him.

"You," said Tony, "haven't been in their city. We were there three days, and never ceased to expect them to walk out any door!"

"After a million years dead?"

"How do we know how it might have been?"

"We know," Jack Taylor reminded him, "how long it must have been at the very shortest. Less than a million years, to be sure; but—plenty long in the dark and absolute zero. They never could have survived it."

Tony looked at him. "Why?"

"Because they couldn't, Tony."

"You mean, because we couldn't have. But we're not—They."

Peter Vanderbilt flicked a speck from his sleeve. "We have no need to be metaphysical," he suggested. "The machine could have come from one source, the pilot from another. The machine could have survived the million years cold; we know that some did. You saw them. But the pilot need have survived no more than a passage from earth—which some three hundred of us here have survived, and a hundred in your camp also."

"Of course," accepted Eliot James practically. "Another party could have got across—several parties; the Germans, the Russians, the Japanese or some others. Two weeks or more ago they may have found another Sealed City with the Other People's aircraft."

"And they," said Tony, "may have got one of the engines going."

"Exactly!"

"All right," said Tony, "that's that. Then let's all sit down again. Why did the pilot, whoever he is, look us over and leave without message or signal? Why—"

They sat down, but drew closer, talking together: "If some of the Other People survived, what would be their attitude to us, would you say? . . . Would they know who we were, and where we came from?"

Tony led a dozen men to the ship in which Eliot and he

had flown; and they bore to the camp the amazing articles from the Sealed City.

Nobody tired. There was no end to their speculations and questions. Tony, seated on the ground and leaning on his hand beside him, felt a queer, soft constriction of his forefinger. He drew his hand up, and the constriction clamped tighter, and he felt a little weight. Some small, living thing had clasped him.

It let go and leaped onto his shoulder.

"Hello!" cried Tony, as two tiny soft hands and two tiny-toed feet clung to him. "Hello! Hello!" It was a monkey.

"Her name's Clara," said Ransdell.

"Yours?" asked Tony. "You brought her over?"

"Nobody brought her over," Ransdell replied. "You know the regulations before leaving earth. I tried to enforce them; but Clara was too good for us. She stowed away."

"Stowed away?"

"We discovered her after things got calm in space," Ransdell said, smiling. "When we were well away from the earth and had good equilibrium. Everybody denied they had anything to do with her being on board. In fact, nobody seemed able to account for her; nobody would even admit having seen her before; but there she was. And she survived the passage; and even our landing. Of course we kept her afterward."

"Of course," said Tony. "Good work, Clara." He extended his finger, which Clara clasped solemnly, and "shook hands" by keeping her clasp as he waved his finger.

"Since we're checking up," added Ransdell, "you might as well know that we brought over one more passenger not on the last lists we made back there in Michigan. —Marian!" he called to the group about them. "You here?"

"Where would I be?" A girl of about twenty-three stood up and walked toward him. Her eyes were gray; her chin was firm; her hair was darkly red. Tony noticed that she carried herself with a boldness different from the others.

"Her name," Ransdell murmured as she approached, "is Marian Jackson. Lived in St. Louis. An acrobatic dancer. Kept her head during the chaos before the destruction. Read about our plans. Crawled into camp the night before we took off. Lived in the woods for three weeks before that—nobody knows what on."

The girl reached the table and took Tony's hand. "I've heard about you," she said. "Often. You don't look anything like I supposed you would."

"I'm glad to meet you," Tony replied.

Unabashed, she studied him. "You look shot," she said finally.

Tony grinned. "I am a little tired."

"You're all in. But then, everybody's tired around here always."

"You better go back to your place," Ransdell said.

"Sure," the girl answered. She smiled buoyantly and returned.

Ransdell looked at her thoughtfully, sipped his coffee, and shook his head. Then he continued privately to Tony: "She's really a moron, I suppose. I doubt if Hendron will approve of having a moron in our company; but her empty-headedness, her astonishment at everything, even her ignorance, which is pretty naïve, have delighted everybody. And she did a big thing for us."

Tony looked thoughtfully at the red-headed girl as she sat down and resumed conversation with those beside her.

"What did she do?" he asked, returning his attention to Ransdell.

"The second night we were here, Eberville went mad. He decided early in the evening that it was against the will of God for us to be here, and that we should all be destroyed. But he quieted down, and he was left alone. Later he got up, got into the ship, started the only generator that would work, and turned on one of the lateral tubes. In the morning you can see a big black patch about four hundred yards to the left of where we were camped. He'd have wiped us out in ten seconds, but Marian jumped on him. She's strong. So was Eberville, insanely strong. But she has teeth and nails. That is why we all escaped annihilation a second time."

Tony shook his head slowly and thoughtfully, without speaking.

The little monkey, Clara, returned to him and squatted before him, peering up at him with its queerly humanlike, puzzled gaze.

She had no business here, Tony recollected. Monkeys were not on the list of necessary or useful creatures to be taken on the terrible transfer from earth to this planet; and a single representative of the tiny monkey clan was particularly impractical and useless. But Tony was glad that Clara was here.

Among the crowd he saw Marian Jackson's red head moving; and he thought: "She had not been selected, either; but all these girls here of higher intelligence, and all the men too, would have been wiped out, but for her."

He did not blame Hendron for the narrowness of the selections more than he blamed himself. He thought: "We must all have become a bit mad in those last days on earth—mad or at least fanatic. We could hope to save so few and became too intent on certain types."

Suddenly Tony got up. Hendron, he remembered, knew none of their discoveries and events. He could delay no longer his return to Hendron.

But when he suggested to Eliot James that they return, others would not allow it.

"Not both of you! . . . You haven't both got to go!"

There was altogether too much yet to tell, and to hear.

"Let Eliot stay here, Tony," Dave Ransdell said. "I'll go to Hendron with you. I ought to report to him; and I want so much to see him."

"Just right," Tony accepted this plan.

"That's the thing to do."

They were in the air, Tony Drake and Dave Ransdell together. In the plane with them, they freighted a fair half of the objects intelligible and unintelligible, which Tony and Eliot had brought from the Sealed City. With them was also Eliot James' record, which he had read to the people in Ransdell's camp.

It was dawn; the slow sunrise of Bronson Beta was spreading its first faint shafts across the sky; and the ground below was beginning to be etched in its pattern of plain and hill and river and estuary from the sea.

The veinlike tracery of roads appeared—the lines left by the Vanished People. Tony gazed far ahead and to each side, searching for another or others of such marvelous, gigantic bubbles which would become, upon approach, other cities. But nothing of the sort came in sight. They spied smears and blotches below which became, when they turned the glass upon them, rows of ruins. They did not stop for these. Already they had much to report; already they were long overdue.

They sighted, far ahead, columns of smoke lifted lazily into the sky. Ransdell pointed and Tony, leaning to his ear, shouted: "Our camp-fires! Our camp!"

He could make out now, in the early morning light, that these were indeed camp-fires ending their duty of lessening the chill of the long night, perhaps, starting their services of cooking. The camp seemed unchanged; it was safe.

Tony compared its crudeness and rudeness with the marvelously proportioned perfections of the Sealed City; and a pang of nostalgia for this encampment suddenly assailed him. Here were his own; here was home.

He glanced aside and surprised his comrade Dave Ransdell, as he stared down. What thousand shattering fragments of thoughts must fill Ransdell's mind! One—and Tony plainly could see it—overwhelmed all the rest. Here, below, was Eve Hendron.

For it was a sudden softness and yearning that was in the eyes of the broad-shouldered, Herculean man at Tony's side. What would be in Eve's eyes when she saw him?

Tony's nostaglia of the moment before was replaced by a jerk of jealousy. Eve always had admired Dave and liked him—and more. More, yes, more than liked him, during those last desperate days on earth. Now he was here; and he had done well.

Yes; any one would say—Hendron himself would declare—that Dave Ransdell had done well indeed to have brought across space the ship intrusted to him with loss of less than half the party. Ransdell would be greeted ecstatically as a hero.

Tony caught his lip between his teeth and tried to establish better control of his inward tumult. If Eve preferred Dave to himself, let her!

He busied himself grimly with his throttles, putting down the ship on the bare soil more than a mile from camp.

They had been seen in the air and recognized; and the camp was outpouring toward them. The tractor was leading, piled with passengers.

Tony and Dave started to run toward them; then they halted. The people from the camp began to see that one figure was not that of Eliot James.

"Who is it? Who's with you?" came the cry from the tractor which was ahead of the runners.

"Ransdell! Dave Ransdell!" Tony yelled; and Dave stopped and lifted high his arms.

"Ransdell! *Ransdell?*" came back.

"Yes! They got over! *The second ship got over!*"

Then the welcome began.

"Tony," said Ransdell later, when for an instant they had a few words together, "how Hendron's changed!"

"Yes," said Tony, "of course he has." But he realized that to Ransdell, who had not seen their leader since the last day on earth, the alteration in Hendron's appearance and manner was more tragic. Indeed, it seemed to Tony that in the few days he had been gone, Hendron had become whiter and weaker.

Never had Tony heard Hendron's voice shake as now it did; and his hand, which clung to the list which Ransdell had given him, quivered as if with palsy.

It was the list of the survivors and of the dead from the second Ark, with which Hendron had insisted that he be supplied.

He had read it several times; but again and again, like a very old man, he went over it.

"It was the tubes, you say, David?" he kept reviewing the disaster at landing, with Ransdell. "Three of the tubes fused! That was the fault of the design—my fault," he blamed himself morbidly.

"Father!" whispered his daughter to him. "Father, you ought to be happier than any other man in the world."

"In the world!" repeated Hendron.

"In all the universe!" Eve quickly corrected. "You brought all the people in our ship over safely; and more than three hundred in the other Ark! Oh, Father, Father, no man in the universe could have done more!"

Hendron shook his head. "These people here, of whom Tony has told us. What metallurgists! They would have made a ship. Ah! Ah! Aha! Tony—David—Higgins! The rest of you! What do you think of this? The People of this planet are not here because they made good their escape through space! They made their own space-ships and better ones and more of them; and escaped when they were passing some habitable sphere as they scraped some star!"

"No, Father!"

"How do you know? I tell you, they probably did it; and accomplished it so much better than I, with my bungling, that I am an amateur—a murderer. How many did I kill, David? How many did you say? . . . What rows of names!"

"Father, you didn't kill them!"

"I tell you I did! The tubes fused—the tubes I figured and designed myself. The human factor did not fail. They piloted it properly. The tubes fused!"

No one could quiet him. His daughter had to lead him away with Tony and Ransdell both helping her. The excitement of Ransdell's news and, on top of it, Tony's had snapped his nerves, drawn too long to extreme tension. It was perfectly plain to all the company whom he had led that his day, as a man of resource, was done.

Tony, thoroughly realizing this, trembled himself as he helped lead his friend to his cabin. Partly it was from pity and compassion; for no one knew better than Tony with what mercilessness Hendron had driven himself and how he had borne so long his enormous burden. But partly this trembling was from an emotion far less worthy. It was jealousy again of Dave Ransdell.

Jealousy more bitter and hard than that which had possessed him when they both were on earth—and rivals. For here they were rivals again and with the conflict between them accentuated.

How Eve had hugged Dave and held to him and kissed him!

To be sure, they had all embraced him—men and girls. Every girl in the camp hysterically had kissed him. But Eve had not been hysterical, Tony knew. Eve—Eve— Well, it had changed this world for her that Dave Ransdell had reached it.

Then there was the talk which Tony had heard: the talk already to-night of Ransdell as the new leader of both camps; the leader of the survivors of earth to replace and follow Hendron.

Tony tingled alternately with hate of Dave, and with shame at himself, as he thought of this talk. He had quieted the talk of himself as leader and he honestly had not wanted it a few days ago; he would not permit himself to be considered a candidate against Hendron; but now that Hendron was surely done, he wanted his people—*his* people, he thought them—to want him for their leader. And some still did; but more, he thought miserably, to-night turned to Dave Ransdell.

This was unworthy; this was childish, this jealousy and hate of his strong, courageous comrade! So Tony told himself; but he could not conquer it.

Now they had come to Hendron's cabin; and Tony felt himself becoming officious in the endeavor to be of more use to Hendron and to Eve than Dave might be.

Ransdell felt this and drew back.

"Thank you, Tony," said Eve, in her gentle voice. "Now you go back to the people."

"All right," said Tony. "Come along, Dave."

"Let him stay here, Tony," said Eve.

"Him—and not me?" Tony stared.

"What more can he tell them?" Eve asked patiently. "He's given them his news, who're living and who"—she lowered her voice carefully so her father could not hear—"who are dead. He has no more to tell. You—you haven't begun to tell them what you must have to tell of the strange city!"

"Don't *you* want to hear it?" Tony persisted.

"I'm staying with Father now," said Eve.

Rebelliously—and yet ashamed of himself for his feeling—Tony turned away and left her with Ransdell.

CHAPTER VIII

THE CITY OF VANISHED PEOPLE

"THE best way to give you some idea of the city," Tony said, facing the entire company except Hendron and Eve, "is to read you extracts from the record made, on the spot and at the time, by Eliot James. Before I begin, however, I ask you to think of a city made of many colored metals built like the spokes of a wheel around a vast central building. Think of a dome of transparent metal over it. And then remember particularly, while I read, that every street, every building, every object in the whole metropolis was in an amazing state of preservation.

"Remember that there was not a single sign of human habitation. I have already told you that the people were human—very much like ourselves—but there was not a sign of them or any remains of them except for statues and paintings and representations which we called photographic for lack of a better word and for record on their remarkable visual machines. Bear all that in mind. Here, for example, is what Eliot wrote on the evening of our first day there. It was the fifty-first day on Bronson Beta. I will skip the part that describes the city in general."

He began to read: "Tony and I are now seated in a bedroom of an apartment in one of the large buildings. The night of Bronson Beta has descended, but we have light. In fact, the adventure of light is the most bizarre which has befallen us since we penetrated this spectacular and silent city. As twilight descended we were about to return to our airplane. We were at the time on the street. We had visited one or two buildings, and the effect of the silence combined with the oncoming darkness was more than we could bear. I know that my scalp was tingling, the palms of my hands were clammy, and when I stood still I could feel my muscles shaking. We could not rid ourselves of the feeling that the city was inhabited; we could not cease looking quickly over our shoulders in the hope or the fear of seeing somebody. As we stood uncertainly on the street the sun vanished altogether, its orange light reflected by low-lying cumulus clouds. The sky took on a deeper green and at a word from Tony I would have run from the place. Suddenly, to our utter confoundation, the city was bathed in light. The light came on without a sound. Its source, or rather, its sources, were invisible. It shone down on the streets from behind cornices. It burst luminously upon the walls of the giant buildings.

"The interiors of many of them were also filled with radiance. All this, suddenly, silently, in the gathering gloom. I shall never forget the expression on Tony's face as he turned to me and whispered: 'It's too much!' My own mind, appalled at this new, marvelous manifestation of the genius of the Other People, was very close to lapsing into unconsciousness for a second. Then I found myself with my hands clenched, saying over and over to myself, 'It's light, just light. It was getting dark, so they turned on the lights.' Then I amended that to—'The lights come on here when it's dark.' Immediately Tony and I fell into an altercation. 'It's just the lights coming on,' I said.

" 'But that's impossible!'

" 'Nevertheless, they're on.'

"Tony, searching frantically for the shreds of his sanity, replied, 'But if the lights come on every night in this city, we'd have seen it through telescopes.'

" 'Maybe we didn't happen to catch it.'

" 'It can't be.'

"Both of us thought of the same thing simultaneously: the lights had come on because the city had been entered. It was true that if the cities of Bronson Beta had been illuminated at night the fact would have been observed before their passing. And a new and utterly irrational feeling struck us. The people were dead, dead a million years—a hundred million years. But in this startling gesture of turning on the lights there was more than mechanical magic. There was hospitality. That was crazy, but it was the way we felt.

" 'It was arranged,' Tony said. 'Arranged for somebody, sometime—so arranged that when they should come here everything would be ready for them. Consequently, unless we do something very stupid, nothing can happen to us.' I repeat that it was utterly irrational; but that was the way it made us feel.

"I was inclined to agree with him, and as my eyes traveled along the brilliant and magnificent streets of this metropolis, I too for the first time felt that the artificial light pouring indirectly upon us had lent to it a humanity that had been hitherto absent.

" 'Let's stay,' Tony said. 'Maybe we can find a place to sleep. We really ought to know more about it before we go back.'

"And so we stayed. We picked a building which we thought contained residences and after some experimenting succeeded in entering it. The ground floor was a hall, or lobby, which was decorated by statuary and bas-reliefs, of animals more fantastic and ferocious-looking than could be contrived in the wildest nightmare. And yet their presentation had a gay note, as if the sculptor had set them as humorous, rather than savage, embellishments in that lobby. At one side of the lobby was another large room which contained the apparatus for what we presently realized was a variety of games. They were like no games on our earth. One of them was played with large metal-like balls, which were extremely light and yet very hard, and with magnets. Another was played over a pool, evidently with jets of water, but we could not turn on the jets and the pool was empty. We did not take the time to puzzle out the technique of these sports, but proceeded by a large staircase to the floor above. There, as we had hoped, we found apartments. One of them, which faced the street from which we had entered the building, was open—and this we have made our own."

As Tony turned a page, his listeners waited almost breathlessly. He continued from the record:

"It is an apartment of indescribable beauty. The living room is more than twenty feet in height. Its walls are decorated with metal figures in various colors. There is no rug on the floor, but the floor is of a texture not unlike that of a very fine, deep rug. There are mirrors on many faces of the walls—the Other People must have enjoyed looking at themselves, or else they must have liked the added effect of distance lent by the mirrors, for large reflecting panels seem to be an important part of their interior decoration. We have also found beds. There were two bedrooms. The beds are very low. We had, I imagine, assumed that they would be of a luxurious softness, but they are rather hard, so that in spite of their comforts the Other People must have been Spartans in some measure. Apparently there are closets and bureaus set in the walls, but we have not been able to get open the panels which cover them. We have also found a bathroom, but we cannot make anything of it. It is a beautiful chamber of all bright metals, the colors of which are gold and azure, but it is filled with fixtures and other gadgets of great intricacy as well as beauty.

"We are leaving the problem of deciphering the Bronson Betans' bathing and toilet-making for experts.

"However, we are quite comfortable in that part of our quarters which we have had the courage to occupy. . . . It is now moderately late in the Bronson Beta night and we have decided to try to sleep. To be sure, we have placed a chair in the door to the hall so it will not magically close upon us, for although we are only one story above the street it is impossible to break these windows. We have also planned to keep our pistols at our sides, although a glance at this world of the Other People makes us quite sure that if there were any survivors and they were bent on our destruction, a revolver would be an extremely useless weapon. However, nobody has survived; of that we are convinced."

Tony looked up and regarded his fascinated audience. They were packed about him, crowding close, eager for his next words. But Eve was not there; nor Ransdell. He tried to dismiss thought of this as he proceeded to read:

"We did sleep, and we slept very well. However, we woke before the actual return of daylight, and feeling sufficiently refreshed, we decided to continue our explorations in the remarkable radiance of the artificial illumination which was so useful though so puzzling to us. You can scarcely understand how this affected us with the conviction that the place must be inhabited, and that around the next corner, beyond the next door, we must find some of the people. But we found no living thing."

Tony looked up again. "I find here a number of pages of notes of the most sober sort. They are Eliot James' attempt to describe and analyze some of the remarkable objects and implements which we examined. Of course neither he nor I are physicists, chemists or engineers, so our notions are probably valueless; those of you who are more expert than either of us will undoubtedly soon have a chance to inspect the engines and implements of the Other People.

"Along with such notes, I find the trivial record of what Eliot and I ate on that amazing morning. I will read that because it will show to you something of our state of mind. We seem to have been so stunned by what we had seen that it never occurred to Eliot that it was ridiculous to describe, along with the wonders of the Sealed City, our breakfast!"

His gaze returned to the notes.

"We got up in what we call the morning," Tony read, "although it was still dark, and we had a breakfast consisting of one bar of chocolate and a rather crumbled piece of hardtack which I had in my pocket, for what reason nobody will ever know. Then an extremely funny thing happened—at least we thought it was funny. We finished the last crumb of the hardtack—for our real food supply was in our ship outside the city—when I, looking for chance provender, felt in a pocket, and produced—to our mutual amazement—a stick of chewing-gum! This we broke evenly in half, and we embarked again on the streets of Bronson Beta chewing gum—a practice which I dare say was unknown on the planet in its earlier days.

"Well, the first thing we investigated that morning was a store. It was a department store in the sense that it contained a great many kinds of things; but it did not contain, for example, clothes or, as far as we could discover, food. It had house-furnishings, and furniture and kitchen appliances—and by the way, cooking must have been a cinch for the Other People, because apparently they cooked things by induced heat and under high pressure with steam, so that it only took a few minutes. The store also exhibited some of those automobile-like vehicles like the one we found wrecked.

"In the store," he continued, "we also found a large department of games and sports, and one of children's toys. The children had very peculiar blocks. Wires extend from their sides and corners so that they look like cockleburs and can be stuck together to make variously shaped figures in which the differently colored blocks are held apart by wires. It was Tony who solved the enigma of those blocks. 'Molecules,' he said, as we stood staring at them. And then I realized that each block was designed to represent an atom and that the children were taught by playing with the blocks the atomic structure of various elements.

"I can give you no idea of the superlative order in which everything in it was arranged. It would be hopeless for me to try to tell you the skill with which those people combined use with beauty. Beauty and use with imaginative intelligence. I can only say two things—first, that you will all see it yourselves, and second, that while the streets, and the buildings, and the apartments of the city of the Other People fascinated us, we had intended to leave that morning."

Again Tony ceased to read. "We appreciated, of course," he observed to his hearers, "that we ought to communicate with you; and after our breakfast, and a brief journey through some of the strange streets, we went out of the city by the way we had entered and returned to our ship where we tried to call you by radio. We failed utterly because of some puzzling interference.

"We argued, then, whether we should return to you with what we had learned or whether we should first try to learn much more. The second argument was overwhelming in its appeal to us. We returned to the city; and on the second day, we discovered that it was not quite so intact as we had supposed. In no less than six places which we observed, the huge transparent dome was pierced and showed great jagged tears or holes and below were marks of demolition exhibiting great violence. Meteors had torn through. But except for the wreckage caused by these, I tell you we found almost nothing out of order in that remarkable city. *They* left it in order, we believe; the meteors probably were met after the city was deserted and during this sphere's long journey through space.

"Now I will give you a few more random details from Eliot's diary:

"One thing we noted on our return to the stores—if they were stores," Tony read, "was that in none of them did there seem to have been a system for collecting money, or a medium of exchange, or of keeping books. Seemingly the Other People just came in and took what they wanted—or individuals must have kept their own books—or some system which we couldn't imagine was used. For at the end of our three days' stay we were pretty certain that they had no medium of exchange to correspond to money.

"A department of that store was given over to musical instruments. Their chromatic scale is different from ours, and their way of writing music entirely different. They had a few stringed instruments, no wind instruments, many percussion instruments, but they had developed a vast variety of instruments which seem to have been operated by the transference of electrical impulses to sound. Unquestionably, music and the science of electricity had existed side by side for so long that the art had developed a science for its expression.

"We found in profusion the small, light vehicles of the type which we first discovered wrecked on the road near our camp. It is plain these were operated by some sort of electric impulse; but we could do nothing with them."

Tony skipped more pages. "Imagine us with the sun rising and the flood of indirect illumination dimming away. Imagine us under that vast transparent bubble in the early morning, having a long look at one marvel after another. We went across bridges and up and down streets. We tramped along ramps and on a dozen levels. We visited civic centers and museums and theaters and recreation-grounds and central kitchens and other places of assembly, the purpose of which was not clear. All we lacked was some one to explain at frequent intervals just what the devil we were seeing, because while we were interested we often could only guess, and sometimes none of our explanations made sense. We never found that some one. One thing was very clear, however: the Other People liked to spend a lot of time together. They had privacy in their own apartments, to be sure, but there were so many things and so many kinds of things for people to do in crowds that we became convinced that they were very gregarious. We felt too that their crowds were not comprised of mobs of unfriendly, unsympathetic, unacquainted individuals—like the crowds that once thronged the streets of New York—but were crowds of people who were associated in a most friendly and coöperative spirit with each other.

"We followed a gallery underground where we found more great machines—engines—which we could not at all understand. We saw further descents into depths we decided not to explore. But we did come upon some of their stores of food—particularly grain."

"Samples of this grain," Tony reminded them, looking up, "already you have examined for yourselves. Eliot and I tasted it; we ate it. It was starchy and not unpleasant. Whether or not it still contains vitamins, at least it has the starch base for nutrition. In the afternoon, we found one other thing of far greater importance to us than any other discovery, if I may except the food supply. This was a school."

"A school?" several voices cried.

"We believe it was a school for their children from their early years up. Can you imagine the benefit of such a discovery to you? We have brought back some of the objects from that school. Some of them seem to be books—books of a different type, to be sure, than our volumes; yet they can be described as books. Other objects, which we believe to have been materials of instruction, are harder to describe. Neither Eliot nor I were able to operate them, but we formed the theory that they probably were mechanisms giving instruction visually or by sound.

"Then we found a sphere. It was in the lobby of the school. It was a sphere about fifty feet in diameter upon which was a relief map which we must assume to be of this planet. Eliot James made a most painstaking sketch of that sphere. There were other maps."

"In short," said Tony, closing Eliot James' book of notes, "we have awaiting us not only an equipment beyond anything dreamed of on earth, but a means of acquiring the secrets of the use of the engines and implements and other knowledge of this planet which we could not have obtained, by ourselves, at all.

"A little study by ourselves as children in those amazing classrooms, a little skill and a little luck in setting in operation their mechanisms of instruction; and their secrets are ours!"

CHAPTER IX

THE MYSTERIOUS ATTACK

LUNCH was very late that day; it was long before the company of the camp could be satisfied that they had heard everything of importance that Tony had to tell them. This included, of course, the report on the finding of the lark-like aircraft of which he had made report to the other camp.

Now Tony sat alone. Many, at first, tried to sit beside him and to talk to him. But he had told them that he was weary and wished to be alone for a little while. When the children came running up to him, however, he talked to them cheerfully. . . . Now they too had left.

Tony had seen meals being sent to Hendron's cabin-like house—watched them being carried past the Ark and the workshop and the lumber-piles. He had stared often at the door of the house. But no one had emerged—and Eve had not sent for him.

He sat alone, on a mound of chips and sawdust. Was Hendron turning over the command to Ransdell, in there now? Was Hendron asleep from exhaustion and were Eve and Ransdell taking advantage of the resultant solitude to express fresh love for each other? His heart was heavy; heavier still because he realized that the torrent of dreads and despairs it held were unworthy of him.

He ached, and stared at his plate. His eyes felt salty and hot. He tried to clamp his mind on present necessities. They should move to the miracle city: they should study the food and machinery there. They should tend their own crops for fresh food. They should learn to run the Other People's vehicles—so that they could all be transported to the new city as rapidly as possible. They should prepare defenses for themselves against the possibility that the people who had flown the lark-like ships might some day attack them. People from earth? Or cautious scouts of the Other People?

His mind jumped incessantly back to Eve—Eve and Ransdell, his two closest friends. They seemed both on the point of deserting him. Ransdell was, of course, a great man. Stronger in character, perhaps. Tony felt the crushing weight of the responsibilities he himself had endured. Still, Ransdell had taken greater risks—held a higher office. And Ransdell had been a new and different sort of man for Eve. She had known plenty of Yale graduates with social position and wealth and superficial culture—plenty—even if the Yale graduates now left alive could be numbered on the fingers of one hand. . . .

"Mr. Drake?" said a voice.

Tony started. "Oh, Kyto!" Suddenly Tony did not want to be alone any longer. The smiling face of the little Japanese was familiar and good. "Sit down here, Kyto."

Kyto hesitated.

"You're not—working for me—any longer!" Tony grinned.

Kyto seated himself with a precise and smooth motion. "That's true," he said slowly. "I'd forgotten for an instant."

Tony was astonished. "You've certainly learned a lot of English in the last few months."

"I always knew more than I pretended to know," the Japanese answered coolly.

Tony smiled. "Really, Kyto? Then why did you pretend not to? Is that one of those things that makes people say the Japs are subtle and dangerous?"

"In a way," Kyto answered. "I pretended not to know much English while I was in your employ, because I was a spy."

"What!"

"It is true."

"But good God, Kyto, what use was my service—to a spy? I didn't know where there was a fort, or a gun—"

"It gave me a respectable character."

"And what did you spy on?"

"It doesn't matter now. I shall tell you some day. You see, I used to be,"—there was scarcely a trace of accent in his words,—"long ago in Tokyo, a professor of foreign languages. I spoke English when I was a baby. Missionaries taught me. I was a patriot. I volunteered for espionage. While I was in America, my ideas changed. I became—before the Bronson Bodies appeared—a pacifist. I had sent in my resignation and offered to give myself up—at the time of the discovery of the approaching planets. My letters were ignored in the subsequent frantic days. So, during those days, I endeavored to reshape my life. You Americans—some of you, at least—stood for the things I desired: A world run by sense and science; a world of peace and fraternity. I wished to go on your ship. But my wish was not exclusively a selfish one. I continued to mingle with my associates in espionage—as one of them. I learned much."

Tony had never been more astonished. As he looked at his former servant he realized that his jaw had literally sagged. "I'll be damned," he murmured.

"You find it amusing?"

"Astounding."

"You were right before." Kyto laughed in a high key. "It is amusing. Delicious! And I was a fool. A blind, patriotic fool."

"I'm glad you told me," Tony said suddenly. "You're a man, Kyto. And we need you here. Need the things your race possesses."

"Thank you," Kyto said solemnly. "You are also a man."

Involuntarily Tony glanced at Hendron's cabin and shook his head.

The Japanese understood perfectly. "I hope you will not mind an expression of my sympathies?"

Tony looked at him—his valet, expressing sympathies on a most personal matter! No—a friend—a professor—a savant. A man who had heroically offered to give up his life for the beliefs that he had gained. "No, Kyto."

"You will need courage," Kyto said. "Courage, restraint. You have both in sufficient quantities."

"I have rats eating my soul," Tony answered stonily.

"It is too big for all the rats on earth."

Tony stared at the little man and said in a curious tone, "Funny."

There was a silence between them.

"I have more to say." Kyto picked up a chip and opened a pocket-knife. He began to whittle as expertly as any country-store porch loafer.

"More?"

"You know that other ships for the trip to this planet were being prepared?"

"Sure. But none of them—"

Kyto shrugged. "Did you know that in what had been Manchuria the most fanatical Japanese, the Russians, and certain Germans combined to build such a ship?"

"No."

"They were mostly extreme communists. But owing to their need of scientific experts, they took into their group many non-communists."

"So?"

"Great men. They were as likely to succeed as you."

Tony stared at his companion. "And you believe they did? You think they are the people who have been flying here—"

"I know." Kyto drew an object from his pocket—a tightly folded piece of paper. On it were drawn Japanese characters. "I found this a few hours ago. I had been walking from camp. It was blowing along in the wind. It was not mine."

"What is it?"

"A prayer—a written prayer. They are in common use in Japan."

"It might have come on the Ark."

"Yes. But it might not. There is no such thing in the catalogue."

"Anybody who had traveled in Japan might have had one—in a pocketbook—and lost it."

"Again, yes. But I know intuitively."

"If they were Russians and Germans and Japanese—why didn't they land, then?"

"My point in telling this! They do not want company here. They came to set up a Soviet. I have the information in detail. They were sworn, if they reached here, to set up their own government—to wipe out all who might oppose them. It is not even a government like that of Russia. It is ruthless, inhuman—a travesty of socialism, a sort of scientific fanaticism. Most of those men and women believe in nothingness of the individual. They believe that love is really only breeding."

Tony shook his head unbelievingly. "Why didn't they wipe us out, then?"

"Your ray-projectors were good protection. They may find a means of making them powerless. They are manifestly ahead of us here in studying the civilization of the Other People—they use their ships already."

"I mean, the first time. Why didn't they annihilate us that first night? It would have been easy. A bomb or two—"

"I have wondered. There must have been a reason—for they are wholly ruthless. And I can find only one explanation: They wish to found a new state—to be alone on the planet—to make it theirs. To found a state takes people; and for people, one needs women. The more the better—the quicker. They will not strike until they can be selective in their killing—so they wipe out all who may oppose them, but preserve all whom they may convert—especially the women."

"Good God!" Tony stood up. "You mean to tell me you think there is a gang of men or people on Bronson Beta planning that?"

"I am positive."

"It's—it's crazy!"

Kyto shook his head. "Conquest was like that, only two thousand years ago—a short time. And there is no more world. Is there anything that can be said to be crazy now—anything we cannot expect?"

"Then why didn't you tell us sooner?"

Kyto fumbled the paper. "I wanted to be sure. This made me sure."

"It's the worst evidence I ever saw. The thing's fantastic!"

"I have warned you as best I can." He bowed his head, and walked away.

Oddly enough, this scene with Kyto had brought back to Tony some of the strength that had ebbed from him. The thought that his new information would be a good excuse to break in on Hendron and Ransdell and Eve occurred to him, but he thrust it aside without effort.

He walked into the group of people who had finished their midday meal. He touched several on the shoulder. "Duquesne, I want to talk to you privately. Von Beitz! Williamson!"

Fifteen minutes later he had explained his command to a dozen picked men.

"I'll have to tell Ransdell and Hendron later," Tony said. "First, we'll double the guard. Second, we'll put out some sentries—far enough out to give a warning of approaching planes. Third, we'll run off a blast on our projectors to make sure they are in order."

Von Beitz scowled. "I can't believe it. Germans? Maybe—some Germans, Heitbrat, for example. But wouldn't it be better if we said nothing to the women? They might get hysterical."

"These women don't get hysterical," Tony answered succinctly.

He had scarcely finished his instructions when a message was brought to him to report at Hendron's house.

He went in. Eve was in the living room—the room that had been headquarters for the camp since the building of the house. She was sitting at her father's desk, and Ransdell stood at a little distance from her. Dodson was there. The faces of all three were serious.

"Hendron has collapsed," Dodson said to Tony. "Whether he will recover or not, I cannot say."

Tony shook his head sadly.

Eve spoke. "The camp must have a leader."

"Yes," Tony answered.

"Election might be unsatisfactory," she continued. "And it would take time."

"Yes."

"Father appointed no second-in-command. Whoever is in charge while he is ill must remain here. You and Eliot James alone can fly our single plane. We'll need it constantly now. A radio must be taken down to the other camp at once, for example."

Tony looked at her with as little sign of emotion as he could show. This was a new Eve to him—a stern, impartial Eve. Grief and need had combined to make her so. "The static we've been having makes a radio useless," he said.

"That static occurs only at night," she answered. "Sundown to sunup."

"The lights in the city—" Tony murmured. He squared his shoulders. "I'll take a radio down at once."

Eve rose and gestured Ransdell into her father's chair. She shook his hand. Dodson shook his hand. Tony shook his hand

—Tony whose soul was at that moment in exquisite torment.

Ransdell looked drawn and bleak.

"One other thing," Tony said, his voice steady. "We may be in a new and to me fantastic danger." Like a soldier making a report, he detailed the knowledge Kyto had given him and told Ransdell what precautions he had already taken. Even as he spoke the air was filled with a hissing thunder and they waited to continue the conversation until tests of the blast tubes had been finished.

"I'll get outposts established at once," Ransdell said. "I scarcely believe that such a thing could be—but we can take no chances."

"I'd like to talk with Kyto," Eve said. She left the room even as Tony turned to bid her good-by.

"That radio—" said Ransdell. Tony could not make his senses believe that the man who spoke to him now was the man with whom he had spent the latter part of the previous night in deep exultation. Rivalry over leadership—rivalry over Eve—they seemed inadequate things intellectually for the breaking of a friendship. Tony remembered the pact he and Ransdell had reached in Michigan, long ago. Now—it seemed broken!

"I'll take it immediately, Dave," he answered.

The use of his first name startled Ransdell somewhat from his barren mood. He rose and held out his hand.

Tony shook it. "So long," he said.

"Good luck."

Tony opened the throttle regulating the supply of minute quantities of fuel to the atomic blast of his plane. The increase of speed as he fled southward took some of the strain from his nerves. His ears roared to the tune of the jets. The ground underneath moved in a steady blur. Beside him on the extra seat was the radio—a set taken from the ark of the air, and still crated.

Tony had lost his hope of being leader. He had lost Eve. Ransdell came first in the hearts of his companions. Tony wondered how other men in the camp would adjust their philosophies to this double catastrophe. Duquesne would shrug: "*C'est la vie.*" Vanderbilt would have an epigram. Eliot James would tell him to hope and to wait and to be courageous.

Far ahead he saw the cantonment.

He lost altitude, dropped in a tight spiral, straightened out, and landed at an unnecessarily furious speed.

A few minutes later he was surrounded, and the radio was being carried from the plane by experts.

James was at his side. "Lord, you look tired! I've got a bunk for you."

"Thanks."

Questions were being asked. "Got to sleep," Tony said, trying to smile. "Tell you later. Every one's all right—Hendron's somewhat ill—Ransdell's commanding up there. See you after I have a nap." They let him go.

He stretched out under one of the shelters. James, after a private question or two, thoughtfully left him. He could not sleep, however. He did not even want to be alone. Then—some one entered the room where he lay. He turned. It was the girl Marian Jackson.

"You're not asleep," she said easily.

"No."

She sat down on the side of his bed. "Want anything?"

"Guess not."

"Mind if I sit here?"

"No."

She brushed back the hair from his forehead and suddenly exclaimed. "You're all chapped and wind-burned!"

He smiled. "Sure. Flying."

"Wait." She was gone.

A moron, Tony reflected. But she was very sweet. Thoughtful! A woman, just brushing back your hair when you were weary, could do strange things in the way of giving comfort. She returned.

"Shut your eyes. This is salve. Make you feel better. You're shot; I can tell. I'll stay here while you sleep, so you won't need to worry about anything."

He felt her hands—delicate, tender. Then he was asleep.

He woke slowly. He was being shaken. Waking was like falling up a long, black hill.

Light hit his eyes. James stood there.

"Tony! Wake up!"

He sat up, shook himself.

"We got that radio working. Were talking to Hendron's camp. Suddenly the man at the other end coughed and yelled *'Help!'*—and now we can't raise any one."

Tony was up again—outdoors—running toward the plane. James was running behind him.

"Give me Vanderbilt and Taylor. We'll go."

"But—"

"What else can we do?"

As Tony descended upon Hendron's encampment, three men peered tensely through the glass windows of the ship: Taylor, Vanderbilt, and Tony himself. Nothing seemed disturbed; the buildings were intact.

"Not a person in sight!" Taylor yelled suddenly.

They slid down the air.

Tony cut the motors so that their descent became a soft whistle.

Then they saw clearly.

Far below were human figures, the people of the cantonment, and all of them lay on the ground, oddly collapsed, utterly motionless.

CHAPTER X

WAR

TONY circled above the stricken camp of the colony from earth. He could count some sixty men and women lying on the ground.

They looked as if they were dead; and Tony thought they were dead. So did Jack Taylor at his side; and Peter Vanderbilt, his saturnine face pressed against the quartz windows of the plane, believed he was witnessing catastrophe to Hendron's attempt to preserve humanity.

The Death spread below them might already have struck, also, the other camp—the camp from which these three had just flown. They might be the last survivors; and the Death might reach them now, at any instant, within their ship.

Tony thought of the illness which had come over the camp after the first finding of the wrecked vehicle of the Other People—the illness that had proved fatal to three of the earth people. He thought: "This might be some more deadly disease of the Other People which they caught." He thought: "I might have brought the virus of it to them myself from the Sealed City. It might have been in or on some of the objects they examined after I left."

This flashed through his mind; but he did not believe it. He believed that the Death so visible below was a result of an attack.

He looked at his companions, and read the same conviction in their faces. He pointed toward the earth, and raised his eyebrows in a question he could not make audible above a spurt from the plane's jets.

Taylor shook his head negatively. The people below them were dead. Descent would doubtless mean their own death.

Vanderbilt shrugged and gestured to Tony, as if to say that the decision was up to him.

Tony cut the propulsive stream and slid down the air in sudden quiet. "Well?"

"Maybe we should take a look," said Vanderbilt.

"What got them," Taylor said slowly, "will get us. We'd better take back a warning to the other camp."

Tony felt the responsibility of deciding. Ransdell was down there—dead. And Eve?

He lost altitude and turned on power as he reached the edge of the landing-field.

Neither of his companions had been in the Hendron encampment; but this was no time for attention to the equipment of the place. The plane bumped to a stop and rested in silence.

No one appeared from the direction of the camp. Nothing in sight there stirred. There was a bit of breeze blowing, and a speck of cloth flapped; but its motion was utterly meaningless. It was the wind fluttering a cloak or a cape of some one who was dead.

Tony put his hand on the lever that opened the hood of the cockpit.

"I'll yank it open and jump out. Looks like gas. Slam it after I go, and see what happens to me."

Either of his companions would have undertaken that terrifying assignment—would have insisted upon undertaking it; but Tony put his words into execution before they could speak. The hatch grated open. Tony leaped out on the fuselage; there was a clang, and almost none of the outer air had entered the plane.

Taylor's knuckles on the hatch-handle were white.

Vanderbilt peered through the glass at Tony, his face unmoving. But he whispered, "Guts!" as if to himself.

Tony slipped to earth. The two men watching expected at any moment to see him stagger or shudder or fall writhing to the earth. But he did not. There was no fright on his face—his expression was locked and blank. He sweated. He sniffed in the air cautiously after expelling the breath he had held. Then he drew in a lungful, deeply, courageously. A light wind from the sea beyond the cliffs fanned him. He stood still—waiting, presumably, to die. He looked at the two men who were watching him, and hunched his shoulders as if to say that nothing had happened so far.

A minute passed.

The men inside the plane sat tensely. Taylor was panting.

Two minutes. . . . Five. Tony stood and breathed and shrugged again.

"Gas or no gas," Taylor said with an almost furious expression, "I'm going out there with Tony."

He went.

Vanderbilt followed in a manner both leisurely and calm.

The three stood outside together watching each other for effects, each waiting for some spasm of illness to attack himself.

"Doesn't seem to be gas," said Tony.

"What, then?" asked Taylor.

"Who knows? Some plague from the Other People? Some death-wave from the sky? Let's look at them."

The first person they approached, as they went slowly toward the camp and its motionless figures, was Jeremiah Post, the metallurgist. He it was, Tony remembered, who first was

and girls and women motionless, sightless, deaf—utterly insensible in their stupor. He could do nothing for them but recognize them; and he went, bending over them, whispering their names to himself and to them, as if by his whispering he might exorcise away this sleep.

He repeated to himself Eve's name; but he did not find Eve. Where was she, and how? Had this sleep dropped into death for some? He wanted to find Eve, to assure himself that she at least breathed as did these others; but he realized that he should first of all locate Dodson. . . . Dodson, if he could be aroused, would be worth a thousand laymen. Then he recollected that he had last seen Dodson in Hendron's dwelling.

Tony rushed to it and flung open the door; but what lay beyond it halted him.

He found Eve. She lay where she had fallen, face forward on the desk; and Ransdell lay slumped beside her. His left hand clasped her right hand; they had been overcome together. Both of them breathed slowly; but they were completely insensible. Dodson had crumpled over a table. There was a pen in his hand, a paper in front of him. Cloth—Tony saw that the cloth was from dresses—had been stuffed around the door. In a bedroom lay Hendron, the rise and fall of his chest almost imperceptible. Tony shook Dodson.

Suddenly he realized that his head was spinning.

He plunged to the door and staggered into the fresh air. He breathed hard. But his head cleared so slowly that his thoughts ran slow as minutes. Gas, after all. The people in Hendron's house had seen it strike the others, and attempted to barricade themselves. They thought it was death. There were still fumes in there.

Dodson—he must get Dodson.

He ran back, and dragged the huge man into the open.

He stood over him, panting. Then he remembered that Dodson had been writing. A note—a record. Tony went for it. So strong had been the poison in the air that he found it hard to read.

"We've been gassed," Dodson had scrawled. *"People falling everywhere. No attack visible. We're going to try to seal this room. They're all unconscious out there. I got a smell of it, closing a window. Nothing familiar. I think—"*

Tony shook Dodson. He brought water and doused him. He found Dodson's medical kit and tried to make him swallow aromatic spirits of ammonia, then whisky. Dodson could not swallow.

Tony jerked about, as he heard some one move. It was Vanderbilt, who had left his post at the tube.

"Nothing's in sight out there," Vanderbilt said calmly. "Taylor stays on watch. I ought to be more use in here."

"What can you do?" Tony demanded.

"I'm two-thirds of a doctor—for first aid, anyway," Vanderbilt said. "I used to spend a lot of time at hospitals. Morbid, maybe." While he spoke his slow, casual words, he had taken Dodson's kit and had been working over the physician. . . . "I gave him a hypo of caffeine and strychnine and digitalis that would have roused a dead elephant. He's still out, though."

"Will any of them come to?"

"Only one thing will tell."

"What?"

"Time, of course," Peter Vanderbilt said. "Then, if it proves my treatment may have helped Dodson,—and not killed him,—we might try it on others."

Tony bent again over Eve and Ransdell; their respirations and their pulses seemed the same; and Hendron's, though much weaker than theirs, had not further deteriorated.

"They don't seem to be slipping," Tony said.

"No. Anything in sight outside?"

"No," said Tony, but he went out for a better inspection, and for another patrol past those that lay senseless on the ground.

He returned to Peter Vanderbilt and waited with him. They pulled Dodson and Eve and Ransdell out into the open air and laid them on the ground; they carried out Hendron too, and stretched him upon his mattress in the breeze and the sunlight.

Nothing remained to do; so they sat watching the forms that breathed but otherwise did not move, and watching the sky. Three hundred yards away, Jack Taylor stood at his tube watching them and the sky, and the scattered, senseless, sleeping people.

"Our other camp!" said Vanderbilt. "What do you suppose is happening there?"

"I've been thinking of that, of course," said Tony. "We ought to warn them by radio; but if we did, we'd warn the enemy too. He's listening in, we may be sure; he'd know we were laying for him here; our chance to surprise him would be gone. No; I think our best plan is to lie low."

Vanderbilt nodded thoughtfully. "I agree. In all likelihood our enemy is taking on only one of our camps at a time. Having started here, he'll probably finish here before beginning on the other."

"We've no idea what forces they have."

"No."

"There might be enough to take on both our camps at once."

"Yes."

Tony and Peter Vanderbilt moved toward their radio-station; and they were debating there what to do, when their dilemma was solved for them: The sound of a plane came dimly to his ears. Both stepped out of the radio-room and lay down on the ground where vision in every direction was unhampered. Tony saw Taylor slumping into an attitude of unconsciousness.

Then his eye caught the glint of the plane. A speck far away. He lay motionless, like the others, and the speck rapidly enlarged.

It was one of the Bronson Betan ships. It flew fast and with a purring roar which was caused not by its motor but by the sound of its propellers thwacking the air.

It came low, slowed down, circled.

Tony's heart banged as he saw that one of the faces peering over was broad, bearded, strongly Slavic. Another of its occupants had close-cropped hair and spectacles. The slip-stream of the plane fanned him furiously and raised dust around him. People from earth! They completed their inspection, and rushed out of sight toward the northwest.

Tony and Vanderbilt jumped up and ran toward Jack Taylor. The three men met for a frantic moment. "They'll be back." Tony shook with rage. "The swine! They'll be back to take over this camp. I wonder if they'd kill the men. We'll be ready. I'll take the west tube. Wait till they're all here. Wait till the first ship lands—I can rake hell out of that field. Then get 'em all! We can't fool. We can't do anything else."

They went to their positions again.

An hour later a large armada flew from the northwest. They did not fly in formation, like battle-planes. Their maneuvers were not overskillful. Some of the ships were even flown badly, as if their pilots were not well versed in their manipulation.

Tony counted. There were seventeen ships—and some of them were very large.

The three defenders acted on a prearranged plan: They did not follow the fleet with their tubes. They did not even move them from their original angles. They could be swung fast enough. They hid themselves carefully.

The ship circled the camp and the unconscious victims beneath. Then the leading ship prepared to land.

Tony fired his tube. The crackling sound rose as the blast began.

The enemy plane was almost on the ground. He could see lines of rivets in its bright metal body. He could see, through a small peephole, the taut face of the pilot. The wheels touched.

Tony heaved, and the counter-balanced weapon described an arc. There was a noise like the opening of a door to hell. The landing-field became a volcano. The plane vanished in a blistering, tumultuous core of light. The beam swung up, left the ground instantaneously molten.

It curved along the air, and broken and molten things

dropped from the sky. Into that armada probed two other orange fingers of annihilation; and it melted, dissolved, vanished.

It was not a fair fight. . . . It was not a fight.

The blasts yawed wide. They were fed by the horrible energy which had carried the Ark through space. Their voices shook the earth. They were more terrible than death itself, more majestic than lightning or volcanic eruption. They were forces stolen from the awful center of the sun itself.

In less than a minutes they were stilled. The enemy was no more.

Tony did not run, now. He walked back to the center of the camp. There he met Vanderbilt and Taylor.

No one spoke; they sat down, white, trembling, horrified. Around them lay their unconscious comrades.

Here and there on the ground over and beyond the landing-place, great fragments of twisted metal glowed and blistered.

The sun shone. It warmed them from the green-blue sky of Bronson Beta.

Jack Taylor, student, oarsman, not long ago a carefree college boy—Jack Taylor sucked in a tremulous breath and whispered: *"God! Oh, God!"*

Vanderbilt rose and smiled a ghastly smile. He took a battered package of cigarettes from his pocket—tenderly, and as if he touched something rare and valuable. They knew he had been cherishing those cigarettes. He opened the package; four cigarettes were left. He passed them. He found a match, and they smoked. Still they did not speak.

They looked at the people who lay where they had fallen—the people who had come through that hideous destruction without being aware of it.

One of those people moved. It was Dodson.

They rushed to his side.

Dodson was stirring and mumbling. Vanderbilt opened his medical kit again and poured something into a cup. Tony held the Doctor's head. After several attempts, they managed to make him swallow the stuff.

He began a long, painful struggle toward consciousness. He would open his eyes, and nod and mutter, and go off to sleep for an instant, only to jerk and writhe and try to sit. Finally his fuddled voice enunciated Tony's name. *"Drake!"* he said. "Gas!" Then a meaningless jumble of syllables. Then "Caffeine! Stick it in me. Gimme pills. Caffalooaloclooaloo. Gas. Rum, rum, rum, rum, rum—headache. I'm sick."

Then, quite abruptly, he came to.

He looked at them. He looked at the sleeping forms around him. He squinted toward the field, and saw what was there. He rubbed his head and winced.

"Aches," he said. "Aches like sin. You—you came back in time, eh?"

"We laid for them," Tony answered solemnly. "We got them."

"All of them," Jack Taylor added.

Dodson pointed at the sleepers. "Dead?"

"All beathing. We wanted to get you around first—if anybody could be revived."

Dodson's head slumped and then he sat up again. "Right. What'd you use?"

"I gave you a shot of caffeine and strychnine and digitalis about an hour ago," Vanderbilt said.

Dodson grinned feebly. "Wake the dead, eh? Adrenalin might be better. Di-nitro-phenol might help. I've got a clue to this stuff. Last thing I thought of." He looked at the sky. "It just rained down on us—out of nothing."

"Rained?" Tony repeated.

"Yes. Rained—a falling mist. The people it touched never saw or smelled it—went out too fast. But I did both. Inside—we had a minute's grace." He struggled and finally rose to his feet. "Obviously something to knock us out. Nothing fatal. Let's see what we can do about rousing somebody else. Probably'd sleep it off in time—a day, maybe. I want to make some tests."

He was very feeble as he rose, and they supported him.

"I'll put a shot in Runciman and Best and Isaacs first, I guess. They can help with the others." Tony located Runciman, the brain-specialist. Dodson made a thorough examination of the man. "In good shape. Make a fine anesthetic—except for the headache." He filled a hypodermic syringe, then methodically swabbed the surgeon's arm with alcohol, squeezed out a drop of fluid to be sure no air was in the instrument, and pricked deftly. They moved on, looking for Best and Isaacs.

As they worked, Dodson's violent headache began to be dissipated. And the persons they treated presently commenced to writhe and mutter.

Hendron was among the first after the medical men. Dodson lingered over him and shook his head.

"Heart's laboring—bad condition, anyway. I'm afraid—"

Vanderbilt and Taylor and Tony knew what Dodson feared.

In two hours a number of pale and miserable human beings were moving uncertainly around the camp. Best entered the Ark and brought other drugs to alleviate their discomfort. Tony had sent a warning to the southern camp. They replied that they had seen nothing, and were safe.

The three men who were heroes of the raid went together to the landing-field. They walked from place to place examining the wreckage. They collected a host of trifles—buttons, a notebook, a fountain pen made in Germany, a pistol half melted, part of a man's coat, fire-warped pfennig pieces—and found more grisly items which they did not touch.

After they had made their telltale harvest among the still-hot débris, they stood together staring toward the northwest. An expedition in that direction would be necessary at once. It would not be a safe voyage.

CHAPTER XI

"TONY, I THROW THE TORCH TO YOU!"

NIGHT came on with its long, deliberate twilight; and with this night came cold.

The sentinels outside stood in little groups together, listening, and watching the sky. No lights showed. Wherever they were necessary within the offices and dwellings of the camp, they were screened or covered. The encampment could not risk an air-attack by night.

Tony found himself continued in command; for Hendron held to his bed and made no attempt to give directions. Ransdell was quite himself again, but like all the others but Tony and Tayor and Vanderbilt, he had lain insensible through the attack and the savage, successful defense the three had made.

Everybody came to Tony for advice and orders. Eve, like all the rest, put herself under his direction.

"You'd better stay with your father," Tony said to her. "Keep him quiet as you can. Tell him I'll keep him informed of further developments; but I really expect no more to-night."

Eve disappeared into the darkness which was all but complete. In the north, toward Bronson Beta's pole, hung a faint aurora, and above it shone some stars; but most of the sky was obscured. There was no moon, of course. Strange, still to expect the moon—a moon gone "with yesterday's sev'n thousand years."

Another girl joined the group of men standing and shivering near the great cannon-like tube aimed heavenward.

"Anything stirring?" asked Shirley Cotton's voice.

"Not now," replied Tony.

"It's cold," said Shirley. "It's surely coming on cold, these nights."

"Nothing to what it will be," observed a man's voice gloomily. It was Williamson, who had been insensible all through the fight, like the rest of the camp. Now he had completely recovered, but his spirits, like those of many of the others, seemed low.

"How cold will it be—soon?" asked Shirley.

"Do you want to know?" Williamson challenged. "Or are you just asking?"

"I've heard," said Shirley, taking no offense, "an awful lot of things. I know we're going out toward Mars. But how cold is it out there?"

"That's been figured out a long time," Williamson returned. "They taught that back in school on earth. The surface temperature of a planet like the earth at sixty-seven millions miles' distance from the sun—the distance of Venus—would be one hundred and fifty-one degrees Fahrenheit. The mean temperature of the earth, at ninety-three million miles from the sun—where we used to be—was sixty degrees. The mean temperature of the earth, if it were a hundred and forty-one million miles from the sun—the distance of Mars—would be minus thirty-eight—thirty-eight degrees below zero, Fahrenheit.

"The earth went round the sun almost in a circle—it never got nearer to the sun than ninety-one million miles, and never got farther away than about ninety-four million; so our temperatures there never varied, by season, beyond comfortable limits for most of the surface of the earth.

"But riding this planet, we aren't going around the sun in any such circle; our orbit now is an ellipse, with the sun in a focus but not in the center. So we'll have a very hot summer when we go close to Venus, where the surface temperature averages a hundred and fifty-one; but before we get that summer, we go into winter out by Mars where normal temperatures average about forty below zero—a hundred degrees less than we're used to. We're headed there now."

"Didn't—didn't *they* know that, too?" Shirley gestured a white-clad arm toward the landing-field where the attackers of the camp had been annihilated.

"They must have."

"Then why—why—"

Peter Vanderbilt's urbane voice finished for her: "Why didn't they spend the last of the good weather trying to capture or kill us? Because they also came from that pugnacious planet Earth."

The reality of what had happened, while they were sunk in stupor, still puzzled some of Hendron's people.

"Why weren't they content to let us alone? There's room enough on Bronson Beta. . . . Good God! Imagine two groups of human beings as stranded as ourselves, as forlorn in the universe, as needful of peace and coöperation—fighting!"

"Men never fought for room," Walters, a biologist, objected. "That was just an excuse they gave when civilization advanced to the point when men felt they ought to give explanations for fighting. There surely was plenty of room in the North American continent in pre-Columbian times, with a total population of perhaps three million Indians in all the continent north of Mexico; but the principal occupation—or pastime or whatever you call it—was war. One tribe would sneak a hundred miles through empty forest to attack another. It wasn't room that men wanted in ancient America—or in medieval Europe, for that matter."

"What was it, then?" asked Shirley.

"Domination!" said Walters. "It's an essentially human instinct—the fundamental one which sets man off from all other animals. Did you ever know of any other creature which, by nature, has to dominate? Not even the king of the beasts, the lion. To realize how much more ruthless men are than lions were, imagine a man with the physical equipment of a lion, among other beasts, and imagine him letting all the weaker ones go their own way and killing only what he needed for food.

"You might imagine one lion-man doing that, but you couldn't imagine all lion-men so restrained. You know they would have cleaned up the neighborhood, just to show they could, and then fought among themselves to the finish of many of them.

"That is the nature we brought with us from the world; it is too much to expect it to desert us all here. It couldn't; it didn't."

"That's certainly clear," Williamson agreed.

"That element in our nature," the biologist proceeded, "scarcely had opportunity to reassert itself because of our difficulties in merely maintaining ourselves. The enemy—the party that attacked us—solved their difficulties, evidently, by moving into one of the Other People's cities. From what Tony told us of the city he examined, their city probably supplied them with everything they lacked, and with more equipment and appliances of various sorts than they dreamed existed.

"They found themselves with nothing to do; they found already built for them dwellings, offices and palaces; they found machinery—even substances for food. They were first in possession of the amazing powers of the original people of this planet. They learned of our presence, and decided to dominate us.

"I have come to believe that probably they would not have killed us; but they wanted us all under their control."

Eve returned to the group. She did not speak, and in the dim light of the stars she was indistinguishable from the other girls; yet Tony knew, as she approached him, that it was Eve.

She halted a few steps away, and he went to her.

"Father asks for you, Tony," she said in a voice so constrained that he prickled with fear.

"He's weaker?" said Tony.

"Come and see," she whispered; and he seized her hand, and she his at the same time, and together through the dark they went to the cabin where lay the stricken leader.

A cloth covered the doorway so when the door opened it

let out no shaft of light to betray the camp to any hovering airman of the enemy. Tony closed the door behind him and Eve, thrust aside the cloth and faced Hendron, who was seated upright in bed, his hair white as the cover of his pillow.

His eyes, large and restless, gazed at his daughter and at his lieutenant; and his thin white hands plucked at the blanket over him.

"Have they come again, Tony?" he challenged. "Have they come again?"

"No, sir."

"Those that came, they are all dead?"

"Yes, sir."

"And none of us?"

"No, sir."

"Arm some of yourselves unto the war, Tony."

"What, sir?"

" 'Arm some of yourselves unto the war,' Tony! 'For the Lord spake unto Moses, saying:

" 'Avenge the children of Israel of the Midianites; afterwards shalt thou be gathered unto thy people.

" 'And Moses spake unto the people, saying, Arm some of yourselves unto the war, and let them go against the Midianites.'

"How many of the Midianites have you slain, Tony?"

"More than fifty, sir," said Tony.

"There might be five hundred more. We don't know the size of their ship; we don't know how many came. It's clear they have taken possession of one of the cities of the Other People."

"Yes, sir."

"Then we must move into another. You must lead my people into the city you found, Tony—the city I shall never see."

"You shall see it, sir!" Tony cried.

"Don't speak to me as if to a child!" Hendron rebuked him. "I know better. I shall see the city; but I shall never enter it. I am like Moses, Tony; I can lead you to the wilderness of this world, but not to its promised places. Do you remember your Bible, Tony? Or did you never learn it?

"I learned whole chapters of it, Tony, when I was a boy, nearly sixty years ago, in a little white house beside a little white church in Iowa. My father was a minister. So I knew the fate of the leader.

" 'And the Lord said unto Moses, Behold, thy days approach that thou must die: call Joshua'—that is you, Tony—'and present yourselves, that I may give him a charge.

" 'Charge Joshua and encourage him, and strengthen him; for he shall go over before this people, and he shall cause them to inherit the land which thou shalt see.' Joshua—my

Joshua, Tony, we must move, move, move to-night. Move into one of their cities. 'Thou art to pass over Jordan this day,' Tony, 'to cities great and fenced up to heaven.'"

Hendron stopped speaking and fell back on his pillow. His eyes closed.

"Yes, sir," Tony said softly.

"The cities I shall never see!" Hendron murmured with infinite regret.

"But, Father—" Eve whispered.

The old man leaned forward again. "Go, Tony! I throw the torch to you. Your place is the place I occupied. Lead my people. Fight! Live! Become glorious!"

"You'd better leave," Eve said. "I'll watch here."

Tony went out into the darkness. He whispered to a few people whom he encountered.

Presently he stood inside the circular room that was all that remained of the Ark. No vent or porthole allowed light to filter into the cold and black night. With him were Ransdell and Vanderbilt and Jack Taylor, Dodson and Williamson, Shirley Cotton and Von Beitz, and many others.

Tony stood in front of them: "We're going to embark for one of the Other People's cities—at once. The night is long, fortunately—"

Williamson, who had once openly suggested that Tony should not become their leader, and who had welcomed the reappearance of Ransdell, now spoke dubiously.

"I'm not in favor of that policy. We have the blast tubes—"

"I cannot question it," Tony answered. "Hendron decided."

"Then why isn't he here?"

There was silence in the room. Tony looked from face to face. His own countenance was stone-like. His eyes stopped on the eyes of Ransdell. His voice was low.

"Hendron turned over the command to me."

"Great!" Ransdell was the first to grasp Tony's hand. "I'm in no shape for the responsibility like that I had for a while."

Tony looked at him with gratitude burning in his eyes.

"Orders, then?" Ransdell asked, grinning.

That was better for Tony; action was his forte in life. He pulled a map from his pocket.

"Copy of the globe James and I found in the Other People's city," he said.

They crowded around it: a rough projection of imaginary parallels and meridians marked two circles.

"Here," said Tony, pointing with a pencil, "is where we are. To the south, Ransdell's camp. West, the city we explored. The Midianites—" He smiled. "That's Hendron's term for the Asiatics and Japs and Germans; it comes from the Bible—the Midianites are camped somewhere to the northwest. You note a city at this point. They doubtless occupy that city. Now—"

His pencil moved south and west of the position where they were camped. "You see that there's another city here. It's west of a line between here and Ransdell's camp, and about equidistant from both. I suggest we go to that city—to-night, by the Other People's road—and occupy it. The distance can't be too great. We'll use the tractors."

He then addressed those who could not see the map: "Imagine that we are camped in New York, Ransdell in Washington, the Midianites in Utica—then this other city is about fifty miles west of where Philadelphia would be, while the city James and I explored is say a hundred miles north of Pittsburgh. That's about correct."

"We'll move?" Vanderbilt asked. "Everything?"

"No. People—necessities. Come back for the rest."

Williamson stepped forward. "Congratulate you, Tony. Glad."

Others congratulated Tony. Then he began to issue orders.

The exiles from earth prepared to march at last from the wilderness. They prepared hastily and in the dark. Around them in the impenetrable night were the alarms of danger. They hurried, packing their private goods, loading them onto the lumber-trucks, and gathering together food-supplies and those items of equipment and apparatus most valuable to the hearts of the scientific men who composed the personnel.

An hour after issuing his orders, Tony stepped into Hendron's house. Eve was there.

"How is he?"

She shook her head. "Delirious."

Tony stared at the girl. "I wonder—"

She seized his hand. "I'm glad you said that!"

"Why?"

"I don't know. Perhaps because I'm half-hysterical with fatigue and anxiety. Perhaps because I want to justify him. But possibly because I believe—"

"In God?"

"In some kind of God."

"I do also, Eve. Have your father ready in half an hour."

"It'll be dangerous to move him."

"I know—"

Their voices had unconsciously risen—and now from the other room came the voice of Hendron: " 'And ten thousand at thy right hand: but it shall not come nigh thee.' "

They whispered then. "I'll have him ready," Eve said.

"Right. I'm going out again."

"Tony!" It was Hendron again. "I know you are there! Hurry them. For surely the Midianites are preparing against you."

"Yes, Cole. We'll go soon."

In the night and the cold again, Tony looked toward the aurora-veiled stars, as if he expected almost to catch sight of God there. To his ears came the subdued clatter of the preparation for departure.

Vanderbilt called him, called softly. It was perhaps foolish to try to be quiet as well as to work in the dark—but the darkness somehow gave rise to an impulse toward the stealth.

"Tony!"

"Here, Peter!"

The New Yorker approached, a figure dimly walking. "The first truck is ready."

"Dispatch it."

"Right. And the second will start in thirty minutes?"

"Exactly."

"Which will you take?"

"Second."

"And who commands the first?"

"Ransdell."

Vanderbilt went away.

Tony watched the first truck with its two trailers—one piled full of goods, the other jammed with people. They were like soldiers going to war, or like refugees being evacuated from an endangered position. They lumbered through the dark and out of sight—silhouettes against the stars. . . . Motor sounds. . . . Silence.

When the second convoy was ready, Tony and Williamson carried Hendron aboard on a litter. The old man seemed to be sleeping. Eve walked beside him.

The motor ahead emitted a muffled din. Wheels turned; the three sections bumbled into the blackness toward the Other People's road. When they had reached it, travel became smooth; a single ray of light, a feeble glow, showed the way to the driver.

The people in the trailer wrapped themselves in an assortment of garments and blankets which they had snatched up against the somber chill of this early autumn night on Bronson Beta. Tony did not recognize a shawled figure who crowded through the others to his side until he heard his voice.

"It is a shame to be driven out like this!"

"It is, Duquesne."

"But by whom—and for what?"

"I don't know."

The Frenchman shook his fist toward the northwest. "Pigs!" he muttered. "Beasts! Dogs!"

For an hour they traveled.

They crossed through the valley where they had cut lumber, and they went over the bridge of the Other People. They reached a fork in the road among foothills of the western range. It was a fork hidden by a deep cut, so that Tony and Eliot James had not seen it on their flight of exploration. Then, suddenly, the light of the truck-tractor went out, and word came back in the form of a soft human shushing that made all of them silent.

CHAPTER XII

A SURPRISING REFUGEE

TONY leaped over the side of the trailer in which he had been standing near Hendron's litter.

He ran forward. "What is it?"

The driver of the truck—Von Beitz—leaned out in the Stygian dark.

"We saw a light ahead!" he whispered.

"Light?"

"Light. . . . Light ahead!" The word ran among the passengers.

"Where?" Tony asked.

"Over the hills."

Tony strained his eyes; and against the aurora and the stars he saw a series of summits. He could even see the metal road that wound over the hills, gleaming faintly. But there was no light.

Not a sound emerged from the fifty human beings packed in the caravan behind.

The wind blew—a raw wind. Then there was a soft, sighing ululation.

Tony gripped Von Beitz' arm. "What was that?"

"God knows."

They strained their eyes.

Tony saw it, then: a shape—a lightless and incomprehensible shape, moving slowly on the gleaming surface of the road—toward them.

"See!" His voice shook.

Von Beitz jumped from his seat behind the wheel. He stood beside Tony.

"Don't see anything."

Tony pointed ahead. "Something. Dipped into a valley. There!"

Again the soft moaning sound. Again the meaningless shape topped a rise and slithered along the road toward them. Its course was crooked, and suggested the motion of an animal that was sniffing its way along.

"Mein Gott!" Von Beitz had seen it.

"It looks"—Duquesne had come up behind them—"like a snuffing dog."

"A dog—as big as that?"

Duquesne shrugged, and murmured to Tony: "It comes this

way on the road. We must meet it. Perhaps it is an infernal machine. An enemy scout."

Tony reached into the front compartment of the truck and brought out two rifles. Then he stuffed three grenades into his pocket. He turned to the trailer.

"Vanderbilt!" he whispered.

"Yes, Tony!"

"Something's coming toward us on the road. We're going up to meet it. You're in charge here. If I fire—one, two, one—that means try to rush through on full power—without stopping for us."

"Right. *Bing—bing-bing—bing*—and we lunge."

Tony, Duquesne and Von Beitz began to hurry along the road.

They went to a point about three hundred yards from the trailers. There they waited. The ululation was louder now.

"Sounds like an animal," Von Beitz whispered nervously.

"I hope to God it is!" Duquesne murmured reverently.

Then it topped a nearer hill. It was a bulk in the dark. It wavered along the road at the pace of a man running.

"Machinery!" Tony said softly.

"An engine!" Duquesne murmured simultaneously.

"Ready!" Tony said. "I'll challenge it when its gets near. If it goes on, we'll bomb it."

They waited.

Slowly, along the road toward them, the thing came. They knew presently that it was a vehicle—a vehicle slowly and crazily driven. It loomed out of the night, and Tony stood up at the roadside.

"Stop or we'll blow you up!"

He yelled the words.

At the same time he took the pin of a bomb between his teeth.

The bulk slewed, swerved, slowed. There was a click, and the curious engine-sound ceased.

"I'll give up!" It was a woman's voice.

Tony shot a flashlight-beam at the object. It was one of the large vans the Bronson Betans had used in their cities. Its strange sound was explained by its condenser-battery-run motor.

From it stepped a girl.

Duquesne switched on another light. There was no one else in the van.

"Sacré nom!" he said.

The girl was in breeches and a leather coat. She began to speak.

"You can't blame me for trying—anyway."

"Trying what?" Tony asked, in an odd and mystified tone.

"Are you Rodonover?" she asked.

Tony's skin prickled. He stepped up to the girl. "Who are you, and where did you come from?"

"You're not Rodonover! You're—*oh, God!* You're the Other People!" she said. Tony noticed now that her accent was British. And he was suddenly sure that she did not belong to Hendron's camp, or to Ransdell's. She had not been in Michigan. She had not come to Bronson Beta with them. But her use of the phrase *Other People* startled him.

"We come from earth," he said. "We're Americans."

She swayed dazedly, and Williamson took her arm.

"Better duck the lights," Tony said.

They were in the dark again.

The girl sniffled and shook herself in a little shuddering way, and suddenly poured out a babble of words to which they listened with astonishment.

"I've been a prisoner—or something like it—since—the destruction of earth. To-day I escaped in this van. I'd been running it. That was my job. I knew you were somewhere out here, and I wanted to tell you about us."

"We'll walk back," Tony said. "Can we pass that thing?"

Von Beitz looked. *"Ja,"* he said. He had never spoken German to them before, but now in his intense excitement, he was using his mother tongue.

Tony took the girl's arm. "We're Americans. You seem to know about us. Please try to explain yourself."

"I will." She paused, and thought. They walked toward the silent, waiting train. "You know that other space-ships left earth besides yours?"

Tony said grimly: "We do."

"You've been attacked. Of course. One ship left from Eastern Asia. Its crew were mixed nationalities."

"We know that."

"They're living in a city—a city that belonged to the original inhabitants of this place—north of here."

"And we know that too."

"Good. A ship also left the Alps. An English ship."

"So—"

"I was on that ship. The Eastern Asiatic expedition came through safely. We came down in a fog. We fell into a lake. Half of us, nearly, were drowned. The Russians and Japs—and the others—found us the next day. They fought us. Since then—they've made us work for them. Whoever wouldn't—they killed."

"Good God! How many—"

"There were three hundred and sixty-seven of us left," she said. "Now—there are about three hundred and ten."

The truck loomed up ahead. Tony spoke rapidly. "We are moving from our camp at night. We intend to occupy a city before morning. You'll come with us. My name, by the way, is Tony Drake."

He felt her hand grasp his own.

"Mine is—or was—Lady Cynthia Cruikshank."

"Peter!"

Vanderbilt sprang from the trailer and ran up the road. "You safe, Tony?"

"Safe. This is Lady Cynthia Cruikshank. She'll tell you her story. I think we'd better move."

"Right."

Von Beitz was already in his seat. Tony vaulted aboard. The train started.

Lady Cynthia began a detailed account of the landing of the English ship. Tony moved over beside Eve.

"How's your father?"

"You can't tell. Oh—Tony—I was terrified!"

He took her hand.

"We could see it—up there in the dark, wabbling toward where we knew you were waiting."

He nodded. "It was pretty sour. Listen to her, though—she's got a story."

They listened. When she had finished, long and dark miles had been put behind. The uncomfortable passengers had stood spellbound, chilly, swaying, listening to her narrative. Now they questioned her.

"Why did the Midianites seize you?" one asked.

"Midianites?"

"That's what we call the 'Asiatic Expedition.' "

The Englishwoman laughed softly. "Oh, Oh, I see. Joshua! Not inapt. Why—because they want to run everything and rule everything on this planet. And because their men greatly outnumber their women." She spoke bitterly. "We'd chosen the pride of England. And pretty faces—"

"Why," some one else asked, "did you wabble so horribly?"

"Wabble?"

"Weave, then. In that Bronson Beta van you drove?"

"Bronson Beta? Oh—you used the astronomical name for this planet. Why—I wabbled because I had to turn my lights out when I saw you coming, and I could only stay on the road by driving very slowly and letting the front wheels run off the edge. When they did, I yanked the car back onto the pavement."

Several people laughed. The van bumbled on toward the promised land. Some one else asked: "What did you call this planet?"

Lady Cynthia replied: "We in our ship—thought— just Britannia. But the people who captured us called it Asiatica. You must realize that when I say captured, I don't mean that in the sense that we were jailed. We lived among them—

were part of them. Only—we weren't allowed arms—and we were forced to live by their laws."

"What laws?"

"German was to be their universal language. We had to learn it. Every woman was to be married. We had been given three months to choose mates. We were to bear children. There was no property. No God. No amusements or sports. No art—except for education—propaganda, you might call it. No love, no sentiment. We were being told to consider ourselves as ants, part of a colony. The colony was all-important, the individual ants—nothing."

"Swell," said one of the younger men from the dark.

Lady Cynthia nodded.

"How did you escape?"

"I'd elected to marry a leader. I was considering—seriously—jumping from a building in one of the cities. But I had a little more freedom than most. I was assigned to truck-driving. I went out every day to the gardens for vegetables. I befriended one of the guards there—I made rather deceitful promises to him; and he let me enjoy what I had told him was a craving of mine—going for a spin alone. I went—and I didn't come back."

Duquesne asked: "You knew where to find us?"

"Vaguely. In our city—the city was called Bergrad, by them—there had been discussions of you. Our captors called you American rabble. They are determined to subdue you."

"Sweet!" said Williamson.

"Of course—in the last days on earth—I'd read about you. I knew two or three of your party. I knew Eliot James. He'd stayed once at our castle. Is he—"

"Very much so," said Tony happily.

"That will be marvelous! And how many of you—"

Tony explained. "We have two camps."

"So I heard."

"A van has gone ahead of us. It will deposit its stores and passengers at the new city, and then start at once to the other camp. We did not dare radio."

"They listen for you all day," said Lady Cynthia. "And at night. But my other friends: Nesbit Darrington? Is he here?"

There was silence.

"I see," she said slowly. "And Hawley Tubbs?"

Again there was silence.

The Englishwoman sighed heavily. "So many people! Ah, God, so many! Why was I spared? Why do I stand here this night with you on this foreign world? . . . I'm sorry!"

Tony jumped. Von Beitz was rapping on the window of his driver's compartment. Tony peered through the window. Von Beitz was pointing ahead.

Tony's eyes followed the German's arm. Far away on the

horizon the night sky was pinkly radiant. At first he thought that it was the aurora. Then he knew. He turned to the others.

"There are the lights of our new home!"

A murmur rose, a prayer, a hushed thanksgiving. . . .

The tractor-truck and its two huge trailers rumbled toward the distant illumination.

Tony bent over Eve. "We'll be safe soon, dear."

"Yes, Tony."

They descended into a long and shadowed cut. At the end was a slow curve.

Then they came out on a valley floor.

In the valley's center was the bubble of the new city. It was not as large as the first one they had seen. But its transparent cover was identical; and like the first, it was radiant with light. Did the lights go on all over Bronson Beta every night? Had Ransdell turned them on? They did not know. They only saw out on the valley floor the resplendent glory of a Bronson Betan city at night, and because none there save Tony and Lady Cynthia had seen the sight before, their emotions were ineffable.

There, under its dome, stood the city, its multi-colored metal minarets and terraces, its spiral set-backs and its network of bridges and viaducts, shining, strong, incredibly beautiful.

"Surpassing a dream of heaven!" Duquesne murmured.

"Magnificent!" Williamson whispered. There were tears on almost every enraptured countenance.

Then a strange thing happened:

Cole Hendron stirred.

Eve dropped a tear on his face as she bent over him. She let go of Tony's hand to adjust the blankets over her father. But Hendron put her hand aside and slowly, majestically, sat up in his improvised cot.

"Father!" she said.

He was staring at the city.

"Cole!" Tony whispered.

The others in the trailer sensed what was happening. They looked at their old leader. And the caravan moved forward so that in the light of the city, faces became visible.

Cole Hendron stood now.

"Tony, my son!" His words rang like iron.

"Yes—"

The greatest scientist earth had ever produced stretched out his two hands toward the city. "The promised land!" Now his voice was thunder.

Eve sobbed. Tony felt a lump swelling in his throat.

Hendron looked up to the cold stars—to Arcturus and Sirius and Vega.

"Father!" he said in a mighty voice. "We thank Thee!"

Then he pitched forward.

Tony caught him, or he would have fallen to the earth. He lifted him back on his pallet and opened his coat. Dodson pushed through the herded people.

The head of the physician bent over the old man's chest. He looked up.

"His brain imagined this," said Dodson. "He brought us here in his two hands, and with his courage as our spiritual flame we shall remain!"

It was an epitaph.

Eve wept silently. Tony stood behind her with his hands on her shoulders—mute consolation and strength.

"Hendron's dead," was whispered through the throng.

The city was now looming in front of them, the buildings inside visible in detail and rising high over the heads of the travelers.

Von Beitz was driving rapidly. This was the most dangerous part of the trip, this dash across the lighted exterior of the city, without protection of any kind.

They could see presently that the great gate was open. Figures stood beside it, motionlessly watching their approach.

Light poured over them. They were inside the city. They slowed to a stop at the mighty portals boomed shut behind them.

Ransdell had been one of those waiting. Tony leaped out, and Ransdell smiled.

"Welcome!"

"Hendron's dead."

"Oh!"

The people began to alight—but they were quiet and made no attempt to celebrate their security.

Others came up.

"We'll take his body into one of these buildings," said Tony. "In the morning we'll bury him—out there, under the sun and the stars—in the bare earth of Bronson Beta."

Behind the voyagers through the night was a wide avenue, and at its center in the city stood a magnificent building. Some one of those who came in the first caravan had brought a large American flag and fixed it on an improvised pole. It was hanging there when they entered the gates. Tony noticed it presently as it was being drawn down to half-mast.

No other symbol of the death of their leader was made that night. There were too many important things to do, things upon which their existence depended.

Dodson, Duquesne and Eve sat in a room with Hendron's body—a room of weird and gorgeous decoration, a room of august dimensions, a room indirectly illuminated. If they had but known, they would have been glad that Cole Hendron lay in the hall of the edifice that had been home of the greatest scientists of Bronson Beta some incalculable age before them.

Tony left the watchers reluctantly and sought Ransdell. The former South African was in a smaller chamber in the building where the Stars and Stripes hung at half-mast.

"He died," said Tony to Ransdell and the other people with him, "standing in the trailer, thanking God, and staring at the city."

"Like Moses," said Ransdell. "A single glimpse of the Promised Land."

"Like Moses." Tony looked with astonishment at the man. He had not imagined Ransdell as a reader of the Scriptures.

"We must go on. He'd want it," said Williamson.

Tony nodded. "The first van has left for your camp?"

"Yes."

"And the second?"

"Fifteen minutes ago."

"It is about four miles from the road to your camp. But I think those tractors can pull all the way in. They'll bring nothing but people—and they'll be able to accommodate every one." He looked at his watch and pondered. "They should be here before daybreak. Now—I don't know about the power and light in these cities. Von Beitz, suppose you take another man and start an investigation of its source. We'll want to know that. The other city I investigated had enormous subterranean granaries and storehouses. Williamson—you search for them. Jack—you take care of housing."

"We've been working on that," said Ransdell. "There's ample room already available—for your people and mine."

"Good. Water?"

"We've located the main conduits. They're full. The water's apparently fresh. We've turned it on in this building. We're running a set of fountains in the rear court and filling a swimming-pool to be sure it is fresh."

"Right.—Shirley, find Kyto and arrange for a meal at daybreak. Prepare for five hundred—we're almost that many."

Shirley left.

Hastily Tony dispatched others from his improvised headquarters. Soon he was alone with Ransdell.

"I got your signal," he said. "You wanted every one cleared out but me. Why?"

Ransdell glanced at the door. "For a good reason, Tony. I've got something important to tell you."

"What?"

"There's somebody else in this city."

Tony smiled. "I know that feeling. James and I had it. You get used to it."

Ransdell shrugged. "I'm not queasy—you know. I don't get those feelings. Here's my evidence: I drove the first caravan. When I reached the gates, I saw something whisk around a distant building. It might have been a man—it might have been the end of one of these little automobiles. . . . Then, after I'd started things going, I took a walk. I found this."

He handed Tony a half of a sandwich. A bite had been taken out of it—a big bite. The other half and the filling were missing. But the bread was fresh.

Tony stared at it. "Good Lord!"

"That bread would be stale in twelve hours, lying as it was on the street."

"Anything else?"

"This building was open. The others were shut. We used your instructions for getting into them. But in here, things were—disturbed. Chairs, tables. There was a ball of paper on the floor of this room. Nothing on it." Ransdell produced a crumpled sheet of paper.

"The Other People had paper," Tony said.

"Not paper watermarked in English."

Tony walked around the room, pondering this. "Well?"

"There can't be many people. Since we arrived, ever since I found the sandwich, I've been conducting a search. So have five other small posses. Nothing was discovered, however."

"I see." Tony sat down. "The Midianites have foreseen our scheme, then, and put watchers here."

"I think so."

"Do you believe that we can find them to-night?"

"You know better than I."

"I doubt it," Tony answered. "It would take months to cover every room, every subterranean chamber."

"Of course," said Ransdell, "it might be some one else. The Midianites might have explored here—and left. The Other People had bread—like ours more or less; and this isn't familiar—exactly. It looks like whole wheat—"

Tony grinned. "You aren't seriously suggesting that the Other People may be alive here?"

"Why not?"

"Well—why not? Anyway—some one is. Spies—ghosts—some one."

It was growing light when the trucks came back from the other camp. They were crowded with cheering people, who grew silent when they heard of Hendron's death. Tony and Ransdell went to greet them. Breakfast was ready; it was served from caldrons borrowed from the Other People's kitchens.

Tony was busy with hot soup when Peter Vanderbilt approached him. "Where's Von Beitz?"

"I don't know."

"Didn't he see you?"

"No."

Vanderbilt scowled. "Funny! Quarter of an hour ago I saw him a few streets from the square here. He was on his way to tell you something about the power. He turned a corner. I thought I heard the first faint part of a yell—choked off. I hustled around the same corner, but he was out of sight. It seemed odd—he'd have had to run pretty fast to make the next corner. So I jammed along looking for him. No sign of him. Thought he was reporting to you. But I went back. Nothing to see at the spot where he'd left me. I—"

Tony was calling. "Taylor—Williamson—Smith—Alexander—look for Von Beitz. Arm yourselves."

But two hours later Von Beitz had not been found.

CHAPTER XIII

FEAR OF THE UNKNOWN

DAY broke with its long, deliberate dawn, while the strange, eerie glow of the night light that illumined the city faded. There was no sound in the streets but the scuffing feet of the sentinels whom Tony had posted, and the echo of their voices as they made occasional reports to each other or called a challenge.

Now the night watch was relieved; and with the brightening day, searching parties set out again under strict order not to separate into squads of less than six, and to make communication, at regular intervals, with the Central Authority.

This was set up in the offices near the great hall in which Hendron lay dead—the Hall of Sciences of the Other People.

So the enormous chamber manifested itself. It had been, one time, a meeting-place of august, noble-minded Beings. The dimensions and proportions of the great hall, its modeling and decorations, declared their character. It was most fitting that the greatest scientist from Earth—he who attempted and triumphed in the flight through space—lie here in this hall.

Thus Hendron lay in state, his face stern and yet peaceful; and his people, whom he had saved from the cataclysm, slowly filed past.

Eve, his daughter, stood at his side.

Dodson had begun the vigil with her, but he had retired to a couch at the end of the great hall, where he had dropped down, meaning to rest for a few moments. Exhaustion had overcome him, and he slept, his huge chest rising and falling, the coat-sleeve of his armless shoulder moving on the floor with the rhythm of his breathing.

As the people filed from the hall, they passed Dodson, gazing at him but never disturbing him. His empty sleeve brought keenly to mind the savage battle in Michigan in the horrible hours when the mob there assailed the camp near the end of the waiting for the escape from earth. Where was Michigan? Where was the earth now?

The people passed more slowly for gazing back again at the catafalque of the Bronson Betans, whereon Hendron lay. . . .

Maltby, the electrical engineer, together with four others was exploring behind the walls of the building. Power was "on." Impulses, electrical in character, were perceptible; and Maltby was studying the problem of them.

Their manifestations were most conspicuous in the glow

which illumined the dome over the city at night, and which so agreeably lighted certain interiors by night and by day. These manifestations resembled those which Tony and Eliot James had reported from the first Sealed City which they had entered.

Maltby and his assistants discovered many other proofs of power impulses.

The source of the power they could not locate; but Lady Cynthia's account of the activities of the "Midianites" suggested to Maltby a key to the secret.

"I believe," Maltby said, "that the Bronson Betans undoubtedly solved the problem of obtaining power from the inner heat of the planet, and probably learned to utilize the radium-bearing strata under the outer crust. They must have perfected some apparatus to make practical use of that power. It is possible, but highly improbable, that the apparatus came through the passage of cold and darkness in such state that when the air thawed out and the crust-conditions approached normal, it set itself in operation automatically.

"What is far more probable is that the Midianites have discovered one installation of the apparatus. We know from Lady Cynthia that they are months ahead of us in experimenting with Bronson Betan machinery. I believe that they have put in order and set going the power-impulse machinery connected with the city which they have occupied.

"The impulses from that installation may be carried by cables under the ground; more probably, however, they are disseminated as some sort of radio-waves. Consequently they reach this city, as they reached the city that Tony and James entered, and we benefit from them."

Behind the wall at the end of the hall, near the couch upon which Dodson slept, one of Maltby's men came upon a mechanism connected with what was, plainly, a huge metal diaphragm. He called his chief, and the entire party of engineers worked over the mechanism.

Suddenly sound burst forth. Voices! Singing! And the thunder of a tremendous chorus filled the hall! Men's voices, and women's! How triumphant, sublime, the chant of this chorus!

No syllable was of itself understandable; the very scale and notes of the music were strange. Strange but magnificent!

It caught all the people in the hall and awed them into stillness. They stood staring up, agape; not frightened at all, only uplifted in their wonder!

Voices—voices of men and women a million years dead—resounded about them, singing this strange, enthralling requiem.

Eve, beside the body of her father, straightened and stood,

with her head raised, her eyes dry, her pulses pounding full again.

Tony, outside in the street, heard the chorus, and he came running in—to be checked at the entrance of the hall as though caught there in a spell. Only slowly, and as if he had to struggle through an invisible interference, could he advance; for the singing continued.

It suggested somehow, though its notes were not like, the Pilgrims' Chorus in "Tannhäuser." It was now like the "Fire Music"—now an exalted frenzy like the "Ride of the Valkyries." Some great Wagner had lived a million years ago when this planet pursued its accustomed course about its distant star!

The chorus ceased.

Tony caught Eve in his arms, lest she collapse in the reaction from her ecstasy.

"Tony! Tony, what a requiem for him! It leaves us nothing now to do for him! Oh, Tony, that was his requiem!"

Down the sunlit streets of the city the children of the earth, Dan and Dorothy, walked hand in hand, staring at the wonders about them, crying out, pointing, and flattening their noses against the show panes.

Though they plainly remembered the thrills and terrors of the Flight, they could not completely understand that the world was gone, that they had left it forever. This was to them merely another, more magic domain—an enthralling land of Oz, with especially splendid sights, with all the buildings strange in shape and resplendent in colors, with tiers of streets and breath-taking bridges. Behind the children, Shirley Cotton and Lady Cynthia strolled and stared; and along with them went Eliot James, who could not—and who did not attempt—to conceal his continued astonishments.

"Isn't this like the other city?" Shirley asked him.

"In general, but not in details," Eliot answered; and he asked Lady Cynthia: "Is it like the city where you were?"

"In general, as you say," the Englishwoman agreed. "But in detail these people certainly were capable of infinite variety. And what artisans they were!"

"And architects!" added Shirley.

"And engineers—and everything else!" said Eliot James.

"Where," demanded Dan, turning to his older companions, "where are all the people?"

"Where?" echoed Eliot to himself, below his breath, while Shirley answered the child: "They went away, Danny."

"Where did they go? . . . Are they coming back? . . . Why did they all go away? . . . What for?"

The questions of the child were the perplexities also of the scientists, which no one yet could resolve.

"Don't run too far ahead of us," Shirley bade the children

in a tone to avoid frightening them. For danger dangled over these splendid silent thoroughfares apparently untenanted, yet capable of catching away and keeping Van Beitz. Was it conceivable that survivors of the builders—the Other People—haunted these unruined remains of their own creation? Or was it that the ruthless men from earth—the "Midianites"—had sent their spies ahead to hide in this metropolis before its occupation by Hendron's people?

Tony called a council of the Central Authority to consider, especially, this problem. The Committee of Authority assembled in what had clearly been a council-chamber near to the great quiet secluded room, and yet illumined by the sunlight reflected down and disseminated agreeably and without glare.

Ten men chosen more or less arbitrarily by Tony himself composed the Committee of the Central Authority—four from the survivors of the hundred who had come from Hendron's camp, six from Ransdell's greater group; and these, of course, included Ransdell himself.

Such was the Central Authority improvised by Tony and accepted by his followers to deal with the strange and immediate emergencies arising from the occupation of this great empty city by five hundred people ignorant of it.

The searching-parties, as they returned or sent back couriers with reports, appeared before this committee.

Jack Taylor, haggard and hungry, made the first report.

"I'm back only to suggest a better search organization," Taylor said excitedly. "I took a truck and toured the widest streets at the lower levels; and some of them at the upper levels. At every corner my driver and I stopped, and yelled for Von Beitz. We didn't see a sign of life or get any reply."

"Did you see any evidence of recent—occupation?" Higgins, of the Authority, asked.

"Nothing."

Kyto brought food for Taylor, and he talked as he ate. "I've been over miles of streets, and covered only a little of the central section. The city's too damned big. If five hundred people had moved into New York when it was emptied—and nobody else was there except maybe three or four people, or a dozen who wanted to keep in hiding—what chance would the five hundred have of finding the dozen?"

"Of course there may be no dozen, or even four or five hiding people to find," Tony responded. "We can't be sure that Von Beitz fails to return because he was captured. He might have fallen when exploring somewhere; or something might have toppled on him; or he might have got himself locked in a building."

Taylor shrugged. "In that case, he'd be harder to find than the dozen who, we think, are hiding from us."

"You feel surer, I see," Tony observed, "that some people, unknown to us, are here hiding from us."

"Yes, I do."

"But without any further proof of it?"

Jack Taylor nodded. "I tell you, there are people here. I can feel it."

Duquesne came in. He had returned from a search in another section of the city.

"Rien!" he made his report explosively. "Nozzing. Except—perhaps I saw a face peering from a window—very high! It was gone—*pouf!* I entered the building. I climbed to the room where the window was. Again—*rien!* Only—as I stood there—I said: 'Duquesne, people have been in this room not long ago.' With the sixth sensation, I smell it." He was excited; but he could add nothing more positive to the account.

He also began to eat, and soon reported himself ready to go out for more investigation.

Ransdell quietly arose. "I'd like to go out again too. You don't need us, Tony," he continued, speaking for the rest of the committee as well as for himself. "It's nice of you to pretend we're necessary; but we know we're not—though we'll be glad to try to be useful when you really want us. We'll all obey you as we would have obeyed Hendron."

"You're going to join the search?" Tony asked.

Ransdell shook his head. "There's enough of us searching now. I want to join Maltby and Williamson and their men, who are working on the Bronson Beta machines and techniques."

Duquesne gestured emphatically, unable to speak for a moment because of the food crammed in his mouth.

"They are mad—mad—all but mad, our technicians! I have seen them!" he presently exclaimed. "It is the problem of the charging the batteries of the Bronson Betans that eludes them—those marvelous, amazing batteries which first we saw in the vehicle wrecked beside the road; and one of which Lady Cynthia herself operated in the vehicle that carried her to us.

"To operate the vehicle, once the charged battery is installed—that is nothing. But the secret of putting power into the battery!

"The Midianites have discovered it, my friends; but they have guarded it so that Lady Cynthia could not even suspect what it is. But if they conquered it, so may we! Ransdell is right," Duquesne ended his declamation. "That secret is far more important than further search. I too will join our technicians!"

Tony found himself alone in the great council-chamber. Now and then some one else arrived to report; but all reports, which had to do with the search for Von Beitz and for the unknown people who might have captured him, were negative. The couriers returned to their exploring squads; and the others scattered in their wondering examination of the marvels of the city.

There proved to be eight gates to this city, and four great central highways which met and crossed in the Place before the Hall of the Sciences, in which Hendron lay, and before also the splendid structure housing the council-chamber.

From right to left, before the Hall, ran a wide roadway, and another equally splendid cut across it at right angles, while obliquely, so that seen from above they must have made a pattern like the Cross of St. George, were two other highways only slightly less majestic. Each of these roads ran straight to the edge of the city, where the huge transparent dome joined the ground; at the eight points where these four roads penetrated were the gates; and at each of these gates stood a squad on watch.

High toward the top of the dome, on towers attained by arduous climbing, others of the men whom Hendron had brought from earth stood on watch, scanning the sky.

Tony strode out into the sunlight of the wide square, and he halted and lifted his head in awe.

He was in command in this city!

He had had nothing to do with creating it. A million years, perhaps, before he was born, this city had been built; and then the light which fell upon it was from some sun to which the sun of the world—the sun which now shone upon it—was a distant twinkling star. Quadrillions and quintillions of miles of space—distances indescribable in terms that the mind could comprehend—separated this city from Tony Drake, who would not be born for a million years. But it had traveled the tremendous reaches of space after it lost its sun until it found the star—the sun—that lighted the earth! So Tony Drake to-day stood here in its central square—in command.

He glanced up toward the orb of the sun; and he saw how small it was; and in spite of himself his shoulders jerked in a convulsive shiver.

"Tony!"

He heard his name, and turned. Eve had come out to the square, and she approached him, quietly and calmly.

"We must—proceed now, Tony," she said.

"Proceed? Of course," he assured her gently. He had ceased to be a commander of a city built a million years before his birth and endowed with marvels which men of his time—if they had remained on earth—might not have made for themselves for another millennium. He became again Tony Drake, recently—not three earthly years ago—a young broker in Wall Street, and friend of Eve Hendron, whose father was a scientist. On earth, Tony Drake had wanted her for his wife; here he wanted her also, and especially in her grief he longed to be her close comforter.

"Your mind doesn't help you much, does it, Tony?" she said.

"At a time like this, you mean. No."

"I went once with Father and with a friend of his, Professor Rior, through the Pyramids, Tony—when we were back on earth."

"Of course," said Tony.

"It was before ever the Bronson Bodies were seen, Tony; when the earth seemed practically eternal. How out of fashion it had become to look to the end of the earth, Tony! Though once it was not. . . . I was saying that Professor Rior was showing us through the Pyramids, and he read us some of the Pyramid Texts. Did you know, Tony, that in all the Pyramid Texts the word *death* never occurs except in the negative, or applied to a foe? How the old Egyptians tried to defeat death by denying! Of course, the Pyramids themselves were their most tremendous attempt to deny death."

"Yes," said Tony.

"Over and over again, I remember, Tony, they declared that he, whom they put away, lived. I remember the words: *'King Teti has not died the death; he has become a glorious one in the horizon!'* And, *'Ho! King Unis! Thou didst not depart dead; thou didst depart living! Thou diest not!'* And *'This King Pepi dies not; this King Pepi lives forever! This King Pepi has escaped his day of death!'*

"Tony, how pitiful those protests seemed to me to be! Yet now I myself am making them.

" *'Men fall; their name is not,'* the Egyptian psalmist of the Pyramid Texts sang, Tony:

> *"Men fall;*
> *Their name is not.*
> *Seize thou King Teti by his arm*
> *Take thou King Teti to the sky,*
> *That he die not on earth,*
> *Among men."*

Tony reminded her, very gently: "Your father did not die on earth."

"No; he escaped to the sky, bringing us all with him. . . . There's the sun. How small the sun has become, Tony."

"We are farther from the sun, Eve, than men of earth have ever been."

"But we're going farther away, yet."

"Yes."

"We're swinging away from the sun; but they say—Father

said, and so did M. Duquesne and the rest of the scientists—we shall swing back again when we have reached almost to the orbit of Mars. But shall we, Tony?"

"Reach almost to the orbit of Mars?"

"Shall we swing back then, I mean. Or shall we keep on out and out into the utter cold?"

"You don't believe your father—or Duquesne?" Tony asked.

"Yes; I believe they believed it. Yet like the old Egyptians, they may have been declaring denials of a fact they could not face."

"But your father and Duquesne and the rest faced the end of the world, Eve."

"That's true; but when they faced it,—and admitted it,—they already had schemed their escape, and ours. For this end, if Bronson Beta drifts out into the cold without return, there is no escape."

"No," said Tony, and combated the chill within him.

"And could they *know?*" Eve persisted. "They could calculate—and undoubtedly they did—that the path of this planet has become an ellipse, that it will turn back again toward the sun; but it never *has* turned back toward the sun, Tony. Not once! This planet appeared out of space, approached the sun and swung about it, and now is going away from the sun. That we *know;* and that is all we do know; the rest we can merely calculate."

"You mean," questioned Tony, "that your father said something privately, during those days he was dying, to make you believe he was deceiving us?"

"No," said Eve. "Yet I wonder, I cannot help wondering. But if we keep on away from the sun, don't think, Tony, I'm—"

"What?" he demanded as she faltered and stopped.

"Unprepared," she said; and she recited:

" '*Thy seats among the Gods abide; Re leans upon thee with his shoulder.*

" '*Thy odor is as their odor, thy sweat is as the sweat of the Eighteen Gods.*' "

"What's that?" asked Tony.

"Something else I remembered from earth, from the Pyramid Texts, Tony. " '*Sail thou with the Imperishable Stars, sail thou with the Unwearied Stars!*' "

She returned to the great Hall of Science of the men a million years dead, the hall wherein lay her father.

Several people crossed the square, some obviously on errands, others curiously wandering. Tony returned the hails of those who spoke to him, but encouraged no one to linger with him; he remained before the great hall, alone.

He had taken completely on faith the assurance which Hendron and Duquesne had given him, together with the rest of the people, that the path of this planet had ceased to follow the pattern of a parabola, but had become closed to an ellipse, and that therefore Bronson Beta, bearing these few Emigrants from Earth, would circle the sun. Tony still believed that; he had to believe it; but the death of Eve's father seemed to have shaken her from such a necessity.

He gazed about at the magnificent façades of the City of the Vanished People—his city, where he had come to the command perhaps only to die in it, with all his refugees from Earth's doomsday, as they drifted out into the coldness and darkness of space.

As this strange world had done once before with its own indigenous people! Where had they gone when the deadly drift began? Where lay the last builders of Bronson Beta?

"Hello! How's every little thing?" said a cheerful voice at his side.

Tony faced about, and confronted the red-haired girl whom he had met in Ransdell's camp, and who had not been selected for the voyage from earth; her name had not been on the lists in Michigan.

Tony remembered her name, however—Marian Jackson. She had been an acrobatic dancer in St. Louis.

She carried on her shoulder the animal stowaway of the second Ark, the little monkey, Clara.

"Can you beat this place? Can you tie it?" Marian challenged Tony cheerfully. "Gay but not gaudy, I'd call it. D'you agree?"

"I agree," acquiesced Tony, grateful for the letdown. The girl might be mentally a moron; but morons, he was discovering, had their points. This girl simply could not take anything seriously.

"But the taxi-service here is terrible," objected Marian.

"We hope to improve it," offered Tony.

The girl walked away. "Don't go into any of the buildings alone!" Tony reminded. "And even on the streets, keep close to other people!"

Marian halted, looking up. "Hello! Hello!" she cried out softly. "Look at the taxies!" And she pointed to one of the wide spiral ramps to the right.

Down the ramp Tony saw descending two Bronson Beta vehicles of the type discovered wrecked beside the first-found roadway, and duplicates of which were stored by the hundred in the first Sealed City. Here there were hundreds or thousands more of the machines.

The two that appeared were followed by two more, and these by two larger and heavier vehicles not of the passenger type, but of truck design.

"By God," cried Marian, "they got 'em going.—Hey! Hey!" she hailed them.

Tony thrilled too, but tempered his triumph by realization that, since the cars came in sight they had been descending, so that they might not be under power at all, but having been pushed to the incline of the ramp, were coasting.

The drivers seemed aware of this flaw in their demonstration, or else they could not yet be content to stop; for when they gained the ground in rapid procession, instantly they steered up the ascending spiral on the other side, and putting on power, climbed even faster than they had dropped.

That ended any doubt of their means of propulsion. Tony felt his scalp tingling. One more secret of the mechanics of these people a million years dead was in possession of his own people!

Now the vehicles, having vanished briefly, swept into sight again, still climbing; then they whirled down, sped into the square, and though braked somewhat raggedly, halted in line before Tony.

Eliot James stepped from the first with a flourish.

"Your car, sir!" He doffed his battered felt hat.

From the second car stepped the English girl Lady Cynthia. Williamson piloted the third; Maltby, Jack Taylor and Peter Vanderbilt were the other drivers.

Williamson, the electrical engineer, made his report to Tony as a hundred others gathered around.

"We discovered the technique of charging the batteries, which are beyond anything we had on earth," he said with envious admiration, "both in simplicity and in economy of power application. There is a station underground which They used. We are using it. All the batteries which we have discovered were discharged or had discharged themselves, naturally, in the tremendous time that the planet was drifting through space; but two out of three batteries proved capable of receiving a charge when placed in sockets of the charging station."

"You mean you found the charging station with its power on?" Tony asked.

Williamson looked at Maltby as if to enlist his support when replying: "We found the power on."

"What sort of power?"

"Something between the electrical impulses with which we were familiar on earth, and radio-activity. We believe the Bronson Beta scientists, before they died—or disappeared—learned to blend the two."

"Blend?" asked Tony.

Maltby took up the task of explanation. "You remember that on earth we didn't even know what electricity was; but we knew how to use it for some of our purposes. Still less did we understand the exact nature of radio-activity; but we used that too. Here we have come upon impulses which exhibit some of the phenomena of electricity, and others of radio-activity. We do not understand it; but we do find ourselves able to use it."

"But the power-station below ground in order and in operation!" objected Tony.

"I think," said Maltby, "it should not have been described as a power-station, but rather as a mere distributing station. The power, I believe, does not originate in the station which we discovered, and in which we charged the batteries of these machines. Our station is, I think, merely a terminus for the generating station."

"The generating station—where?"

At this, Maltby and Williamson, the technicians, both gazed at the English girl; but she, without making direct reply, nodded to Maltby to proceed.

"She believes that the chief generating station is under the city of our Midianites. It is a far larger city than this, and was probably the metropolis of the planet—or at least of this continent. She knows that the technicians with the Asiatic party got much of the machinery of the city going weeks ago.

"We believe that their technicians are employing the power-generators of the ancient civilization here without thoroughly understanding it—or without understanding it at all beyond having learned how it works, and what they can do with the power impulses.

"We believe that we get the power here because they cannot use it themselves without giving us some of it. Probably much of the power is disseminated without wires or cables. Undoubtedly the light-impulses are—those that light this city at night and illuminate interior apartments by day.

"These impulses probably are spread in a manner similar to radio waves. Williamson feels sure that power in the charging station cannot be so explained. He feels sure that the charging station below this city must have a cable connection—underground, undoubtedly—with the generating station.

"Now, if that generating station is under the city of the Midianites, either they know they are sending us that power—or they don't know it. If they know it, they may be unable to cut off our power without also cutting off their own; but if they don't know they are now giving us power, they may find it out at any moment—and cut us off. Duquesne thinks the latter; so he has remained below with all the men he needs to keep all the charging sockets busy, while we"—Maltby smiled deprecatingly—"allowed ourselves this celebration before busying ourselves above."

"At what?" asked Tony, half stupidly, half dazedly. "At

what here above?" Too much was being told him at once; too much—if one had to think about it.

Marian Jackson, who had remained beside him, had heard it all; but it had not confused her. It had merely amused her. She went to Eliot James and teased him to show her the controls of his machine; and she sat in it and started it.

"Easy! Easy!" Eliot yelled, and running beside her, shut off the power. "It's perfectly easy and obvious in its steering and controls. Anybody can run it; but from the little I've seen, it must do over two hundred miles an hour, or three hundred, if you open it up. *So don't open it up!*"

The other drivers argued only less emphatically with other experimenters, and the crowd followed the machines.

"You see," Maltby was explaining to Tony, "now we know how to use their power, we ought to get other things going besides the vehicles; we ought to get a part of the city, at least, in some sort of operation."

"Of course," Tony comprehended. "Of course." And he led Lady Cynthia aside, with Williamson and Maltby. "When we have power," he challenged the English girl, "how much of its use can you show us?"

"I know how to get in and out of the buildings which have doors operated by electricity—or whatever it is. I know how they run the kitchens and the lights and baths, and things like that."

Tony said: "Then you had better take these men through a few buildings. Show them everything you've seen in operation—how it seemed to work. . . . Williamson,—Maltby,—you choose the party to go with her. When you're through with her, please ask her to come back to the Council Hall."

As Tony turned away, Jack Taylor approached him.

"You don't want a ride," he tempted his friend, "in one of the new million-year-old machines through the city?"

"Not yet," Tony said.

"Why not yet?"

"You," said Tony, "you take it for me, Jack."

"All right," said Jack, staring at him almost understandingly. "Sure. I'll take the ride for you!"

Tony retired to his deserted Hall of the Central Authority. He would have liked nothing better than to feel free to ride the ramps to the highest pinnacles as, in the square below him, others—many of them no younger than he—were preparing to do. Those allowed to experiment with the vehicles were as eager and excited as children with their first velocipedes. Tony watched them for a time enviously. No one but himself stopped him from rejoining them and claiming his right to ride the amazing highroads of this city. But not yet!

"Why?"

He glanced up toward the sun, the small, distant sun, warm

enough yet when the sky was clear, warm enough especially under the splendid shield spread over the city.

He dropped back from the window and slumped down before the beautiful desk which had served its original purpose countless years ago when this world whirled about some other star. He still was alone.

Two tiny images of men—men not of the world, but of this planet—decorated the desk, one standing at each of the far corners of the desk-top. They were not secured to the metal top, but could be plucked from their fastening without breaking. Tony toyed with them; they reminded him of little images brought from Egypt. There had been a name for them in the world. *"Ush—ushab—"* He could not quite recall it.

Some one entered. It was Eve; and he arose, awaiting her. His mood had returned to readiness for her; and she was calmer than before, and quite collected.

"What are those, Tony?" She gazed at the exquisite little images in his hand.

"You tell me, Eve."

"Why, they look like *ushabtin,* Tony."

"That's it! The *'answerers,'* weren't they? The *Respondents."*

"Yes," she said. "The *Answerers,* the *Respondents for the Dead.* For when a man died, the Egyptians could not believe that he would not be called upon to continue his tasks as always he had done them in his life. So they placed in his tomb the *'Answerer'* to respond when he was called to perform a task after he was dead. *'O Answerer!'* the soul appealed to the statuette: *'If I am called, if I am counted upon to do any work that is to be done by the Dead . . . thou shalt substitute thyself for me at all times, to cultivate the field, to water the shores, to transport sand of the east to the west, and say "Here am I; I am here to do it!"'* "

"I see," said Tony. "Thank you. I remember. I hope your father can feel I am his *Answerer,* Eve."

He knew, then, why he had not left the Hall of Authority to ride the ramps of the city: Cole Hendron would not have done it.

CHAPTER XIV

THE FUNERAL OF COLE HENDRON

"WHAT weapons did the Midianites find in their city?"

"Practically none. None at all, that I know of," Lady Cynthia corrected.

She had returned from her tour with the technicians, having demonstrated all she had learned of the manner of manipulating electric locks, taps, pumping-apparatus and other mechanisms which now were capable of being operated.

Duquesne had delegated to other competent hands the continuous charging of the batteries; and he sat with Tony, as did also Eliot James in the office of the Hall of the Central Authority. So the three men listened to the girl and questioned her—to learn, with least delay, of the discoveries of the Midianites.

"We found no weapons in the city we entered," Eliot James reminded Tony. "We have come on nothing like a weapon—except some implements in what must have been a museum—here."

"The people of Bronson Beta," pronounced Duquesne, "seem to have had no need of war in their later development. Why? Because morally they had passed beyond it? I do not believe it. Other causes and conditions intervened. No greater authority upon human development than Flinders Petrie lived on earth; and what did he say?

" 'There is no advance without strife. Man must strive with Nature or with man, if he is not to fall back and degenerate.' Certainly these people did not degenerate; there is no sign in this city but of a struggle, *magnifique*—epic. But not of man against man. It was, of course, of man against Nature—even against the drift into the darkness of doom which they saw before them.

"In comparison with this struggle, strife between themselves became puny—imbecile. Long ago, long before the drift into the dark, they ceased to wage war; and so they left to our enemies none of their weapons."

"They left material, however, which could be used as weapons," the English girl corrected.

"Most certainly; the gas—gas that was merciful anesthetic for the Vanished People, probably."

"How much progress," Tony asked the girl who had been a prisoner in the other city, "did your captors make in reading the records of the Vanished People?"

"Very considerable, I am sure. They brought over from earth an especially strong staff of linguists. They seemed to have realized, even better than did our party—or perhaps than did you," the English girl said, "the importance of solving quickly the secrets of the original civilization. And they went right at it."

"How did they learn?"

"From repairing and putting into operation what seems to have been instruction-machines for the children of this planet—machines which in form are very unlike but in effect are like talking motion pictures. The machines illustrate an object, and print and pronounce a word at the same time. I have shown M. Duquesne similar machines found here."

"Maltby and Williamson together," said Duquesne to Tony, "are working on them now."

Tony arose. Again the implications of what he heard were so tremendous that he could not think of them without confusion. He put them aside for the moment.

He paced up and down. "What was on that lake where your space-ship fell?" he asked the English girl.

"Nothing. It seemed to have been burned over all around the border. The water was fresh."

"Half of you, you said, were drowned?"

"Nearly half."

"All the survivors of the crash were captured?"

"Yes; and when I escaped, I figured that three hundred and ten of us were living." She repeated the figure she had given in her first account.

"And how many were *they*—your captors—our 'Midianites'?"

"More than our number, considerably. They never said how many they were, nor gave us a chance to count them. They were always on the move."

"Where to?"

"Everywhere."

"You mean they visited several other cities?"

"Oh, yes."

"How many?"

"As many as they could find and reach. And I believe they could have found all within reach. For they had a globe of this planet. I heard about it; but they never let any of us slaves see it."

"Every city of course has a globe—or several," Tony said to himself, aloud, and asked her: "What did you pick up from them as to their opinion of the different cities?"

"They believed they had the best one."

"Did they say why they believed it the best?"

"No."

"What else could you pick up?"

"They said that one city was a good example of every other. They're all complete, and all similar in a general way."

Tony gazed out of the window. More and more of the vehicles of the Vanished People were appearing on the ramps and the streets. The sun, the small clear sun, shone down through the huge transparent dome. He swung back.

"Did they find how the air was kept fresh in the cities when they were fully—populated?"

"Yes; and they even operated some of the ventilators, though it was not necessary with so few people in the city, of course. The Original People had huge apparatus for what we would call air-conditioning, and for heating the air. The Asiatics of course were especially interested in that."

"The heating, eh? Did they think the planet was drifting again into the cold?"

"That," said Lady Cynthia, "surely worried them. They had their own computations, but they repeatedly asked what ours were. They were—and are, I am sure—especially careful with our scientists. They aren't sure, you see, that this planet will stay livably near the sun."

"Were your scientists—the English, I mean—sure?" asked Tony.

"They said they were. We'd go out into the cold nearly as far as Mars—and then come back."

"Yes," said Tony.

"That's what you think here, isn't it?" the girl appealed.

Intentionally Tony waited until Duquesne replied. "It is upon that," said the Frenchman, "that we rely. Now may I ask something? Did these people—your captors, these Midianites—find any trace as to where the builders of these *magnifique* cities and the other inhabitants went?"

"No! Constantly they talked about it. Where were they? Where did they go? And did any—survive?"

"Precisely," said Duquesne.

"We shall name this city," said Tony suddenly, "Hendron. *Hendron.* I am sure no one objects. . . . I thank you," he said to the English girl, "for all you have told us. Of course we will have much more to ask; but not now."

He left them and went out. Now he had need, as he had not before, for an inspection of the city.

Jack Taylor, seeing him, stopped one of the cars and took Tony in with him. Dizzily they spun up a twisting ramp and shot out upon a wide boulevard. They pulled up after a couple of miles, which had been coursed in barely a minute, beside a building at one of the guarded gates. On the far side of its entrance-lobby was a dining-room where a score of women were setting out upon tables the square metal plates upon which the Other People had dined perhaps a million years before.

Tony got out and went in. He smelled the aroma from a caldron of stew, but he was not hungry.

Higgins was there eating—excited to be sure, but eating.

"Tony!" Higgins called. "Tony!" he beckoned, rising.

Tony sat beside him. "I've been two miles underground!" Higgins reported. "Two miles! Maltby got the lifts working. I took a chance on one. Two miles down. Wonderful. Temperature rises all the way."

Tony whipped his thoughts to this problem. "Temperature rises? How could it? Didn't this planet cool—ages ago?"

"Not to the core. Only the crust. Two miles down, it was a hundred and six degrees Fahrenheit. I brought back—well, you will see."

"What?"

"Samples of what they tried to preserve below, or store for themselves. Some of it preserved, some of it not; some sealed in naked rock close to the surface and allowed to get terribly cold; some stored in metal containers and placed at strata where some heat would have endured—and did. There is enough stuff under this city to feed a Chicago for years—generations. I can't estimate how long—that is, if the stuff remained edible. The meat must be decidedly questionable."

"Meat!"

"From what animals I can't say; the vegetables from what plants I am unable to guess. Some of it may not be digestible by us. Some may be poison, we'll discover. But some must be edible, for I've eaten some and I still feel fine."

Tony went down the staircase to the hall with Higgins. In the hall a half-dozen square glasslike containers, each about two feet high and a foot in its other dimensions, had been set on tables. Covers sealed them hermetically. Their contents were visible; meat indeed—a reddish lean meat not unlike beef, and a lighter meat in small fragments; and vegetables—one appeared as long yellow cylinders, another as pink balls not unlike radishes, a third streaked with yellow and green and of an indeterminate lumpy shape.

Tony regarded the exhibit thoughtfully. "They covered their cities. They stored food-supplies for a prodigious time. They must have prepared for the journey into space."

"Of course," said Higgins.

"But where are they?"

"I do not know."

"And the heat increased with depth?"

"Exactly."

"Probably the same system that lights the cities heated the storerooms, so the precious food there would not at first freeze, crack its containers and spoil."

"Possibly," said Higgins. "I am a plant biologist, not an engineer. But I would venture to disagree, even so."

"Why?"

"I saw no evidence of heating-mechanisms. Ventilation—yes. Heat—no."

"But the air—it's warmed," Tony persisted.

"It wasn't. Observation showed the air on Bronson Beta was frozen solid—as it approached."

"We couldn't make observation under the domes."

"True. But you will find ample evidence in fractures and wash-marks to show that the air in the city was frozen. Yes—it is not heated air from the domed city which has kept these immense subterranean warehouses warm." Higgins shook his head. "Radium."

"Radium?" Tony repeated.

"Radium. Deep in this planet. Only radio-active minerals could maintain heat inside a planet during untold ages of drift through frigid space. So we may conclude that the interior of Bronson Beta is rich in such minerals."

"Then it must be dangerous—"

Higgins shrugged. "The presence of heat does not mean that rays are also present. They are doubtless absorbed by miles of rock. Hundreds of miles, maybe. But the heat is there, the activity of radium; and the rocks carry the heat almost to the surface."

There was silence in the group. Tony addressed a bystander. "Jim, get Duquesne. Tell him to turn the power-station over to Klein, and investigate this. Take Higgins with you." Then: "If the interior of Bronson Beta is warm still—then it is quite possible—"

"That the original inhabitants still persist somewhere? How? They melted air from the frozen lightless desert above them on the surface, and lived down in the radium-warmed bowels of their planet? I found no living quarters underground. But—who can say!"

Tony squared his chin against his imagination. "They are all dead," he said.

Higgins started away with Jim Turnsey, talking excitedly.

Before noon, people began to collect for their next meal. No one brought any information about Von Beitz. He had vanished. But another clew to the possible existence of living people in Hendron had been discovered. Williamson, exploring with a searching-party, had found three beds that had been slept in. He had been led to the find by an open window in a building on the northern edge of the city. Whether the beds had afforded resting-places for the Other People after the city was built, or for scouts from the Midianite camp, he could not be sure.

Three beds, with synthetic bed-covers rumpled upon them. No more.

The vast dining-room was filled as the sun came directly

overhead. Twenty of the women waited on table. Plates of stew were served, then coffee in stemmed receptacles which had handles for five fingers—five fingers a little different from human fingers, evidently, for they were awkward to use.

After that, Tony rose and spoke.

"My friends," he said, "we are safe. Our security is due to the courage and intelligence of our dead leader. No praise is adequate for him. I shall not attempt to reduce what is in your hearts to words. Prodigious labors, great dangers, even the dangers of battle and peril of annihilation at the perihelion of our orbit, lie ahead of us. Unknown conditions, diseases, poisons, threaten us. Enemies may lurk among us. An evil and powerful aggregation of fellowmen is striving and planning now to conquer us. Mysteries of the most appalling sort surround us. Still—Cole Hendron faced calmly both hazards and enigmas as awesome. We must endeavor to emulate him. And on this afternoon we shall pay a last homage to him.

"I have prepared the earth to receive him. I have named this city for him. I shall ask you to remain inside the protecting dome of this city—standing on the ramp of the western skyscraper—while Cole Hendron is buried. I do not dare to expose you all. The following will accompany me to the grave." He read from a paper: "Eve Hendron, David Ransdell, Pierre Duquesne, Eliot James and Doctor Dodson. His pall-bearers to the gate will be the men whose names I have just read, and also Taylor, Williamson, Smith, Higgins and Wycherley.

"We will march from here to the gate. You will follow; Eve will open the gate."

Once more, before Cole Hendron—Conqueror of Space—was borne from the Hall of Science, the music of Bronson Beta burst forth. Maltby once more made rise the tremendous tones from the throats a million years silent to sing Cole Hendron's requiem. Then the bearers of the body descended the staircase of the majestic building.

Cole Hendron had no coffin. Over the body was an immense black tapestry—a hanging taken from the great Hall in which he had lain.

The procession reached the street, amid muffled sobs and the sound of feet.

At the gate, Eve pulled the control lever. Hendron's closest friends and his daughter marched into the open.

It was cold.

The mourners filed up a great spiral ramp and stood watching.

Tony beside Ransdell, at the head of the bier, walked with his head down. Eve came last, a lone regal figure.

They surmounted the knoll. The body was lowered. They stood around the grave, shivering a little in the cold.

"The greatest American," Tony said at last.

"The greatest man," said Duquesne, weeping openly.

Dodson, a person of expletives rather than of eloquence, looked down at the dark-swathed and pathetic bundle. "I doubt if ever before so much has depended upon one man. A race, maybe—or a religion—or a nation; but never a species."

Eliot James spoke last. "He did not make mere history. He made a mark across cosmos and infinity. Only in memory can adequate honor be paid to him. . . . Good-by, Cole Hendron!"

Then, from the city, came suddenly the sound of earth's voices raised in Rudyard Kipling's "Recessional":

God of our fathers, known of old. . . .
The tumult and the shouting dies,
The captains and the kings depart. . . .

Earth's voices singing to the skies, where never earth people had been before.

Tony sprinkled earth upon Hendron—earth not of the earth, but of the planet that had come from the edges of infinity to replace it. The grave was filled.

At the last Eve and Tony stood side by side, while the others rolled a great bowlder over the spot as a temporary marker.

Tony heard Eve whispering to herself. "What is it?" he said. "Tell me!"

"Only the Tenth Psalm, Tony," she whispered: *"Why standest thou afar off, O Lord? Why hidest thou thyself in times of trouble?"*

And in the far sky a speck passed and vanished beyond the hill, an abrupt and vivid reminder of the exigencies of the present.

CHAPTER XV

VON BEITZ RETURNS

ELIOT JAMES sat in the apartment which he had chosen for his residence, and looked from its unornamented gray walls out over the city of Hendron. Presently he began to write. In a cabinet at his side were drawers filled with notebooks upon which was scribbled the history of the migration from earth.

"In summary," he began, "since there has been no time for detail, I will set down an outline of our conditions since our perilous removal to this city of the ancient people.

"We have shelter, the gorgeous shelter of these buildings rising in a hundred hues under their transparent dome. We have warmth, for although we are moving out into the cold at a prodigious speed, the air sucked into the city is heated. Around the rim of the dome are situated eight tremendous ventilating and air-conditioning plants. We have light in abundance—our city in the long dark of night is like day. Underground is food enough for us for unmeasured generations. Some of that food disagrees with us. Some is indigestible. In some there is no nourishment which our gastric juices can extract. Two varieties of vegetables are definitely poisonous to us. But the vast bulk of the stored produce is edible, delicious and healthful.

"We have a plethora of tools and machines. In the development of electricity the Other People have far outstripped us. Also in the extension of what we called 'robot-control.' They manufactured almost no machinery which needed human attention. A technique of photo-electric cell inspection and auxiliary engines makes every continuous mechanical process self-operating. The vast generators which run underground to supply light, the powerful motors of the ventilators, and the pumps which supply processed water from the river for our consumption, not only run by themselves but repair themselves.

"The northwest ventilator cracked a bearing last week—and in the presence of Tony and Ransdell it stopped itself, took itself apart, removed the cracked metal, put on a new bearing, reassembled itself and went into operation again. They said that the thing reminded them of the operation of one of those earthly phonographs which stops automatically and has a moving arm to take off played records and put on new ones. Only—the ventilator motor was thirty feet in height and proportionately broad and long.

"We have clothing. In our first camp there is still much clothing from earth, but we have not reclaimed it. The Bronson

Betans wore very light and very little clothing. We know so much about them now, that we can follow their clothing trends over ages of their history. With domed cities, always warm, they needed clothes only for ornament—as do we—in reality. But they left behind not only vast stores of garments and goods, but the mills in which the materials were fabricated. We are using the materials now. No one has yet appeared, except for amusement, in a Bronson Betan costume. Their shoes, of soft materials, are all too wide for us. Their garments were like sweaters and shorts,—both for men and women,—although the women also wore flowing robes not unlike negligees. However, we do wear portions of their garments, and we use their materials—all intermingled with the remains of the clothes we brought from earth, so that we are a motley mob.

"All Bronson Betan clothes were of the most brilliant colors —they must have loved color to live in a paradise of it. I saw Tony yesterday, for example, in a pair of old brogans, old corduroy trousers and a shirt (made by Shirley Cotton, who is now in charge of textiles) crimson in color, ornamented with green birds about a foot high—by all odds a more strident and stunning garment than I've ever seen on one of New York's four hundred. Ransdell has been running around in jade green Bronson Beta shorts, and Lady Cynthia has remodeled one of the 'negligees' I mentioned into a short metallic gold dress.

"We have baths of every temperature—private and public. The Bronson Betans were great swimmers. Jack Taylor made a study of their athletic records—and found them superior in almost every kind of event to ourselves. We have ray baths— ultra-violet and infra-red, and others we cannot use until they have been more thoroughly studied.

"We—and when I say we, I mean a score of our number— have mastered the language and much of the science of the Other People. Of course, we have not delved into their history deeply as yet, or into their fiction, or their philosophy or their arts—into their biography or their music. And their poetry is still quite incomprehensible to us.

"We fly their planes now. We run their machines."

Here Eliot James paused before continuing:

"Our personal relations are interesting at this point. I have given them little time in my diary hitherto, because of the pressure of my activities.

"Our most notable romance—the love of Tony and Dave Ransdell for Eve Hendron—has reached a culmination.

"Tony is going to marry Eve.

"There was a period shortly before our desertion of our original camp when it appeared for a little while that Eve would marry Ransdell. That was immediately after his dramatic return to our midst. Eve indubitably still holds Ransdell in high esteem, and even has a place of sorts for him in her heart. But

Tony is her kind of man. Tony is nearer her age. Tony is our leader—and she was the daughter of the greatest leader of all time. Tony worships her. They announced that they would celebrate the first wedding on Bronson Beta in the near future. And it will be the first. The Asiatics have, according to Lady Cynthia, made a complete mockery of marriage—and marriage was apparently unknown to the Other People.

"Ransdell, I think, knew always that Eve was not for him. He is a silent person, usually; but I believe that occasionally his love for Eve must have been very nearly indomitable—that he was more than once on the verge of asserting it wildly and insisting on it. He has that kind of passion—but I believe it will never be seen uncontrolled. Now he is resigned—or at least calm. And he has been not only one of Tony's ablest men, but one of his closest friends—if not his closest.

"Shirley Cotton, the siren of the city, is still in love with Tony. She talks about it in public, and tells Eve that when the biologists eventually decide that because of the larger number of women than men, two women will have to marry one man, she is going to be Tony's second wife. An odd situation—because some day that may be a necessity—or a common practice. There are now nearly ninety more women than men in our city. Eve is so brave and so broad-minded and so fond of Shirley, that if the situation ever became actual, I almost think that she would not mind. We have passed through too much to stoop now to jealousy. And all of us feel, I think, that we belong not to ourselves but to the future of man. The emotion rises from the spirit of self-sacrifice that has marked our whole adventure—rather than from such a cold, cruel and inhuman law as that which attempts to set up the identical feeling among the Midianites.

"Dan and Dorothy, under Westerley, are going to Bronson Beta school—learning the language by the talking-picture machines, just as the Other People's children did. And they are the only ones who are beginning to be able to speak it naturally. In two or three years they would be able to pass as Bronson Betan—except for their minor physiological differences.

"Dodson is having trouble with the language. He goes about the city talking to friends, eating in the central dining-room and mumbling that 'you can't teach an old dog new tricks.' He never was a good linguist—as Duquesne has proved by talking in French with him for the amused benefit of all who spoke the language. But Dodson is frantic to learn, because from illustrations in the metal books and in the screened lectures on the subject, he has found that surgery on this planet was a science far beyond terrestrial dreams. Working with him are five women and eleven men doctors.

"Jack Taylor is the sheik and Romeo of Hendron. About

twenty of our handsome girls and women (they are handsome again, the long strain of our first rugged months having ended) are wildly vying for his attention. The tall red-headed oarsman takes his popularity with delight—and he is seldom seen without a beautiful lady companion. When he was absent on a mission for Tony, the number of blue damsels was appalling. They could not even write to him, which seemed to distress them enormously.

"Duquesne has moved next door to the German actress who joined us in Michigan. He is working on the mystery of our power source—and 'cementing the bonds of international amity,' he says.

"Higgins has found some carefully preserved seeds in the radium-warmed cellars of the city, and he has planted them. He keeps digging them up to see if they have sprouted—which, so far, they have not; and he goes about in a perpetual daze."

Again Eliot James paused. Again he wrote:

"All those factors are on the pleasant side of our ledger. We are a civilization again. Love and clothes and cosmetics and fancy desserts and gossip and apartment-decoration have returned to us. Our animals have been collected from the encampments, and they are installed in a 'barn' made from a very elaborate theater. We have harvested and dried a quantity of the spore vegetation as hay for them. They thrive. We are wakened by a cock's crow in the morning, and we serve fresh eggs as a badge of honor with great ceremony at the rate of four or five a day. Dan and Dorothy have milk. We've made butter to go with the eggs. We should be perfectly happy, perfectly content. But—

"Where is Von Beitz?

"He vanished the day Cole Hendron died—the day we arrived here. That was sixty Bronson Beta days ago. And nothing has been seen of him or learned about him since then.

"And—

"Who dwells secretly in our city? Who stole one of our three roosters? Who stole Hibb's translation of a book on electricity? Who screamed on the street in the dead of night three days ago—turning out the people in Dormitory A to find—no one? Do the Other People still live here—watching us, waiting to strike against us? Do the Midianites have spies here?

"We are virtually agreed upon that theory. Yet we cannot find where they hide. But we do know—to our sorrow—that they have spies in other cities.

"After learning to fly the planes, we armed them. Then Tony dispatched a fleet of six to make a thorough inspection of the surrounding country and the neighboring cities. He wanted full information on the Midianites, and on the territory around us.

"There are two cities south of where Ransdell landed his ship. There are several inland. All were entered and explored. In the southernmost city the crew of a plane commanded by Jack Taylor was sniped upon, and two of his men were killed.

"In the nearest vacant western city Ransdell fought hand-to-hand with twelve or fourteen Midianites, who attacked his party as it came through the gate. Ransdell is a deadly shot. His five men took cover, and in a battle that lasted for three-quarters of an hour, one was wounded. Six Midianites were killed. I should say—three Japs and three Russians.

"A third plane did not return. It was subsequently sighted near the northern city occupied by the main Midianite colony—shot down and wrecked completely.

"We have been spied upon several times by planes flying over the city. A request for surrender to the Dominion of Asian Realists' was dropped twice, and our failure to reply brought one tremendous bomb—which, however, did not penetrate our tough, transparent envelope, although it was unquestionably intended for that purpose.

"It is not safe to leave the city. Twice parties on foot exploring the geology and flora outside the gates have been fired at by the enemy planes which appeared from the north and dived at them.

"It is evident that the Midianites are engaged in a war of attrition. They mean to conquer us. They mean to have Bronson Beta for themselves—or at least to insure that all human beings upon the planet will be governed by them and will live by their precepts. And Lady Cynthia has left no doubt in our minds about their desire for our women. They need what they call 'breeding females.' I think that 'need' in itself would be sufficient to cause every man and woman here to fight to the death.

"Yes, we could and should be happy here now. But—

"More than three hundred Englishmen and Englishwomen are living in subjugation, and we are unable to set them free. They are our own blood and kin. They are living under conditions at best odious, at worst horrible to them. We cannot be happy while they are virtually slaves.

"And also—Bronson Beta moves ever into cold. Bitter cold! Sixty days ago the surface of the planet was chilly. Then, for a while, it warmed again, so that we enjoyed a long fall or Indian summer. But now the chill is returning. Our seasons are due not to an inclination of our axis, as on earth, but to our eccentric orbit. The earth in winter was actually nearer to the sun than in the summer, but in winter the earth's axis caused the sun's rays to fall obliquely. Here on Bronson Beta we move from a point close to the orbit of

Venus to a point near that of Mars—and the change in distance from the sun will bring extremes of temperature.

"That is not all. That is not the only problem—anxious problem—which faces us in these autumn days. Shall we turn back toward the sun? Our scientists say so; but shall we? This planet has not done it yet. Its specialty seems to be a drift out into space.

"Our astrophysicists and mathematicians burn their lights far into the night of this new planet in order to anticipate the possibilities in our state. They are not romantic men.

"Meanwhile as we move out into space toward Mars, that red world increases in size and brilliance. Already it is a more vivid body than was Venus from the earth, and its color is malevolent and ominous.

"So the days and nights pass.

"Yes, our colony is returning to the happy human pursuits of love and knowledge and social relationships. But we are surrounded by mysteries, terrors, spies within our city, enemies who would conquer us; and always the red planet draws nearer—as not long ago the two bodies from cosmos drew toward the condemned and terrified earth."

As Eliot James finished that entry in his diary, he was interrupted by a knock on his door.

"Come in!" he called.

Shirley Cotton entered. She said something that sounded like *"Hopayiato!"*

"Hopayiato yourself," Eliot James answered.

"That's a Bronson Beta word," she said. "It means, 'How the devil are you?'—or something like that."

"Sit," said the writer. "I'm fine. What's news?"

Shirley grinned. "Want a nice mauve-and-yellow shirt? Want a pair of red-and-silver shorts?"

"Any rags? Any old iron? What's the trouble? Your clothing-department running out of orders?"

"Nope. And when we do, we'll revive fashions—so you'll have to patronize Shirley Cotton's mills, whether you want to or not."

"My God," said James with mock anger, "you'd think that after managing to abolish styles for a couple of years, people would be glad enough to give them up forever!"

She shook her head. "This year we're going in for light clothing with animal designs. Next year I plan flowers. Higgins is going to present some patterns—"

"He never will, I trust."

"I'll bribe him with a waistcoat in Bronson Beta orchids and mushrooms. By the way—how long have you been sitting in this cramped hole?"

"All morning. Why?"

"Then you haven't heard about the green rain."

James looked at her with surprise. "Green rain?"

"Sure. Outdoors. Didn't amount to anything—but for about ten minutes it rained green."

"I'll be damned! What was it?"

Shirley shrugged. "Search me. A green sky is bad enough. But a green rain—well, anything can happen. Higgins has bottles full of whatever it was—more like snow than rain—only not frozen. It misted the dome a little. And then—you probably haven't heard the rumor about Von Beitz that was going around."

"News?"

"Not news. A rumor. Scandal, I'd call it. People have been saying this morning that the spies hiding here are undoubtedly from the Midianite gang. Some of them are Germans. Von Beitz was a German. So they say that he wasn't kidnaped, but that he had always belonged to them, and merely joined them at the first opportunity."

Eliot James swore. "That's a lousy libel. Why—Von Beitz is one of the whitest men I know. A great brain. And nerve! I fought side by side with that guy in Michigan, and—why—hell! He's practically a brother of mine. Why do you think I went out scouring the other cities last month, and why do you think I've been in every corner of this burg looking? Because Von Beitz wouldn't turn us in for his life—that's why."

The handsome Shirley Cotton nodded. "I agree. But everybody's nervous these days."

"The Lord knows there's enough to make them nervous—"

They were interrupted by a banging on the door.

"Come in!" James called.

The door swung inward automatically. On the threshold stood Duquesne. He was ordinarily of ruddy complexion, but now his face was white. "Have you seen Tony?" he asked.

"No. What's the trouble?"

The Frenchman stepped into the room, and the door closed behind him. "I have searched everywhere."

James leaped to his feet. "You don't mean that Tony—"

"Oh—no, not lost. Just busy somewhere." Duquesne regarded the man and woman for a moment. "I was in a hurry to find him, because I have some very interesting information. I shall tell you. It is for the moment confidential."

"Sit," said the writer, as he had to his previous guest. "What's it about?"

"The source of our power."

James leaned forward. "You found it?"

"Not specifically. I have clung to the theory that power was generated under the city. When we learned that the interior of the planet was still warm, it seemed plausible that the power was generated from that heat—deep in the earth.

So I explored. It was difficult. All the electrical connections are built into the very foundation of the city. They cannot be traced. My assistants meanwhile studied the plans of the city—we found many. The clew in them pointed always toward a place in the earth. We finally—this morning—located that place. It is far underground. But it is not a generating plant. No."

"What is it, then?" James asked.

"A relay-station. A mere series of transformers. Stupendous in size and capacity. From it lead the great conduits—out, underground, deep down—toward the north. The station for this city is not here. It is as we suspected, in some other city—or place. And all the cities near here derive their power from that place. That is the explanation of why, when the lights came in one city, they came in all. It was a central plant which had been turned on—and which supplied every city."

"That's a very interesting confirmation," James said.

Duquesne snorted. "My dear young man! Can't you think of more to say than that it is interesting?"

James leaned back. "I see. You mean that now it is sure that they have control of our power."

"Exactly."

"And they can shut it off whenever they wish."

"Precisely."

"So that—when it gets colder—they can cut our power and not only put out our lights, but stop our heat."

"Right."

James tapped on his desk with the pencil he had been using.

"How much chance," he asked, "have we of setting up a power-station of our own—a station big enough to heat a couple of buildings, and light them, all winter?"

Duquesne shrugged. "What do we use for fuel?"

"Not coal—we've seen none. Or oil. How about wood? Those forests?"

"And how do we get wood here?"

"Trucks."

"And if our enemies are trying to freeze us into submission, would they let us save ourselves by running trucks day and night to distant forests for fuel? No. They would blow up the roads and bomb the trucks. It would take much wood to keep us warm. We could not run any sort of blockade—or cut wood under fire from an enemy. No."

"The river, then?"

Duquesne spread his hands. "You have imagination, my boy. But already it is too cold. And to build a dam and a hydro-electric plant takes months. I have thought of those things."

"In other words," Shirley said slowly, "if you are right about the Midianites being in possession of the power-plant, we'll have to take it way from them—or beat them somehow. Or else—"

James grinned bitterly. "Why not just leave it at, 'or else'?"

The Frenchman rose. "That is told in confidence. I may be mistaken in my conjectures. I shall now search for Tony further. He will in any case appear for luncheon." He left them, and they heard the nervous click of his heels as his short legs carried his large body down the hall.

"Not so good," said Shirley Cotton.

James went to the window. Down on the street below, people moved hither and thither. A few of the Bronson Beta automobiles shot back and forth on their roadways, and wound the spiral ramps of buildings. Overhead in the green sky the sun shone, brightening the city, touching with splendor its many-colored facets.

Then a mighty bell sent a rolling reverberation over the district. James turned from the window. "Lunch," he said.

He went with the girl to the dining-room. The five-hundred-odd inhabitants of Hendron were gathering. They came together on the street outside the dining-hall in twos and threes, and moved through the wide doorway to their appointed places. They talked and laughed and joked with each other, and on the faces only of a minority was an expression of unalterable apprehension. The rest were at least calm.

In ten minutes the hall was a bedlam of voices and clatterings, and the women on duty as waitresses hurried from the kitchens with huge trays.

Higgins invaded this peaceful and commonplace scene in great excitement. Instead of taking his place, he went to Tony—who was engaged in earnest private conversation with Duquesne—and spoke for a moment. Tony stood, then, and struck a note on a gong. Immediate silence was the response to the sound.

"Doctor Higgins," said Tony, "has made a discovery."

Higgins stood. This ritual had been followed in the announcement of hundreds of discoveries relative to Bronson Beta, and the life, arts and sciences of its original inhabitants.

"It concerns the greenness of the sky," Higgins said. "We have all remarked upon it. We have agreed that normal light polarization would always produce blue. We have agreed that any gases which would cause a green tint in atmosphere—halogens, for example—would also be poisonous.

"This morning at seven-eighty, Bronson Beta time, we had a green rain of nine and a half Bronson Beta minutes' duration. I collected the precipitated substance. It proved to be the explanation of our atmospheric color." He took a vial from his pocket and held it up. Its contents were green. "The color is caused by this. A new form of life—a type of plant unknown on earth. You are all familiar with the algæ in the sea—minute plants which floated in the oceans of earth in such numbers as to change the color in many places. Very well. The higher atmosphere of Bronson Beta is crowded by plants in some ways similar. These plants are in effect tiny balloons. They germinate on the surface of the earth apparently, in the spring. As they grow (the ground everywhere must be covered by them), they manufacture within themselves hydrogen gas. They swell with it until, like small balloons, they rise. Their hydrogen holds them suspended high in the atmosphere during the summer and fall—trillions upon countless trillions of them. They make a level of thin, greenish fog overhead. Examined microscopically, they reveal their secret at once.

"There is sufficient carbon dioxide and moisture to nourish them. They live by simple photosynthesis; and it is the chlorophyll they contain which makes them green—a characteristic of all terrestrial plants except the parasites. These plants reproduce from spores."

Higgins sat down.

His brief description was greeted by applause in which the botanists and biologists were most vehement.

Carter stood up. "About their precipitation, Higgins?"

Again Higgins took the floor. "I have only a theory to offer. Temperature. I believe that, although they are resistant to cold, an adequate drop in temperature will cause them to crack and lose their hydrogen. Then, naturally, they fall to earth."

"So you anticipate more green rain?"

"I do—a tremendous volume of it. And I may add that these plants fix nitrogen, so that their dead bodies, so to speak, will constitute a fine fertilizer, laid annually upon the soil of the entire planet."

Carter nodded. "Excellent, Higgins! Have you made calculations relative to the possible and probable depth of 'green rain' we may expect?"

"Only the roughest sort. I shall work on that at once, of course."

Again there was applause. Other questions were asked. The bottle began to pass from hand to hand. The meal was resumed. It did not continue long without interruption, however. While the five hundred people saved by Hendron dined in the city named for him, they were guarded by a perpetual watch. Not since the first glimpse of a strange plane flying over the original camp, had vigilance been relaxed. In Hendron, day and night, men and women stood guard—at the gates, in the top of the tallest building, and underground in the central chambers.

During that noonday meal the guards on the north gate saw one of the Midianite planes moving toward the city.

It was not uncommon for an enemy plane to pass across their range of vision. This plane, however, was evidently headed for the city of Hendron. When that fact became assured, the alarm was sounded.

In the dining-hall there was an orderly stampede.

A swift car from the north gate brought news of the danger.

Arms were taken from racks, and at vantage-points near the gates, men and women—some still carrying hastily snatched bits of food—took their posts.

The plane, meanwhile, had reached the dome of the city. It did not fly over, however. It did not drop bombs, or a message. Instead, it circled twice to lose altitude, and from a hatch in its fuselage a white flag was run up on a miniature mast.

Then it landed.

By the time it touched the ground, more than two hundred persons were on hand to see. The transparent cover of their city gave them a feeling of security. However, the flag of truce upon the plane did not encourage them to any careless maneuver.

The ship was expertly brought down to the ground, but afterward it behaved badly. It slewed and skidded. Its engine died and then picked up as it started to taxi toward the gate. It did not cover the intervening stretch of ground. Instead, it lurched crazily, hit a rock, smashed a wheel, dragged a wing —and its motor was cut. Then, half wrecked, it stopped.

There it stood, like a bird shot down, for five full minutes. No one moved inside it. No one made an effort to descend.

By that time every one in the city had rushed to its edge.

Tony gathered his lieutenants and advisers together.

"Ruse to get the gate open," Williams said.

"I think so," Tony agreed.

They waited.

Dodson, standing near Tony, murmured: "The Trojan-horse gag."

Tony nodded. . . .

Ten minutes.

"Let me go out there," Jack Taylor said finally. "Just open one gate a crack. They can't get a wedge in at that distance. It's some sort of booby trap—but I'll spring it."

Tony said no. They sat.

A thought moved through the mind of Eliot James. He went to Tony. "It might be Von Beitz. He might be hurt—"

Tony lifted a pair of powerful glasses to his eye. He saw several areas of holes on the plane's side. Machine-gun bullet-holes.

"Open the gate a crack—and lock it behind me," he commanded. He stalked to the portal. It yawned for an instant. He went out. Jack Taylor, winking at the men who manipulated the gate, followed close behind Tony.

Tony turned after the gate clanged, and saw Jack. He grinned. The people inside the city who watched, were deeply moved. Tony's decision to accept the danger—Jack's pursuit of his leader into peril—those were the things of which the saga of Hendron's hundreds were made.

They went cautiously toward the broken ship. No sound came from it. They were ready to throw themselves to the earth at the first stirring.

There was none.

The crowd watching held its breath. The two men were under the shattered wing. . . . Now they were climbing the fuselage.

Tony looked cautiously through a window.

Inside the plane, alone, on its floor, in a pool of blood, lay Von Beitz.

Tony yanked the door open. Taylor followed him inside.

Von Beitz was badly wounded, but still breathing. They lifted him a little. He opened his eyes. A stern smile came upon his Teutonic face.

"Good!" he mumbled. "I escaped. They have the power city. They plan to cut you off as soon as it is cold enough to freeze you to terms. I do not know where the power city is—it is not like the other cities."

He closed his eyes.

"Did they kidnap you here?" Tony asked.

He thought that Von Beitz nodded an affirmative.

From the outside came a yell of warning from many throats. Tony looked. The gate was open. People were pointing. In the north was a fleet of enemy planes winging toward the spot.

"Hurry!" Tony said to Taylor. "Take his feet. Gently—and fast! They're going to try to bomb us before we get Von Beitz' information back to the others!"

As he spoke, he and Taylor were carrying the inert man to the door of the shattered ship.

CHAPTER XVI

HISTORY

THE watchers at the gate of the city ceased to be mere spectators, and poured out. Many were useless; they merely endangered themselves to no purpose. Eliot James, who had the local command, shouted for all but one other, besides himself, to keep under the shield of the city; and he and that other ran forward as Tony and Jack Taylor emerged from the half-wrecked plane and pulled out the limp form of Von Beitz.

The two uninjured men, bearing Von Beitz, began to run across the open space between the city and the ship; and Eliot with his companion, Waterman, ran toward them.

From the north the swarm of pursuing planes approached —the planes of the Other People, of the Vanished People of this planet, which had been appropriated by the "Midianites."

At least, that was what Eliot believed as he glanced up and saw the great metal larks in the sky. It must be men from the earth who piloted them; yet deep in his thoughts clung the fantastic idea that it might be Bronson Betan hands which piloted these splendid planes, even as Bronson Betan hands and brains had built them a million years ago before the Other People began their frightful drift into the cold and darkness of space between the stars.

Bullets, or some sort of projectiles, splashed up dirt before him and left Eliot no illusions as to the attitude of these pilots, whoever they might be. But he was unhurt; his comrade also was unhurt, and neither Tony nor Jack Taylor stumbled.

The attack from the air ceased; the planes veered away and dispersed so suddenly that it seemed to Eliot that they must have been signaled.

Waterman and he reached Tony and Taylor, and the four bore Von Beitz within the gate, which swiftly was shut behind them.

Women, as well as men, surrounded them. Tony turned at Eve's touch, and he stared at her dazedly.

"Tony," she implored him, "are you hurt too? Did they hit you?"

He shook his head; he was panting so violently that any expression of his feelings, as she held to him, was impossible. For a brief moment he caught her hand and held it, but gasped only: "Get Dodson—for—Von Beitz."

The command was unnecessary. Dodson was already kneeling over the German.

Eliot pressed back the people who crowded too close. The surgeon opened his kit, which had never been far from his hand during the perilous months on this planet. He began to administer drugs. "Half starved," he muttered. "No bones broken. Exhaustion. In terrible fight. Fists. Knife—at least some one had one in the fight. Wait!"

The German opened his eyes and sat up. *"Danke schöne,"* he said.

"Not yet!" Dodson warned, pushing his patient back into a reclining position.

"Take your time," Tony begged him, though he himself jerked with impatience for Von Beitz' report. He gazed up through the shield over the city into the sky, for the airplanes which had pursued, and which so suddenly had abandoned attack.

"Where are they?" he said to Eliot James.

"Gone."

"What scared them off?"

"What happened to their other planes before, I guess," said Eliot.

"Would they all have remembered it together just at the same second?" Tony asked.

Eliot shook his head; the planes were gone, whatever had turned them back; thought of them could engage neither Eliot nor Tony—nor Eve, since they had spared Tony.

She clung close to him in tender concern. They were in the inner edge of the circle, watching the German, who lay now with eyes shut and a scowl on his face.

The spasm of pain appeared to pass; he opened his eyes, and looking up at Tony, he winked.

It was the most reassuring thing he could have done. "Good stuff!" Tony whispered to Eve.

"Where was he, Tony?"

The German seemed to have heard; he spoke to the Doctor. "I should not sit up, eh?"

Dodson reminded: "You've had a terrible beating, Von Beitz. You're half starved. When you've had some hot soup, and when I've dressed your various cuts and bruises, you'll be able to talk."

"Pooh!" said the man on the ground. "You've been searching for me, eh? And now you want to know why I come dramatically in a ship from the north? Well—I will tell you. I can eat later. But I lie down. You must know at once.

"I rounded a corner in this city as you know; and to you, I vanished. To myself—four men seized me. A cord about the neck, a sack over the head. It gave me no fear that my assailants might have been men from Bronson Beta," Von

Beitz added sardonically. "The technique was too much of our world as we have known it. I was down and helpless, knowing no more of my attackers than that they must be men from earth.

"We spent I do not know how long hiding high in a building in this city. My eyes were taped shut. I was gagged much of the time, but I was given food, and—except on occasions which I will come to—I was not badly treated.

"At first they spoke between themselves in tongues I could not understand, but it was not language of another planet. It was speech from our old world—Russian sometimes, I am sure; sometimes, I think, Japanese."

Von Beitz rested a moment.

"Did you discover how many they were?"

"Here in this city watching us," Von Beitz proceeded after a moment, "there were four at least. I am sure I heard four different voices speak. Sometimes it seemed to me that more moved back and forth; but I cannot be certain that more than four actually were here."

"Men?" asked Tony.

"They were all men. I heard no woman speak; it was never a woman's hand that touched me. But they talked a great deal about women as they watched us," Von Beitz said.

"You mean, you heard them talking about our women? They talked in some language you understood?"

"No; not then. They talked about our women in their own tongues. But I did not need to understand the words to know they were talking about—women."

"I see," said Tony.

"They did talk to me in English later—two of them did."

He stopped again.

"What did they tell you?"

"Tell me?" repeated Von Beitz. "Nothing. They asked me."

"Asked you what?"

"About you—about us. They wanted to know what we knew, how far we had progressed in mastering the secrets of the Old People."

"Ah!" said Tony.

"They were here—those four—before we moved into this city. They were sent here as similar squads of them were sent to every other city accessible to them. You see, they moved into their city—which apparently was the old capital of this planet or at least of this continent—long before we made any move at all."

"Yes," said Tony. "That's clear."

"Our delay," breathed Von Beitz, "laid on us a great handicap." He did not continue that criticism, but observed: "For *they* grasped the essentials of the situation almost at once. It lay, of course, in mastery of the mechanics of the ancient civilization. So they seized at once and occupied the key city; and they dispatched a squad to each of the other cities, to explore and bring back to them whatever might be useful."

Again he had to rest, and the others waited.

"Particularly diagrams."

"Diagrams?"

"The working plans of the cities, and the machinery and of the passages which, without the diagrams, you could not suspect."

"Underground passages?"

"Precisely. That is how they took me out of the city. They laughed at us guarding all the gates! When they decided to take me away, two of them escorted me underground and led me on foot to a door that was opened only after some special ceremony, and which communicated with a conduit."

"Conduit for what?"

"I could only suppose what. My eyes were taped, and during this journey, even my ears were muffled; but I am sure from my sensations during the journey that I was underground, and carried through a long, close conduit like a great pipe."

"Carried?" repeated Tony, as the others in the group excitedly crowded closer to catch the weak word. "How did they carry you?"

"In a car. They sat me up in some sort of small car which ran very rapidly—and, I am sure, underground. I could feel enough of it with my hands to be sure it was not what we would call a passenger-car. I am sure now, from what I felt at the time, and what I learned later, that it was a work-car, built by the Old People for their workmen in the conduit. I was taken into a power tunnel, I believe, and transported in a work-car through the conduit to the other city. Certainly when, after a time I can only estimate as hours, I was brought up to daylight, it was in the city occupied by Russians and Japanese, and with them, on the same terms, some Germans. There are also English there, men and women; but not on the same terms as the others."

"Go on!" begged several voices.

"They let me see the city—and themselves," said Von Beitz. "It is a great city—greater than this, and very beautiful. It offers them everything that they could have dreamed of—and more! It makes them, as they succeed in mastering its secrets, like gods! Or they think so!"

"Like gods!"

"Yes," said Von Beitz, "that is our great danger. They feel like gods; they must be like gods; and how can they be gods, without mortals to make them obeisance and do them reverence? So they will be the gods; and we will be the mortals to do their bidding. Already they have taken the English and set themselves above them, as you have heard. They tried to take us—as you know. We killed some of them—some of the most ruthless and dangerous; but others remain. They know they need not endanger themselves. They wait for us confidently."

"Wait for us? How?"

"To come to them."

"But if we don't come?"

"We must."

"Why?"

"We have no help for ourselves—and they know it. For the truth is as we feared. For all these great cities of the eastern section of this continent," the German declared solemnly and slowly, "there is a single power city—or station. It is located deep underground—not directly beneath their city, but near it. Of course they control it, and control, therefore, light and power— and heat. Any of these we can enjoy only as they ration it to us.

"We move out, as we know, toward the cold orbit of Mars where heat will mean life in our long dark nights. They wait for that moment for us to admit their godship, and come and bow down before them."

Tony stared silently at Von Beitz, biting his lip and clenching his hands. He remembered the exaltation which he had felt—which he could not help feeling—when he realized that he was in command in this single city. *They* felt themselves in command—in absolute power—over this planet. He could comprehend their believing themselves almost gods.

The weakened man went on: "In the cavern city where are the engines which draw power from the hot center of this planet, a guard of the 'gods' stands watch. It is the citadel of their authority, the palladium of their power. I have not seen the station; but yesterday I learned its location. I stole a diagram and traced it before I was discovered. I escaped my guards. I fought my way into a ship this morning."

"You have the tracing?" Dodson whispered.

The German smiled. "I have it."

He shut his eyes and gave a sigh that was partly a groan. Dodson leaned over him. "We'll carry you to the center of the city now. You've taken a terrible beating."

Von Beitz opened one eye, then, and a grin overspread his battered features. "My dear Dodson," he replied spiritedly, although in a low tone, "if you think I've taken a terrible beating, you ought to see the other fellows. Three of them! One I left without so many teeth as he had had. The one who had the knife, I robbed of his weapon, and I put it between his ribs—where, I fear, it will take mortal effect. The third—alas, his own mother would neither recognize nor receive him!"

With those words the courageous Von Beitz quietly fainted.

Tony told Jack Taylor to post a call for a meeting, in the evening, of the Council of the Central Authority; and he himself accompanied those who bore Von Beitz to Dodson's hospital.

It was, of course, really a hospital of the Other People which Dodson had preëmpted. The plan of the place and its equipment delighted Dodson and at the same time drove him to despair trying to imagine the right uses of some of the implements of the surgery, and the procedures of those Vanished People.

Von Beitz' case was, however, a simple one; and Tony left, fully assured that the German would completely recover.

Tony went home—to the splendid, graceful apartment where he knew he would find Eve, and which they called their home because they occupied it. But they could never be free from consciousness that it was not theirs—that minds and emotions immensely distant from them had designed this place of repose.

Minds far in the future, Tony always felt, though he knew that the Other People actually pertained to the epochal past; but though they had lived a million years ago, yet they had passed beyond the people of earth before they came to gaze on the dawn of their day of extinction. So, strangely, Tony knew he was living in an apartment of the past, but felt it to be like one of the future. Time had become completely confusing.

What were years? What had they been? A year had been the measure of an interval in which the earth circled the sun. But the earth, except in fragments, no longer went around the sun. This planet had taken its place; and earthly time ceased to have significance. You lived in the time of this strange planet; its eons and epochs were behind you; and the incalculable accomplishments of its people.

The soft illumination of interiors, to which he had now become accustomed, glowed in the hallway. It was agreeable, soothing, never harsh; and the soft pastel colors of the walls showed patterns pleasing to the eyes, though they were eyes from earth, and earth never had seen anything similar.

Taste, thought Tony, reached through the universe; and beauty; and happiness—and peace. And cruelty also? When had these Other People been cruel? Had they cast it off only at last?

He was very tired, but excited too; he was glad to find Eve alone, awaiting him.

He kissed her, and held her, and for a moment let himself forget all else but the softness of her in his arms, and the warmth of her lips on his.

"Lord of my love," she whispered, in her own ecstasy. "Lord of my love," she repeated; and holding him, went on:

> *"To whom in vassalage,*
> *Thy merit hath my duty strongly knit."*

"Oh," said Tony.

"I memorized it as a child, Tony, never guessing at its meaning till now. How could Shakespeare have found words, dear, for so many feelings? . . . This place was planned for love, Tony."

"Yes."

"*They* loved here, Tony; some couple very young—a million years ago. We lie on their couch. . . . Where are they?"

"Where we, sometime, shall probably be; but why think of that? *'From fairest creatures'*—finish that for me, Eve, can you?"

"The first sonnet, you mean?"

"I don't know the number; but I knew it once—at Groton. I had to learn it to get into Harvard for the college board examinations. Wait: I've got more of it:

> *'From fairest creatures we desire increase,*
> *That thereby beauty's rose might never die.'*

"Where are Harvard, and Groton, now, Tony?"

"With Nineveh and Tyre; but you're here—and beauty's rose shall never die. . . . And by God, no one will take you from me—or freeze you in the cold, if I don't let you go."

"You've the diagram that Von Beitz brought?"

"I've seen it—studied it. He did well; but not enough. We know now where is the great central power-station: but we don't know how to get to it. We don't know even how they get in and out of this city."

"You think they still do?"

"We can't say that they don't. Undoubtedly Von Beitz was right; he was taken out by way of some conduit. We'll have to find that first, and stop it up or guard it; and then there may be a dozen underground doors leading anywhere, for purposes we've not progressed enough to guess. We've got to catch up on the old records of this place—though it's plain that some of them have been removed by the men who captured Von Beitz. Yet we've an awful lot to learn that we can learn."

"Tony, it's perfectly fascinating—and terrible, some of it. I met Professor Philbin when I was coming here. I never saw him so excited. He didn't know anything about what had just happened; he didn't even know that Von Beitz had returned. When I told him, he only stared at me; he wondered why I'd mentioned it. He was living in something far more exciting. He'd found the record, Tony, of the Other People when they first discovered the star of their doom approaching! He was looking for you; he wants to report to you what happened here, Tony, a million years ago!"

But Tony not yet could leave her. "If it's waited a million years, it can wait," he said, "ten minutes more."

CHAPTER XVII

AT THE MERCY OF THE MIDIANITES

TONY found Philbin with Duquesne, to whom the linguist had brought his version of the records he had decoded.

The French astronomer strode about the table in his excitement.

"We may picture now, with some confidence," he proclaimed to Tony, "the original situation of this planet—the place which it occupied in the universe when the people, who have provided these cities for us, lived.

"Its star—its sun—was, as we know, in the south. Eleven planets, of which this was one, circled that sun. This planet, and the one which we called Bronson Alpha, were the fifth and sixth in order of distance away from their sun. They were more closely associated than any other two planets; in fact, this planet revolved about Bronson Alpha almost like a moon. But it was not like our moon, which was always a dead world. It was Bronson Alpha, the greater planet, which bore no life; it was this planet—the smaller of the two—which bore life. And what a splendid order of life it bore at the end of its time!

"It seems to have been about two hundred years before the end that the people on this planet began to appreciate that a star was approaching which was to tear them away from their sun and cast them out into utter darkness and cold. There appear to have been living on this world, at that time, about one billion people."

"One billion people!" Tony exclaimed.

Philbin nodded. "One thousand million—about two-thirds of the population of our earth before our destruction began. I have found reference to earlier conditions of this planet which indicates that at one time the total population here might have been similar to ours. They had solved sanitation problems, and health and nutrition difficulties, at least a thousand years earlier; and for centuries their population grew rapidly; yet I believe that they never had quite the total population of our earth.

"After they became scientific and gained control of their living conditions,—and the conditions of birth,—they seem to have reduced their total number to about a billion. They seem to have stabilized at that figure.

"For centuries there seems to have been little change, except locally; they kept their birth-rate approximately level with their death rate. The thousand millions of people were spread fairly evenly, in cities, towns and villages, over the best parts of this planet. Civilization seems to have spread and been established everywhere, though the people were not everywhere homogeneous. It is perfectly plain that they had developed at least six different races of men, with some forty or fifty subdivisions distinguished by what we called 'national' characteristics. I have not yet been able to make out the form of their government at the time prior to the approach of the destroying star; but it is clear that war either was very rare or had been completely abandoned.

"They had come to provide for themselves a very high quality of life; they seemed to have established throughout their globe both peace and comfort—when their scientists saw their fatal star approaching."

"Go on," said Tony, when Philbin halted. "Or can't you?"

"Yes. I know a little more of what they did at that time—or at least how they felt—that billion people who used to live on this earth."

Yet he halted again while he gazed about the hall at their handicraft, their lovely sensitive art and decorations. They were gone—the billion of them—but they had been people who strived and struggled, and who had undergone an ordeal surpassing, in its prolonged torture, the agonies of the end of the earth. Philbin, the linguist and translator, tried to put some of this into words.

"You will pardon me, my friends," he said to Tony and Duquesne, "and understand that I can give you facts in fragmentary manner only, at this moment. My source is an autobiography of a man called Lagon—Lagon Itol. Lagon was what we would consider his surname. He was an artist and an architect of the time I speak of—the period of their discovery of, or their realization of, their threatened extinction from the approach of the star.

"With this autobiography of Lagon Itol, I found a volume about him by one of his contemporaries—one Jerad Kan. Lagon was a genius; he was, I think, the Michelangelo of this planet; and with this enormous artistic and architectural ability, he had an insatiable curiosity and interest in personalities. He kept a most careful diary, which is like nothing so much as Samuel Pepys'. Think of this remarkable man—Lagon Itol—as an amazingly vital, vigorous blending of our Michelangelo and Samuel Pepys.

"He records on this page,"—Philbin spread it before Tony and Duquesne,—"his first fear, if you will call it that, of the star.

"This is how I translate his words:

"'Colk called to-day. He says the star Borak will certainly

disturb us—or rather the great-grandchildren of our great-grandchildren. It presents us a pretty problem for survival.'

"Now the inspiring, and the exciting thing," exclaimed Philbin, "is to follow how this Lagon Itol immediately set to work to plan a scheme of survival for these people—though the need for that scheme would not come until the time of his great-grandchildren's grandchildren."

Duquesne, with Tony, was staring at the page, the words of which they could not read; but there was a sketch there which fascinated them.

"It looks," cried Duquesne, "like a first imagination of this city!"

"That's what it was," said Philbin. "It is perfectly clear that cities of this type were Wend, Strahl, Gorfulu, Danot and Khorlu.

"None of these names appear anywhere in the records of the time of which I am speaking; no such cities existed. Here Lagon Itol first began to dream of them, and he and his friend Jerad Kan began to write, educating the people to plan for what lay ahead of their grandchildren's grandchildren.

"For what happened to them—what, at that time, was threatened and had not yet occurred—was a widely different doom from that of our earth. When we discovered our destroyers, we knew that we ourselves must face the destruction, and that very soon."

"Precisely!" Duquesne had to exclaim. "Time for us was more merciful! For them—for two hundred years, at least, they must have looked at their doom! Tell me—tell me, friend, how a mind like Michelangelo's—this Lagon Itol—met it."

"In the most inevasive way. It is plain from his diary that, in his time, there was doubt—or at least the best scientists were divided—over the point as to whether the approaching star would tear this planet completely away from its sun, or would merely alter its orbit so as to make the climate, for part of the year, very much colder. Lagon Itol considered both of those possibilities. He made a plan for survival under colder conditions; he also speculated on the possibilities of survival even in the dark and cold of space.

"Lagon Itol himself did not believe that was the probability. The approach of the star was not to be a near passing, except in astronomical terms; it would not come within a billion miles of the sun of Bronson Beta. It was certain to effect the orbit of this planet; but would it make that orbit wholly unstable?

"Lagon Itol seems to have proceeded on the assumption it would not. On this day, on this page, he discusses that. On this next page, he is discussing the effects of the uses of *klul.*"

"Klul?" asked Tony.

"Apparently it was a drug they used to make the air more exhilarating—or intoxicating. It seems to have been one of the dearest vices, or indulgences, of the Other People. They let *klul* evaporate in a room; then they came in and breathed it. It appears to have been extraordinarily pleasant; both sexes indulged in it, but it was forbidden to children. Lagon Itol records the formula, as he did all things that interested him."

"But," said Tony, "you found no actual diagram of the engineering arrangements under the cities?"

"At the time in which I now find myself," said Philbin, "these cities existed only in Lagon Itol's fancy. His diary either was missed by our friends the Midianites, when they tried to remove all diagrams that would have been useful to us; or else they considered this book harmless."

No one found more useful diagrams, during the days which swiftly were becoming colder.

Steadily the sun diminished in size; blue shadows stole across the plains of the adopted planet as the long, late afternoons dwindled to dark, and in the night, the outer temperature dropped far below zero.

Under the shield of the city, heat remained, and was renewed from the huge transformers fed from impulses far away.

By mercy of the Midianites!

By mercy, or by policy?

They argued this under the great glass shield of the city of Hendron—known to its builders long ago as Khorlu—while their world slipped farther and farther from the sun.

Hourly they argued this, especially at night, when the needed lights burned bright, and the ventilators spun, circulating the warmed currents of air to combat the bitter cold that settled on the shield. And machinery moved, because the power impulses sent from the station in control of the Midianites continued.

The enemy made no attack. Indeed, only at a distance did they reappear at all; and then it was in the sky. Larks hovered but far away—watching; that was all. And Tony told his pilots, who also were flying larks, not to molest them, or even appear to attack them.

What if they sent down a few flyers from the sky? Attack upon the city with a few planes would be absurd; attack from the ground would be fantastic. The defense, established in any of these great metal cities, must be impregnable; the advantage of cover was overwhelming. The Midianites themselves appreciated this. After the pursuit of Von Beitz, they made no move which even suggested an attack upon Hendron. To the contrary, they continued to send through the conduits under the ground the power-impulses which kept lighted and warm the city of Hendron, much as it had been when it was Khorlu, a million years ago.

Khorlu, Wend, Strahl, Gorfulu, and *Danot*—so the Other People had named the five cities they had built in defiance of the destruction stealing upon them—the five cities forecast in the sketches of Lagon Itol.

Wend was the great shielded metropolis which Tony and Eliot James first had visited; *Strahl* and *Danot* were the two similar cities seen, and mapped, to the south.

Gorfulu was the greatest; and not only that—it was the control-city of the group; for it dominated the underground works which generated the power for the entire group of cities. It was *Gorfulu* that the Midianites had seized for themselves, and to which they had brought the survivors of the English space-ship, as captives.

It had been easy enough to promise to the English girl who had escaped—Lady Cynthia, met on the road to Hendron-Khorlu—that Hendron's people would rescue the English from the Midianites. But that promise appeared only more and more wild and fantastic as the new inhabitants of Hendron-Khorlu became more familiar with the peculiar strength of the shielded cities.

Attack upon the city, with the weapons at hand and transportable, would be folly; every feature and material of construction of the cities gave overwhelming advantage to the defense.

No one offered any scheme of attack that suggested any chance of success.

Jack Taylor and Ransdell, and Tony and Eliot James and Peter Vanderbilt (for though he was not of the younger men, he remained of the boldest) met often and planned attack; but while they talked, they knew they were helpless.

"The fact is," said Eliot James once, putting frankly in open words what they all were feeling, "so far from being able to conquer *them,* we're at their mercy this minute; and they know it."

Peter Vanderbilt nodded. "And as regards them, I have little illusion that the quality of mercy is much strained. Let us adjourn for a walk in the square, or—what have you?"

"Tony, did you know that the portrait bust near the north gate is of Lagon Itol? Philbin assured me of it, quite positively, yesterday. He looked a good deal like Goethe, don't you think?"

"I'll take another look at it," said Tony; but he did not go out with the others. He sought Eve in the delightful apartment fitted for other lovers a million years ago, and lighted by the small distant sun whose heat was reinforced by warmth from power-impulses from machines engineered and prepared by the minds and hands of a million years ago, which had been repaired and were operated by the Midianites.

For the power-impulses continued to come; and this fact persuaded many, in the city of Hendron-Khorlu, that a change of heart must have affected the party of men from earth who held control of the capitol of the Vanished People.

They had come to their senses, some were sure as they worked, under the shield of the city of Hendron-Khorlu, at the emergency measures which the council of the Central Authority had ordered.

But if some believed in the mercy of the men who had taken over the capital that controlled the conditions in all the cities, others did not become so credulous.

"When are *they* going to shut us off?" they asked each other; and when they did not utter the words, they wanted to. The waiting had become an obsession.

They felt themselves teased and tantalized by this unceasing, silent provision of light and heat and power which kept them comfortable—indeed in luxury—under the dome of the great transparent shield when the world without was frozen.

The long rivers had turned to ice; the lake became a sheet of ice which the sun at noonday scarcely affected. Floes filled the seas, the pilots of the larks reported. Frequently at noonday, when the small sun stood nearly overhead, surfaces thawed, but when the world began to turn away, and long before the darkness, it was bitter cold again.

It was at night that It came—at dinner-time.

The company under Tony's command were assembled in the great hall where meals were served. A few of the men stood at salient posts, always on watch. There was a watch at the top of the tallest towers, and at the eight gates. Guards were posted also at the passages to the chief channels below the city. . . .

The lights went out. Later it was realized that, simultaneously, the movement of the currents of warmed air ceased; but at first this was appreciated only by those stationed near the fans, which whirred to a stop in a humming diminuendo.

Not only the great halls were blackened, but the streets became tombs.

It was an overcast night; and no single star showed even to the watchers on the towers. Light died and was buried; and all in silence.

In the unbreathing, Stygian oppressiveness of the dining-hall, Tony arose—an invisible figure. He felt blotted out. He wondered whether his voice, when he spoke, could be heard.

"They've done it, my friends. This is no accident, no failure which they will repair. They have shut off our power-source. So immediately we put into effect our plans for this emergency! we go under the power-loss orders which you all already know."

Matches were struck and applied to torches previously fixed on brackets about the hall. Everybody pretended to like it; everybody sat down again. Dinner went on in a medieval gloom.

Ransdell, charged with the security of the streets, went out and inspected the guard positions where he was challenged by his sentries, who examined him in the glare of flashlights attached to condenser batteries; but the stored electricity was to be used but sparingly. The company had charged the batteries by the thousand; but what were they against the darkness and cold to come?

Combustible substances must be used for light wherever possible, and always for heat.

"It's begun," said Dodson, the surgeon, to Eliot James.

"I won't worry about putting it down in my book to-night," the diarist replied. "I'll not forget it before to-morrow!"

He was aware of an anger within him which had no parallel in his experience—a smoldering anger that grew and grew.

"*They're* doing this," he said, scarcely more to Dodson than to himself. "They're doing this deliberately to freeze us out to them—to take their terms."

"What terms exactly, d'you suppose?" some one inquired calmly.

Eliot turned, and in the flickering glow of a flare, he faced Peter Vanderbilt.

"We'll hear soon enough, I'd say."

CHAPTER XVIII

THE FATE OF THE OTHER PEOPLE

BUT no terms came.

No proclamation, no communication at all, arrived from those in control of the capital city—and in control, therefore, of the five shielded cities.

Gorfulu maintained its illumination, as Eliot James and Ransdell ascertained by flying at dawn and sighting the great glowing dome of the ancient capital. Light pervaded that city as before; and beyond question, heat was there.

Ransdell circled the city and turned back, as larks, piloted by the Midianites, rose into the sky. Ransdell had promised Tony neither to seem to offer attack, nor to provoke it. He flew directly home.

Other pilots inspected the three other cities—Wend, Strahl and Danot, the shields of which, like the dome of the capital, remained aglow; and these pilots flew back also to Hendron-Khorlu, which alone of the five cities lay lightless and cold in the winter morning.

In the great Hall of the Council, these pilots joined James and Ransdell and completed their reports:

"They've cut us off—and us alone."

"Why not, then," some one said, "move to another city? To Wend?"

"Then wouldn't they cut us off there?" countered Ransdell practically. "The only reason those cities aren't cut off is because we aren't there."

"But they're not occupied, are they?"

"Not in force," replied Ransdell. "But they've an observation group in each of the other cities—as they had here."

"Then how about some other cities—elsewhere?"

"Where else?" questioned Ransdell; for he had done much observation flying.

"On some other continent—perhaps in the other hemisphere."

"There are no other cities suitable."

"Nowhere else in this world?"

"None. The old globes which we found do not show them; and we have never found any others."

"But why were there only these five?"

"Well," said Ransdell, "why were there even as many as five cities at the end?"

"But we have been told that the old population of the planet was one billion people!"

"Not at the end, however!"

"What happened?"

Dave Ransdell, for reply, turned about to Tony.

"We can give to-day at least a partial answer to that," Tony said, looking about the little group of his Council. "And I think it can be considered pertinent to our discussion of our own emergency, for we are dealing with a mechanism of living —or of dying—created not by ourselves but by the original people of this planet. It certainly can only be of help to us to understand what they did. Professor Philbin," he said, "please tell us."

The little linguist arose.

"You have all heard, I may assume, something of the state of this planet at the time when the studies of the star approaching convinced the scientists of this planet that it was certain to disturb life here greatly."

Peter Vanderbilt arose quietly; when Philbin stopped, Vanderbilt suggested:

"Should not every one hear this?"

"Certainly," said Tony. "Open the doors." And into the great room hundreds came and stood. For the halls without had been crowded. Nearly everybody was there, except men on watch or detailed to definite errands. Men, women and girls crowded as close as they could to the council-table; even the children came—the two children saved from the doom of earth on the first space-ship.

"I can assume," the little linguist repeated, "that you all have learned what we, who have been interpreting the books, learned and reported some days ago of the time of Lagon Itol, which was approximately two hundred years before this planet was torn from its sun.

"Lagon Itol—who was certainly a very great man, one of enormous perceptions and imagination—considers in his diary the fate facing one billion people; so we may put that as a rough figure for the population of this planet in his time. But he astutely observes that there would be nothing like that number finally to face their fate; and he was right. From his time, the people of this planet rapidly reduced themselves in number by diminishing births. In fact, before he died, he observed it and recorded it; he even speculated on the probable number who would be alive to face the catastrophe.

"I have now discovered an official record of their year 16,584, Ecliptic."

"Ecliptic?" a woman, close to the table, questioned.

"Ecliptic—reckoned, I mean, from the first eclipse. The old people here," Philbin explained, "had a very accurate and rational way of reckoning. For thousands of years, their determinations of time were exceedingly precise; but as on earth, of course their history went back through ages of rough record and without record into oral traditions. Undoubtedly they once had scores or hundreds of arbitrary points from which they reckoned the years locally—as our Egyptians reckoned years from the start of the reigns of each Pharaoh. As we all recollect, most of our civilized world finally agreed upon a year which we called the Year of Our Lord, from which we reckoned backward and forward.

"The people of Bronson Beta chose a year of a famous eclipse. For this planet, and its huge companion Bronson Alpha, circled their sun in such a way that eclipses sometimes—though rarely—occurred. They were not so frequent as with the earth; they happened, on the average, about once in fifty years. Each was, therefore, more notable; and early in the history of man on this planet, there was a special eclipse which was noted by many nations of the primitive people. Later civilized ages could identify that eclipse with certainty and assign it a definite date. It offered itself as a very convenient and logical point from which to reckon the start of rational processes—the first recorded eclipse.

"Lagon Itol first mentions the disturbing star in the year 16,481, Ecliptic. He died in the year 16,504—before which time, as I have told you, he saw the population of the planet rapidly being reduced.

"For the year 16,584 I have, I say, the official census figures; they total slightly over two hundred millions of people—a reduction of four-fifths in approximately a century, or a loss of eight hundred millions of people."

Many gasped aloud. "What happened?" voices asked. "A world plague? The Black Death?"

"No plague, no unusual death," the little linguist continued. "Merely a cessation of births—or what must have been, for a time, almost a cessation. Would we have done differently? Who of us brought babies into the world, in our last two years, only to be destroyed? How many of us would have wanted children against a destruction if it was still a hundred years away?

"What happened to this planet was one of the things that might have happened to our earth—"

Duquesne broke in: "In fact, my friends, what happened here was the commoner occurrence in the cosmos. The fate of our earth was one of the ends of existence which always was possible, but yet exceedingly rare. The fate of this planet was much more typical of the ends of the earths which have been happening, and must continue to happen, until the termination of time. What is the first state of a star? Loneliness. At last another star approaches; and from its own substance, streamers are torn forth. The disturbing star passes on; but it has begot—planets. For it is from the substance that streamed from the sun, when another sun came close, that worlds are born.

"They circle their solitary parent, the sun; they cool and grow old; and upon one or two, not too large or too small, or too near or too far away from the sun, life begins—and grows and changes, and becomes man.

"Through millions of years!

"And what saves him, through all these ages? Nothing but the solitary situation of his sun; it is the loneliness of the Life-giver—the loneliness of his sun in space—that permits man and his world to endure.

"But at last the sun suffers it no longer; once more, it must speak to another star; and at last—for always sometime it must be so, even in the loneliness of the sky—another sun approaches; and before fresh material is sucked out to start another set of worlds, the spheres already old are drawn away and cast out into space. Such is the circle of life—and death—of worlds, to which all must, in the end, submit. Sometime one of those cast-off worlds may find another sun, as this has done."

The Frenchman bowed to Philbin. "You were, monsieur, in the year of this planet the sixteenth thousand, five hundred and eighty-fourth, Ecliptic. I return you to it."

"It was a remarkable year," said the little linquist, thrillingly, "if for no other reason, because of the production of the tremendous pessimistic poem 'Talon.'

"I translate the original title—*Talon,* a claw. The Talon of Time was meant. The people here understood the awful circle of the life, and death, of worlds as M. Duquesne has just sketched it. The poet of 'Talon' was the Omar Khayyám of their days of facing their fate. So in a poem of marvelous power he pictures man pursued by Time—a great tantalizing, merciless bird of prey which waits for him through the ages while he rises from a clod without soul to feel and brain to know, until he can appreciate and apperceive the awful irony of his fate; then the bird reaches out its great talon and tears him to pieces.

"I despair adequately to render in our words the ironic tragedy of this poem; but Fitzgerald, translating our Omar, has rendered two lines like two of these:

'And lo!—the phantom Caravan has reach'd
The nothing it set out from. Oh, make haste!'

"Like Omar, the poet preached pleasure; and he laughed at the ghastly futility of those who defied and fought the fated drift of their world into eternal darkness and cold.

"Clearly he presented the prevailing mood of the period; but clearly, also, there was another mood. The spiritual and intellectual heirs of Lagon Itol had proceeded with his plans for these cities.

"There was yet no complete agreement among the scientists that this world must be torn away from its sun. Its orbit was on the edge of the critical area of disturbance. Every one agreed that the five outer planets would surely be torn away; they agreed that the next planet inferior—that is, nearer its sun than this one—probably would not be torn away.

"The name of that planet was Ocron; and by the way, these people knew that it was inhabited.

"They agreed that this world on which we now stand would be severely altered in its orbit; yet they considered there was a chance it would not be torn away.

"Yet that chance did not appeal to many. By the year 16,675 Ecliptic—which is the last year for which I can find a census—the total population was under twelve million, and many of them very old. The number of children under ten years is given separately; they were less than a hundred and fifty thousand. At the rate they were allowing themselves to die, probably there were barely ten millions of people of all ages when the disturbing star—which they called Borak—came its closest and cast them off into space.

"The best of the energies of the dwindling millions had been put, for two generations, into these five cities which were planned, located and created and equipped for the final defiance of extinction. They abandoned all older habitations and adopted these."

"But where did they go, in the end?"

A dozen demanded it, together.

"Of that mystery, we have not yet," Philbin confessed, "a trace. They had reduced themselves, we know, from a billion in number at the time of Lagon Itol—two hundred years before—to about ten millions. Barely one per cent of them, therefore, were spared up to the time of the catastrophe to attempt the tremendous task of further survival.

"Throughout at least the last five thousand years of their history, cremation of the dead was universal among them. We will find no cemeteries or entombments, except perhaps a very few archaic barrows from a very early age. The people throughout their civilized period disposed of their dead in a systematic, orderly and decent way.

"Now, did the last ten million also die, and as they went, were they also cremated by their survivors, so that we will find, at the end, only the bones of some small group who, enduring to the last, had disposed of those immediately before them? Or somehow, did some of them—escape?"

The great chamber of the Council was tensely silent, close-crowded as it was.

It was Tony, presiding, and having the advantage of having heard most of these facts before, who first found voice:

"Returning to our present problem," he recalled them to that which had gathered them together, "it is clear that we can find no other cities of the shielded type, and equipped to combat the cold, except the five we know; for no others ever were built. We know also that there is no other generating station providing light and heat and power, except that close to Gorfulu; for no other ever was planned or built."

CHAPTER XIX

THE PIONEERS PLAN REPRISALS

JACK TAYLOR's post, when on watch, was the northern gate.

"The Porte de Gorfulu," Duquesne had dubbed it, recalling the fashion in Paris of naming the gate after the city to which, and from which, its road ran.

There was not at this gate, or at any of the seven others, any actual guard station. What Philbin had read had made certain, if it had been doubtful before, that the builders of these cities had acted in complete coöperation and unison; they had been banded together in their desperate attempt to defy their fate of dark and cold.

However, the structural scheme and the materials chosen had made each gate exceedingly strong. It would have required artillery to reduce it; and artillery here did not exist, except perhaps in some museum of archæology of the Vanished People.

The blast of the atomic tubes, which had transported the Arks through space, of course could reduce any of the gates; but first they must be brought to the vicinity and placed in position; and if this could be done without danger, there was the problem of the lining of the tubes. Those in the second space-ship from Michigan, commanded by Ransdell, actually had burnt out at the end of the passage, and had contributed to the disaster which overtook that party.

Little, indeed, had been left of the lining in the tubes of the Ark which Hendron himself, more successfully, had piloted. So it was fairly certain that the propulsion tubes in the possession of the Midianites must be in similar state.

"What they have left of the lining, they'll save for their own defense—as we used ours," Jack expressed his opinion to Eliot James, who to-day was standing watch with him.

Eliot nodded. "I think so. At least, I'm sure they'll not attack us with the tubes; they'll not think it necessary. They figure, of course, we've got to come to them."

"Well," challenged Jack, "haven't we?"

Eliot gazed out the gate along the road where the shadow of a post placed by the Ancient People lay long and faint upon the ground.

"There goes the sun," he said. "And gosh, it's cold already! But we can burn things to keep warm. It's humiliating as hell; but we can burn old wood or grain, or a thousand things, and keep warm for a while, anyway. Physically, we're not forced to go to *them;* but can we be men—and stay away?"

"That's it," Jack commended his friend. "That's it exactly."

"I know," said Eliot. "I was never so mad in my life as the night when they cut off our light and heat. I could have done anything—if I could have got to them, for it. It was the most infuriating thing I ever felt."

"Are you telling me?" said Jack. "You thought you were alone in that feeling?"

"Of course not; but I can't laugh at it yet. Can you?"

"No; and I never expect to—until I can fix that feeling."

"But how can we fix it?"

"Exactly. How can we? How in the world—how on Bronson Beta, Jack, are we going to be able to get at *them?*"

"Tony'd like to know; but it's got to be without too great a risk. He won't have us killed—not too many, anyway."

"Well, how many of us would he think it worth while to lose, if we took Gorfulu?"

"Do you think you know how to do it? . . . Whew, that chill certainly comes on."

"Sun's gone; and damn' little of it there was to go. We simply weren't made to be this far away from the sun."

"Half a year from now, you'll be saying we weren't made to be as near the sun as we'll be."

"If we live till then."

"Yes; and if this cock-eyed world decides to do a decent orbit really around the sun, and not go sliding off into space, as it's done before."

"What makes you say that? Do you think Duquesne and Eiffenstein are giving us a run-around? They say we're coming back, and too close to the old sun for comfort."

"Yes," agreed Jack. "But do they *know?* Does anybody know until the old apple does it—or doesn't do it? Somebody certainly must have told the people who built these cities that they were going to stay in sight, at least, of some sun; and they certainly took a long ride in the dark. . . . Hello, here's our relief." And Jack hailed the pair who appeared in the twilight of the street; he passed them his report, *"Everything quiet,"* and he started up the street with Eliot toward his quarters.

"What's the hurry, soldiers?" some one softly hailed from the darkness of a hooded doorway. It was a girl's voice, teasing, provocative.

Both halted. "Who are you?"

"Please, soldiers, we're only friends caught out in the dark and needing protection."

Jack laughed, and knew her before he turned on his flashlight. "Marian," he demanded, "what are you doing here, and who's with you?"

Then her companion, Shirley Cotton, made herself known.

"We were hoping," Marian Jackson said, as the two girls walked along with the two young men, "for somebody to come by who knows how to turn on the heat again, not to speak of the lights."

"Were you in that building?" Eliot asked her.

"We were; and I tell you, it's hard to open doors now that the power's off. They stick terribly."

"What were you doing in that building? You know you shouldn't have gone in from the street alone."

"Sure I know," agreed Marian blandly. "But where have we got by obeying all your nice orders?"

"What were you doing, Marian?"

"Shall we tell them, Shirley?"

"Why not?"

"Well," said Marian, speaking carefully as though she might be overheard, "we decided we'd see what we could do as baits."

"Baits?"

"Baits. The chunks of meat trappers used to put in traps, and like minnows on hooks—baits, you know. My idea."

"Then," said Jack generously, "it must have been a pippin. Baits. I've got the general underlying scheme of you girls now; go on."

"But there's nothing to go on to; nothing happened."

"The fish didn't come?"

"No nibble. No. But give us time, boy. There's some way, we know, by which somebody still gets in and out of this city. The idea is, we hope he—or they, if they're two of 'em—will try to grab us. We'll go along."

"Sabine-women stuff, Eliot," Shirley put in.

"What?" asked Marian Jackson.

"I'll tell you later, dear," Shirley offered.

"Oh," sniffed Marian. "Deep stuff! Well, anything they didn't teach in the first six grades of the St. Louis grammar schools is lost on me. Still, you got me curious. What did the Sabine women do, Shirley?"

"They went along," Shirley told her, "with the men from the other city that grabbed them."

"And then what did they do, darling?"

"They stayed with them as willing little wives."

"No stabbing after they found the way in and out?"

"No," said Shirley. "That's where the Sabine women were different."

Jack Taylor whistled softly. "So that's what you little girls were up to?" he said. "Perhaps it's just as well we came along. But they rather show us up, eh, Eliot?"

Dinner was a moody meal in the evening of that prolonged day. The natures of the people from earth had not adjusted themselves to the increased length of both day and night; most of the people still slept, or at least went to bed, for eight hours of each twenty-four, so they dozed by day and were awake, on the average, sixteen hours of each period of darkness.

Philbin had learned that this had not been the custom among the ancient people; they had passed through the stages of evolution adapted to the long day and night; but it appeared impossible for the people from earth to acquire this adaptation.

Accordingly, after dark, there were long, restless periods; and to-night Eliot James, Jack Taylor and Peter Vanderbilt, with two more of the younger men—Crosby and Whittington—met for a midnight discussion.

Tony was not called to this informal council of his friends; nor was Ransdell; for Tony, though personally the same with all of them, yet was Chief of the Central Authority; he bore the responsibility; and if he forbade the enterprise on foot, his friends could scarcely proceed. So it was agreed not to let him know. And Ransdell, too—being charged with the security of the city—had better learn about the plan much later.

The five gathered in Vanderbilt's quarters, which were not cramped, to say the least. There was no need in that city, constructed on its splendid scale for some two millions of people, for any one now to be niggardly of room. Each of the emigrants from earth could choose his own dwelling-place, so long as it was approved for its security.

Peter Vanderbilt had chosen what would have been called, on earth, a penthouse—a roof-dwelling, built, he was sure, by some connoisseur of living.

The place delighted Peter; it was on a roof but near an edge of the city where the shield sloped steeply down; so the roof there was not high, and was easily reached by foot, after the power failed.

Also it was especially well adapted for habitation in the present emergency when the heating apparatus prepared for the city had failed or rather, had been cut off. For the original builders had allowed for no such emergency; they had been dealing with elements in respect to which they had no reason to figure on that factor of failure—the internal heat and radioactivity of the core of the planet. Stoppage of that was unthinkable; and so, to them, was the cutting of the power-conduits to any of the cities. Therefore they had supplied no alternative heating arrangement.

As a consequence the present tenants had to employ the most primitive methods of keeping themselves warm in these lovely supercivilized chambers. They were driven to build bonfires in some of the great halls; but they spared those of exceptional splendor.

Peter Vanderbilt, being on the roof in his "penthouse," had contrived a chimney and a fireplace which gave him heat without much smoke or soot.

It was before this fire that the five gathered.

"Wonderful place you have, Peter," said Whittington, looking around. He had not visited it before, and he went about examining the metal panels of mountain, woodland, marsh and sea, all splendid in the colors of enamel paints baked on.

Peter asked him: "Are you complimenting me? All I've done is to choose it. . . . Do you know, not a thing was flecked or rubbed, not a thing was worn. The man who made it never used it."

"It seems so with most of the buildings," said Whittington. "It seems they must have gone on building them to complete their plan, after they knew they themselves would never fill them."

"What else could they do," asked Eliot, who had thought much about this, "while they waited? Could they just wait—for slow annihilation?"

"Philbin," said Vanderbilt, "rendered a couple of lines of his poem 'Talon.' He says it gives no idea of the enormous melancholy of the original; but as he said modestly, it is better than no translation at all:

" '*And now the winds flow liquid,*
The sole cascades to seek the sea.
At last these awful streams themselves are hardened.
The air that once was breath is metal, frozen.
Where, then, are we?' "

Nobody spoke until Taylor, after a moment, put wood on the fire.

"Did you hear, Peter," he questioned, "what those girls—Marian and Shirley—were out to do?"

"Yes," said Vanderbilt; and the five got immediately at the problem of how to gain entrance and control of Gorfulu.

"Seidel is in command, Von Beitz is sure," Eliot James said. "Cynthia agrees that is most probable. He was pushing aside Morkev, who was nominally chief Commissar—he called himself that—when Lady Cynthia escaped.

"Von Beitz says that Seidel supplanted Morkev but did not kill him, Morkev had too many friends. It is perfectly certain that there are two factions among our friends the Midianites, which is complicated, of course, by their racial mixture. Their position is further complicated by the English, who obey them only because they must.

"Cynthia has told us, and Von Beitz has confirmed it, that the mixture on top is constantly afraid of what they call 'a rising of the serfs'—that is, the English. They guard against it. The English are allowed to gather—even for work—only in very small groups, and always under supervision."

"It looks like a set-up," observed Whittington, optimistically, "if once we get in."

Vanderbilt shook his head. "Eliot specialized, in that speech, on their elements of weakness. Their strength is utter ruthlessness. I believe that, when they attacked your camp," he said to Eliot James, "you killed a good many of them, and some of the most violent fell. But enough were left. Von Beitz says that Seidel keeps himself surrounded by them. He has no use for the milder men. He has a despotism which he completely controls by intimidation; and no form of government is more merciless and efficient—at least at first. And this is very early in the life of this particular despotism."

"There is a building which they call the Citadel," Jack Taylor said, as if he had heard none of this. "It held the offices of administration of the Old People. Seidel occupies it with his inner ring.

"If three of us could get in—or two of us—and kill ten of them,—the ten top men, including Seidel,—we'd—"

"What?"

"We'd at least be able to start something," Jack ended somewhat weakly.

"But the two of you would have to kill the ten of them and the top ten—before you could really begin," said Peter Vanderbilt quietly. "How simple you make it seem!"

Taylor swore, then laughed. "We don't know what we could do; or what we'd have to do. But we do know this: some of us, somehow, have got to get into that city, and that Citadel of that city. Then we can trust to God and what chances He may offer us. But first, and whatever's before us, we're going to get in! Agreed?"

"Agreed!" said all voices, and Vanderbilt's was distinct among them.

"Now how? We've no chance to advance against them by air or on the ground—or under the ground from the direction of this city. We know they've got guarded all the conduits and passages which we've discovered; and probably some we don't know about. But would they guard the conduits from the other cities?"

"That's something, Jack! Say—"

"See here. There's Danot—on the other side of them from us. They've a guard in there; we've nobody. They'd never look for us to come from that quarter. We get into Danot and go underground! We—"

That night was long, but not long enough for the five conspirators.

CHAPTER XX

JUSTICE TIPS THE SCALES

RANSDELL, on the evening of the third day later, reported to Tony:

"Five men have not returned—three of our best friends, Tony," he said, dropping formality. "Eliot, Jack Taylor and Peter Vanderbilt—and Whittington and Crosby with them. They left, you know, in two 'larks' about two hours before dusk yesterday. They said they were only going to have a look around. I thought it was a good idea; I told them to go."

"No word from them at all since?" Tony asked.

"Not a syllable. Marian Jackson is missing too."

"She went with them?"

"No. Entirely separately; and she went on the ground, not in the air. The gate watch who let her go out—it was Cluett—was ashamed of himself and did not report it promptly. It appears that she drove to the gate in one of the small cars, and wheedled Cluett into letting her take a turn outside. It was near noon, and the sun was shining. He saw no harm and let her pass. Then she turned the battery on full, and streaked away.

"Still he thought she was just fooling with him, and would return, probably by another gate; so he sent no one after her. But as far as we're concerned, that was the end of her."

"Which gate?" asked Tony briefly.

"The northern gate. Duquesne's Porte de Gorfulu."

"She disappeared down that road?"

"Yes. And the only word she left behind with the girls she knew was that she was tired of being cold; she thought she'd try being warm again. She commented, further, that she sees now she pried herself into the wrong party."

Tony nodded; he knew what that meant. Marian frequently reminded everybody that she hadn't been selected among the original company for either Hendron's or Ransdell's spaceships; she had pried herself into the party. Obviously, she meant she wished she had chosen the ship of the Asian Realists who now held the capital city, Gorfulu.

"Have you searched for her?" asked Tony.

"I've flown myself," Dave said, "along the road more than halfway, to be sure she wasn't wrecked by the road."

"Probably," said Tony, "she went right on. But do you think the others were up to anything foolish?"

"I'm sure of it," Ransdell answered.

"Why? Did they tell you?"

"Not me—Higgins. And he's just told me. Tony, they're dead now; or they're trying to get into Gorfulu from Danot. From what they told Higgins,—who swore to keep it until to-night,—we can't possibly help them now, except by being ready to respond to their signal that they're in Gorfulu and will have a gate open for us."

Tony rose excitedly.

"From what they told Higgins, and he told you, is the signal—overdue?"

"It is, Tony; that's the trouble. I don't know in detail what those—those glorious idiots tried to do; but the signal, Tony, is overdue!"

Four of them, at that moment, were alive. Crosby was dead; they had his body with them. Of the four alive, not one was unwounded; and they were lying in the dark in the tube of the power-conduit between Danot and Gorfulu, and with both ends of the tube closed against them.

They had taken Danot; at least, they had surprised one gate and got in. For they had grounded their larks in the valley beyond Danot, and accomplished this in the twilight, unseen. Then they had crept to the western gate, surprised the guard and got in.

Two of the other side fell in this fight; and Crosby and Taylor were shot. Jack still could walk, but the others had to drag Crosby with them.

Once inside, they met their bit of luck—or they thought it that. Four men had been at the gate they surprised; and the two that fled separated. James and Whittington took after one of them, leaving Vanderbilt with the wounded men. The luck was that the man they pursued fled to the conduit-tube which supplied Danot from Gorfulu.

They caught that man in the tube, overpowered him; and Whittington went back to guide Taylor and Vanderbilt and help him with Crosby. Meanwhile, Eliot had found the work-car which traveled in the tube beside the great cables to the transformers. It was part of the equipment made by the Other People which the Midianites were using when they traveled back and forth.

The five had hardly got into the tube; and Vanderbilt was helping Crosby to the car, when the man who had escaped led another group of the guard underground. Eliot and Whittington turned back to fight them; and Vanderbilt and Taylor turned too.

It was revolvers and knives and iron bars—anything was a weapon at close quarters.

Everybody was wounded; but the five got away on the car, with Crosby dying. Power was on; and lights were on. The whole tunnel was illuminated; and the track of the car in the huge conduit was clear.

Eliot James put on the power, full. He saw the chance to surprise Gorfulu; he saw the probability, too, that some signal might be sent ahead by the survivors of the fight in the tube.

But there was a chance—a chance!

So Eliot opened it wide, and they sped on—the four living men wounded, and one dead, on the car to catch by surprise the city that controlled the continent and which the enemy from earth held. For two hours thus they traveled.

Then—the lights were extinguished; the car rushed on in a Stygian cave. But the car's speed was slowing; the power that propelled it was shut off.

It did no good for Eliot to thump the control; the power was gone; the car slid to a stop.

So there they lay underground in the tube, without light or food or water; one dead, four wounded. It seemed senseless; yet the only thing left to do was for the wounded to crawl the rest of the way to the chief city held by the enemy.

Marian Jackson's situation was not in the least like theirs. Marian had driven by broad daylight to the chief gate, and shown herself and begged admittance.

Marian was exceedingly good-looking; and the guard who parleyed with her had the good sense to take her at once to his superior, who knew that his business was to show her to Seidel.

Seidel spoke English; Marian's "line," as well as her appearance, pleased him.

She pointed out that the American parties—both of them from both ships—were composed of fools. She congratulated herself that she had not been chosen by them to join them; she had made them take her.

This was true; and Seidel had learned that it was true, from his spies in the city. Marian was tired, she said, of ninnies from America who had chosen themselves to people this planet. They couldn't even keep themselves warm!

Seidel had Marian assigned to quarters close to his in the Citadel.

During the second day, she got a good view of the local situation, learning, among other things, that Seidel had taken very clever measures to protect himself against the always-feared uprising of the serfs: All the other rooms surrounding his suite were equipped with sprays which, upon pressing a lever, spread stupefying and paralyzing gas—the same gas which the Midianites had used in the attack on Hendron's camp.

Also, Seidel had learned the use of *klul.* Indeed, he was addicted to *klul,* but he had let no one but the chemist who supplied him with the drug, know it.

However, he let Marian know.

Marian pretended she had never heard of it before. How would she, among the Americans, who were only fools? The fact was, Marian had tried it out pretty thoroughly, and was proud of the fact that she had a pretty good "head" for it.

Seidel thought it would be very amusing to induct Marian into the uses of *klul.* It was most pleasant and effective, he had found, when breathed in a warm, almost steamy atmosphere. He liked to let it evaporate beside the bath, then to lie in the bath, breathing the *klul*-drenched air. He had a marvelous bath in his suite in the Citadel. The Ancient People had built a pool which could be heated to any temperature—a beautiful, enamel-tiled pool with gay decorations.

Seidel insisted that Marian swim with him alone in the lovely pool and breathe *klul.* He dismissed his attendants and led her in.

The *klul,* in its big basin, was rapidly evaporating in the warm, steamy air. Marian kept herself covered with a single garment like a kimono.

He ordered her to throw it off and bathe with him. She asked, first, to breathe more *klul;* and she pretended that she was very intoxicated.

She danced and delighted Seidel, who ordered her to throw off her garment and dive into the water with him.

"Why do you keep it clutched about you?" he demanded.

In a moment, she showed him; for he tried to tear off her kimono, and she let go with her hand, which had been holding, under the cloth, a knife.

She stabbed him as he reached for her. She left the dagger in him as he staggered back. He cursed her, and found his alarm signal before he pulled out the knife, threw it at her—and died.

Marian heard them at the door. For a moment she was dizzy; perhaps the *klul* was affecting her. She picked up the knife, with which she had killed him, and armed herself with it again. Then she remembered the protection he had prepared for himself against the uprising of the serfs.

She pulled the lever that sprayed all the outer rooms with the stupefying gas—the rooms filled with his friends, the most dependable and trustworthy of those who had supported him.

The signal promised by the five—if they succeeded—did not come to Hendron-Khorlu. It was longer and longer overdue.

At dawn Ransdell set out to fly toward the capital city and toward Danot beyond it; but on the way he met another plane.

A lark, it was—one of the machines of the Vanished People flown by another pilot from earth; and Ransdell, not seeking encounter, was avoiding it when he saw that the passenger—or observer—in that plane was standing, waving to him.

Ransdell swung about, and curiously, yet keeping a cautious distance, pursued the plane, which was making straight for Hendron.

It landed on the field outside the city; and Dave followed it down.

Two men stepped out; and it was evident that the passenger was watching the pilot; the passenger was armed; the pilot was not.

Ransdell and Waterman, who was with him, approached the pair; and the passenger, forgetting his watch of the pilot, hurried to them.

"You're the Americans?" he hailed them in English; more, he spoke like an Englishman.

"Yes!" called Ransdell. "Who are you?"

"Griggsby-Cook! Once Major Griggsby-Cook, of the Royal Air Forces!"

"Where from?" challenged Ransdell wonderingly.

"Where from?" repeated the Englishman. "Out of slavery, I'd say! I came to tell you. We've taken over the city, since that girl of yours stabbed Seidel and gassed the rest of the ring! We've taken over the city!"

"Who?' demanded Ransdell; and answered himself: "Oh, you mean the English! Then Taylor and James and Vanderbilt and the five of them got in!"

"The five?" repeated Griggsby-Cook. "It was a girl that got in! She did for Seidel in his bath—like Charlotte Corday with Marat!

"Then she gassed a lot more. . . . There was nothing to it when we got wind of that, and rose against them. I say, we've quite taken over the city! I buzzed off to tell you chaps. Didn't take time to learn the trick of this plane myself; so I pistoled one of their pilots into taking me. But he's good now, isn't he?"

Ransdell nodded; for the pilot was meekly waiting.

"Oh, they'll all be good!" said Griggsby-Cook confidently. "They'll have to be."

"But the five—the five men that went from here?" Ransdell persisted.

"Know nothing of them!" said the Englishman. "Sorry."

Then no one spoke; but the four of them stared, as in the dim gray dawn, the great dome of Khorlu began glowing, and illumination showed in the streets too.

"The lights are coming on!" Ransdell exclaimed incredulously.

"Yes," said the Englishman. "We were working at that; they hoped to get the power to you before I got here!"

It was only a little later that the same English engineers restored the power-supply to Danot, which had been cut off for reasons unguessed, until they had searched the tunnel and found one dead and four wounded Americans.

Tony Drake, on entering the capital city, went first to the hospital rooms where Eliot and Jack Taylor and Whittington and Peter Vanderbilt lay. They would all "pull through," the English surgeon promised; but he could not say so much of others under his care; for the uprising had cost, on both sides, thirty lives; and ten more of the wounded would not recover.

But battle on Bronson Beta was over—at least for the present. Further contest was unthinkable; yet it was prevented only by the overpowering numbers of the Americans and English together, when compared to the still defiant few of the "Asian Realists." Some score of these had to be confined; but all the rest were reconciled to the government that was being arranged by the Americans and the English.

They were gathered all together in Gorfulu; and they were going to have a great meeting to discuss and agree upon the form of government.

Marian Jackson sat with the men on the committee; for surely she had earned the right; but she had not, as she herself proclaimed, "the first ghost of a glimpse of government."

What was it to be?

Some suggested an alternate dictatorship, like the consuls of Roman republic, with an American consul alternating in power with an English. Others declared as positively that all rivalries and jealousies of the shattered earth should be forever banished and denied.

There were a score of other schemes.

And more debate than ever before on manners and morals—especially about marriage. Should there be laws for love? Cast off conventions and taboos! All right; try to get along without any. . . .

Tony retired to the lovely apartment provided in the capital city for Eve and himself; he was very tired. The day had been dark and long, and outside the shield of the city, very cold.

It was neither dark nor cold within; for the power-plant more than supplied needed heat and light. The people were provided with every material thing.

"And to-day," said Tony to his wife, "we ascertained beyond possible question that this planet stays with the sun. To-day we passed aphelion, and have definitely begun to approach the sun again. Life here will go on."

"Our life together, Tony!"

He kissed her more tenderly for his child within her.

"I've not dared think too much of—our son, Eve. But now it seems certain he'll come into a world where he can live. But what strange, strange things, my dear, he is sure to see!"

THE END

MOST DAZZLINGLY PROPHETIC NOVEL EVER WRITTEN IN AMERICA. THE ALL-TIME GREAT WHICH RANKS WITH BRAVE NEW WORLD AND 1984

WHEN WORLDS COLLIDE

by Philip Wylie
and Edwin Balmer

The classic story of Earthman's fight for survival against nearly impossible odds.

64-360 75¢